# *Abigail's Promise*

## VIVIAN BELLE

STERLING RIDGE PRESS LLC

Cover designed by Sterling Ridge Press LLC

Published by: Sterling Ridge Press, LLC www.sterlingridgepress.com

ISBN: 978-1-966093-19-0
Printed in the United States of America

First Edition: March 2025

For permissions, contact: support@vivianbelle.com or visit www.vivianbelle.com

# Dedication

*For all the dreamers who see beyond what is, to what could be,*
*For the menders of broken things who believe in second chances,*
*And especially for you, dear reader, who understands that sometimes*
*the strongest foundations are built on the ruins of what came before.*
*With profound gratitude for allowing my words into your world,*
*Vivian*

# About The Author

**V**ivian Belle is a talented author known for her sweeping **Historical Christian Romance** novels set against the untamed beauty of the American frontier. With a deep love for history and storytelling, she brings to life **resilient heroines, steadfast heroes, and faith-filled journeys** in the vast, rugged landscapes of the past.

Nestled in the **majestic mountains of northern West Virginia,** Vivian finds endless inspiration in the rolling hills, winding rivers, and boundless sky that mirror the spirit of her stories. When she's not writing, she enjoys **kayaking on tranquil waters, hiking through breathtaking mountain trails, and, of course, getting lost in a good book.**

Vivian's novels capture the heart of **faith, love, and perseverance**—where strong women and honorable men overcome life's trials to find hope, home, and happily-ever-after. Whether she's exploring the great outdoors or crafting her next frontier romance, Vivian's passion for adventure and storytelling shines through in every word she writes.

You can find out more about Vivian and her latest releases at www.vivianbelle.com or follow her on social media for updates and behind-the-scenes glimpses of her writing process. Stay connected—you won't want to miss the heartfelt stories of love and family she has in store!

# Also by Vivian Belle

Where the Heart Finds Home

Faith on the Frontier

Love in Hopewell Creek

Abigail's Promise

# Contents

# Chapter 1

Abigail Whitaker gripped the worn leather strap as the stagecoach lurched violently over another rut. The impact sent her slight frame bouncing against the hard wooden seat, jostling her bonnet askew. She winced, her fingers instinctively reaching for the small scar below her right earlobe, a permanent reminder of a devastating carriage accident.

"Almost there, miss," the driver called down through the open hatch above. "Clear Springs just ahead."

The words sent a flutter of anxiety through her chest. After six grueling days of travel from Denver, preceded by a seemingly endless train journey from Boston, her destination was finally at hand. She smoothed her wrinkled skirt with trembling fingers, grateful that none of the other passengers from earlier legs of the journey remained to witness her nervousness.

The stagecoach rounded a steep bend, and Clear Springs appeared below them, nestled in a valley between craggy mountains. The humble collection of weathered buildings seemed insignificant against the vast, untamed wilderness surrounding it. From this distance, Abigail could see the layout clearly: a main street flanked by various establishments, several side streets with scattered homes, and a small white structure set slightly apart that could only be the church.

The Clear Springs Church. Her parents' financial contributions had made its construction possible. Now it would be her church to restore, both physically and spiritually.

"Lord, give me strength," she whispered. "I am here as You called me to be."

The stagecoach descended rapidly into the valley; the horses picking up speed as they approached more level ground. Abigail steadied herself against the jostling, trying to maintain her composure. She was a missionary's daughter, after all. The daughter of Samuel and Eleanor Whitaker, respected, devoted servants of God who had dedicated their lives to bringing spiritual light to dark places.

Until that rainy Boston evening six months ago when their carriage had overturned on the way home from a missionary fundraiser. The memory struck her with physical force, and she closed her eyes against the sudden pressure of tears.

The stagecoach thundered into the outskirts of Clear Springs. Abigail craned her neck to look through the small window, taking in her first close view of the frontier mining town that would now be her home.

What she saw made her heart sink. The buildings were more weathered than she had expected, many with boards haphazardly nailed over broken windows. A layer of dust seemed to cover everything: the street, the buildings, even the few people visible on the wooden boardwalks. Two men stumbled out of what was clearly a saloon, though it was barely past noon. A wiry dog darted across the road, narrowly avoiding the stagecoach wheels.

The stagecoach came to an abrupt halt before a small building with "Clear Springs STAGE & POST" painted in fading letters across its front. The driver jumped down and opened the door.

"Clear Springs, miss. End of the line."

Abigail gathered her reticule and stepped carefully down onto the dirt packed street. The bright midday sun hit her with an intensity she wasn't prepared for, and she blinked rapidly, grateful for her bonnet's modest protection.

The air smelled of dust, horses, and something metallic she couldn't quite place, likely from the silver mine nearby. The sounds were equally foreign: the sharp clang of metal on metal from somewhere down the street, the braying of a mule tied outside the general store, rough laughter from the saloon. The constant, underlying bustle of a town built on hard work and harder living.

Her fine Boston walking dress, once crisp and elegant, now hung limply on her frame, creased from days of travel. She felt conspicuously out of place as the driver unloaded her trunk and two valises, placing them unceremoniously on the boardwalk.

"That'll be the last of your things, Miss Whitaker," he said, tipping his hat. "Good luck to you."

"Thank you," she replied, reaching into her reticule for a modest tip. "Can you direct me to the boardinghouse? Mrs. Hale's, I believe?"

The driver pointed down the street. "Three buildings past the general store, on your right. Can't miss it, only place with flower boxes."

He climbed back onto the coach and, with a sharp whistle and snap of reins, continued down the street to what she assumed was the livery stable, leaving Abigail standing alone with her luggage.

A sudden commotion from across the street caught her attention. A group of miners, faces smudged with dirt and clothing worn from hard labor, trudged past, their voices carrying in the still afternoon air.

"McGrant's pushing too hard," one man was saying. "Aaron nearly lost his arm yesterday when that support gave way."

"Quiet," another hissed. "You want to lose your job? We're lucky to have work at all."

Abigail watched as they passed, their weary, defeated postures telling a story more eloquent than words. This, then, was what her parents had seen. The need for hope, for spiritual sustenance in a place where physical demands consumed nearly everything.

Her attention was diverted by the unmistakable sound of a hammer striking an anvil. Down the street, partially visible through an open doorway, stood a large man, his powerful arm rising and falling in a steady rhythm. Even from this distance, she could see that his shoulders were broad beneath his simple cotton shirt. A leather apron protected his chest as sparks flew from whatever he was fashioning.

As if sensing her gaze, the man paused and looked up. Though the distance was too great to clearly see his features, something in his stance, a certain rigidity, perhaps, gave Abigail the impression of wariness.

The moment lasted only seconds before he returned to his work, but it left Abigail with an odd sensation of having glimpsed something significant, though she couldn't have explained what.

She shook off the feeling and turned her attention to the immediate problem: her luggage. The trunk alone was far too heavy for her to manage, and she looked around for assistance. The street, however, seemed suddenly deserted.

The door to the building marked "SHERIFF" opened, and a man of medium build with a neatly trimmed beard and a silver star pinned to his vest emerged. He glanced around, then did a visible double-take at the sight of Abigail standing alone with her luggage.

"Ma'am?" he called, approaching with quick strides. "May I help you?"

Abigail smiled with relief. "Yes, thank you. I've just arrived and need to reach Mrs. Hale's boardinghouse."

"You must be Miss Whitaker. We've been expecting you." He touched the brim of his hat. "Caleb Mansfield, deputy sheriff. Mrs. Hale mentioned you'd be arriving today."

"It's a pleasure to meet you, Deputy Mansfield."

"Likewise, ma'am. Let me help you with these." He effortlessly lifted her trunk. "I can carry this if you'll manage the smaller bags."

Abigail gathered her valises, grateful for the assistance. As they walked, Deputy Mansfield maintained a respectful distance while offering a running commentary on the town.

"General store there. Mr. Paulson's fair with his prices, though supplies can be limited depending on when the wagons come through. Doc Carpenter's office is next door to the boardinghouse. He's a good man, that doctor. Church is down at the end of Main Street, though I reckon you know that already."

Abigail nodded, trying to absorb everything. "And the silver mine? I understand it employs most of the men here."

The deputy's expression tightened almost imperceptibly. "Yes, ma'am. McGrant Silver Mine. Been operating for about three years now under Mr. McGrant."

They arrived at a two-story clapboard building distinguished, as promised, by modest flower boxes beneath the front windows.

The deputy set down her trunk and knocked on the door. Almost immediately, it swung open to reveal a plump, pleasant-faced woman in her fifties, her gray-streaked brown hair pulled back in a practical bun.

"Well, there you are at last!" the woman exclaimed, her face break-ing into a warm smile. "I was beginning to worry the stage had run into trouble." Her gaze shifted to the deputy. "Thank you kindly for escorting her, Caleb."

"My pleasure, Mrs. Hale." He tipped his hat to both women. "Miss Whitaker, welcome to Clear Springs. If you need anything, don't hes-itate to call on the sheriff's office."

As he departed, Mrs. Hale ushered Abigail inside. The interior of the boardinghouse was modest but scrupulously clean, with simple furnishings.

"You must be exhausted, poor dear," Mrs. Hale said, leading her into a small parlor. "Sit down and catch your breath while I fetch you some tea. Then we'll get you settled in your room."

Abigail sank gratefully into an upholstered chair, suddenly aware of just how tired she truly was. "Thank you for your kindness, Mrs. Hale."

"Margaret, please. We don't stand on ceremony here in Clear Springs." The older woman bustled about, pouring tea from a pot that had been keeping warm on a small stove in the corner. "Now, tell me about your journey. Was it terribly difficult?"

Accepting the offered cup, Abigail managed a smile. "Long and dusty, but not unbearable."

"And you came all the way from Boston? Such a distance for a young woman alone." Margaret's eyes reflected genuine concern.

"Yes. After my parents passed, there was nothing to keep me there. And their work here was unfinished."

Understanding softened the older woman's features. "Yes, I heard about your loss. The whole town did. Your parents were well-respected here, even by those who never met them. That church wouldn't exist without their support."

A lump formed in Abigail's throat. "Have you been inside recently? The church, I mean. The correspondence I received suggested it's been standing empty."

Margaret's expression grew troubled. "I'm afraid it's been neglected these past few years. The last circuit preacher came through months ago, and he only stayed a couple of weeks." She hesitated. "It's not just the building that needs attention, Miss Whitaker. This town... well, you'll see for yourself soon enough."

"What do you mean?"

Before Margaret could respond, heavy footsteps sounded on the porch, followed by a sharp knock. The boardinghouse keeper frowned slightly.

"Excuse me, dear." She rose and went to the door.

Abigail heard a deep male voice, though she couldn't make out the words. Margaret's replies were equally indistinct. The conversation lasted only a moment before the door closed and Margaret returned, her expression troubled.

"Is everything all right?" Abigail asked.

"Oh, yes. That was just Jonah Brooks. He's our blacksmith. Wanted to know if I needed any repairs." Margaret smiled, but it didn't quite reach her eyes. "Now, let me show you to your room. You'll want to rest before supper."

Abigail followed her hostess up a narrow staircase to the second floor. The simple room contained a single bed, a small dresser, a washstand, and a chair near the window that overlooked the main street.

"It's not fancy," Margaret apologized, "but it's clean and comfortable."

"It's perfect. It will do for one night before I move into the parsonage tomorrow," Abigail assured her. And it was a solid roof, clean linens, and a safe place to sleep were luxury enough after days of travel.

"The washroom is at the end of the hall. Supper's at six sharp. I'll have the boy bring up your trunk shortly." Margaret said.

Left alone, Abigail sank onto the edge of the bed. She reached into her satchel and withdrew her Bible, its leather cover worn smooth by years of handling from her parents.

Opening it to a familiar passage in Isaiah, she read silently: "Fear not, for I am with you; be not dismayed, for I am your God; I will strengthen you, I will help you, I will uphold you with my righteous right hand."

The words blurred as tears filled her eyes. "I'm trying to be brave," she whispered. "But I'm so very far from home."

She allowed herself a few moments of quiet weeping, for her parents, for her old life, for the uncertainty ahead, before wiping her eyes and squaring her shoulders. Self-pity would accomplish nothing. She had come to Clear Springs with a purpose, and tomorrow she would begin.

Rising, she moved to the window and gazed out at what would now be her home. The afternoon sun cast long shadows across the dusty street. People moved about their business. A woman with a basket of laundry, two children chasing a hoop, and a man leading a heavily laden mule. In the distance, she could see the white steeple of the church standing like a silent sentinel at the edge of town.

Her church now. Her responsibility. Her mission.

# Chapter 2

Abigail awoke later than normal the following morning to the unfamiliar sounds of a frontier town coming to life. The distant ring of the blacksmith's hammer, the clatter of wagon wheels on the hard-packed dirt off the main street, and voices calling greetings and instructions. For a moment, disorientation gripped her, the simple room foreign compared to her bedroom in Boston.

Reality returned swiftly. This was Clear Springs. This was her new home.

She rose quickly and performed her morning ablutions at the washstand, grateful for the clean water. Donning a practical day dress of navy-blue cotton, she twisted her blond hair into a simple knot at the nape of her neck. The looking glass above the dresser reflected a young woman with determined blue eyes and a stubborn chin—her father's chin, everyone had always said.

Downstairs, Margaret greeted her with a warm smile and a hearty breakfast of flapjacks, bacon, and strong coffee.

"You'll need your strength today," the older woman said, pouring a second cup of coffee into Abigail's cup despite her protests.

"I'd like to visit the church first thing," she explained. "Then perhaps meet with whoever has been keeping the keys... Reverend Blake?"

Margaret nodded. "Thomas Blake. Used to preach regular until his health failed him. Lives in a little cabin just beyond the church. Good man, but getting on in years." She hesitated. "The church hasn't been used since the last circuit preacher passed through. I'm not sure what condition you'll find it in."

"I'm prepared for the worst," Abigail said, though her stomach tightened at the thought. "Whatever state it's in, it can be restored with enough faith and hard work."

Margaret's expression softened. "You sound just like your father in that letter he sent when he first decided to support our little church. 'With faith and work, all things are possible,' he wrote."

Emotion threatened to overwhelm Abigail, but she swallowed it back. "Yes, that sounds like him."

After breakfast, she set out toward the church. The morning was cool, and the air crisp. As she walked, she took care to observe the town more thoroughly than she had upon arrival.

Clear Springs was larger than it had first appeared, with the main street featuring all the essentials of frontier life: the general store, a small bank, the post office that doubled as the stagecoach stop, the sheriff's office, the doctor's practice, and various other establishments, including the blacksmith's forge. Side streets branched off, lined with modest homes. Beyond these, she could see scattered cabins and small homesteads extending toward the foothills. In the distance, the silhouette of the mining operation was visible against the mountainside, a constant reminder of the industry that gave the town its purpose.

People stopped to watch her pass, some nodding politely, others merely staring with undisguised curiosity. Abigail smiled and offered greetings, determined to begin establishing connections immediately.

"Good morning," she called to a woman hanging laundry outside a small house.

The woman looked startled, then gave a tentative smile in return. "Morning, miss."

A group of children playing with hoops in the dusty street scattered as she approached, then regrouped behind her, whispering and giggling. Abigail turned and smiled at them.

"Hello there."

A bold-faced boy of about ten stepped forward. "You the new preacher lady?"

"William Thatcher!" A sharp female voice cut through the air as a harried-looking woman hurried from a nearby house. "You mind your manners!" She approached Abigail with an apologetic expression. "I'm sorry, miss. The boy means no disrespect."

"None taken," Abigail assured her. "And yes, in a way, I am 'the preacher lady.' My name is Abigail Whitaker. My parents helped establish the church here."

Recognition dawned in the woman's eyes. "The Whitaker's? Why, everyone knows that name. I'm Clair Thatcher." She gestured to the boy and two smaller children who had crept up beside her. "These are my children—William, Sarah, and little James."

"It's lovely to meet you all," Abigail said warmly. "I hope to see you at services once the church is ready."

Clair's expression became guarded. "Well, we'll see. My husband works six days a week in the mine. Sunday's his only day to rest."

"I understand," Abigail said. "Perhaps we can talk more another time."

Continuing on her way, she reached the end of the main street, where it intersected with a smaller lane. Ahead, set slightly apart, stood the Clear Springs Church and the parsonage, where she would live.

Abigail's steps slowed as she approached, her heart sinking at the sight. The small white clapboard building with its modest steeple had once been a beacon of hope and faith. Now it stood forlorn, its paint peeling, one shutter hanging askew, the small cemetery beside it overgrown with weeds. The sign that should have proudly displayed the church's name lay on the ground, its lettering faded nearly to illegibility.

"Oh, my," she whispered. "There's so much to be done."

Taking a deep breath, she continued up the path to the church steps. The wooden stairs creaked ominously beneath her weight, and she tested each one carefully before proceeding. The double doors at the entrance were secured with a heavy padlock.

Abigail stood for a moment, uncertain how to proceed. As she hesitated, the sound of approaching footsteps caused her to turn.

An elderly man with a shock of white hair and stooped shoulders made his way slowly up the path, leaning heavily on a carved wooden cane. Despite his obvious physical frailty, his blue eyes were sharp and clear beneath bushy white eyebrows.

"Miss Whitaker, I presume," he called out in a surprisingly strong voice. "Thomas Blake. I was the shepherd of this little flock before the rheumatism got the better of me."

Abigail hurried down the steps to meet him, extending her hand. "Reverend Blake, it's an honor. Thank you for coming to meet me."

The old man's handshake was firm despite his age. "Couldn't very well leave Samuel Whitaker's daughter standing on the doorstep, now could I?" His eyes twinkled. "Besides, I have what you need." He patted his pocket, producing an iron key.

They ascended the steps together, Abigail offering her arm for support. He accepted with a nod of thanks.

"Hasn't been opened in months," Reverend Blake explained as he worked the key into the rusty lock. "The Last circuit preacher was Reverend Withers... decent fellow, but more interested in fire and brimstone than building community."

With a grunt of effort, he turned the key, and the lock clicked open. He removed it and pushed one of the double doors inward. It swung open with a protesting creak as the door shifted, a hinge breaking.

"Welcome to Clear Springs Church," he said with a hint of irony. "Such as it is."

Abigail stepped inside, and her heart sank further. The interior was in even worse condition than the exterior had suggested. Dust lay thick on every surface. Several pews were damaged, one missing its back entirely. The small pulpit stood askew, as if someone had collided with it and left it where it fell. The altar cloth was gray with dust and spotted with what appeared to be candle wax. Most distressing of all, one of the modest stained-glass windows behind the pulpit was cracked, with several pieces missing entirely, allowing birds access. Evidence of their presence was scattered across the altar and floor.

"Oh my," Abigail breathed, unable to hide her dismay.

Reverend Blake sighed heavily beside her. "I know it looks dire, Miss Whitaker. The truth is, this town's been struggling in more ways than one. McGrant's mine keeps most folks fed, but it takes everything they have to give. Not much left over for spiritual matters." He gestured around the sanctuary. "This is just the physical manifestation of a deeper neglect."

Abigail walked slowly up the center aisle, taking inventory of the damage. Despite everything, the essential structure seemed sound. The roof appeared to have a leak in two spots. Most of the floor seemed solid beneath her feet, and the pews could be salvaged with some repair.

"It's not as bad as it could be," she said. "With some help, I can have it ready for services within a week or two."

Reverend Blake regarded her with a mixture of admiration and skepticism. "That's the spirit, young lady. But where will you find this help? Most men work from dawn to dusk in the mine, and the women have their hands full, keeping homes together and children fed."

"God will provide," Abigail replied simply, though privately she acknowledged the challenge. "He always does."

The reverend's weathered face creased in a smile. "Your father said much the same thing when he first wrote about supporting our little community and helping us build this church. 'The Lord will make a way,' he said."

Abigail felt a surge of connection to her father, as if he were standing beside her at that moment. "And He did, didn't He? The church was built."

"That it was." Reverend Blake's gaze grew distant with memory. "This was a different town then. More hopeful. Before McGrant consolidated his hold on the mine and everything else."

"Tell me about Mr. McGrant," Abigail said, sensing the undercurrent of tension whenever the name was mentioned.

The reverend's expression darkened. "Silas McGrant arrived about four years ago with money from back east. Bought up mining claims, merged them into one operation. Made himself indispensable to Clear Springs's survival." He paused. "He's not a man who appreciates competition—of any kind. Including the spiritual."

"Surely, he doesn't oppose the church?" Abigail asked, surprised.

"Not openly. But he makes it clear that a man's loyalty should be to the mine first. Sunday work is common. Those who refuse find themselves with reduced hours or worse positions." The old minister sighed. "It's not just that, though. There's something... wrong... about how he operates. Accidents in that mine have increased threefold in the past year or so. Men injured, some killed. Always blamed on carelessness or bad luck, never on the conditions McGrant provides."

They completed their inspection of the church, Abigail making notes of everything that needed attention: the broken windows, damaged pews, tilted pulpit, dusty altar, bird-soiled floors. The list was daunting, but not insurmountable.

"This door leads to the side yard, with the parsonage just beyond," Reverend Blake said, indicating a small door near the pulpit. "It's modest, just a few rooms, but it should meet your needs once it's tidied up."

"Perfect. I'll clean that today as well so I can move in immediately," Abigail decided.

# Chapter 3

Abigail attacked the thick layer of dust on the pulpit with vigorous strokes, her scrub brush creating small clouds that danced in the shafts of light streaming through the broken windows. Sweat beaded on her forehead despite the cool morning air, and she wiped it away with her sleeve, leaving a smudge of dirt across her cheek. Her once-pristine blue dress was now spotted with dust and cobwebs.

After Reverend Blake had departed, promising to spread word of her arrival and need for assistance, Abigail rolled up her sleeves and set to work immediately. She'd found a broom, dustpan, and scrub brush in a small closet off the sanctuary, along with a cracked bucket that still held water if she didn't fill it more than halfway.

"This is Your house, Lord," she murmured as she dipped her brush into the now-murky water. "I won't let it remain in disrepair a moment longer than necessary."

The task before her was overwhelming. Bird droppings stained the altar cloth beyond salvation. Dead leaves and twigs littered the corners where the wind had blown them through the broken windows. Several hymn books lay scattered and water-damaged, their pages warped and mildewed.

The rough brush handle bit into her soft palms, already reddened from work, as she scrubbed. Her parents had raised her with the firm belief that no work was beneath a person when done in service to God.

A sudden gust of wind rattled the broken windows, sending a shower of dust and debris onto the freshly cleaned pulpit. Abigail bit back a sigh of frustration.

Setting her brush aside, she approached the damaged stained-glass behind her. The window depicted a simple cross surrounded by lilies, nothing elaborate like the grand windows of Boston's churches, but beautiful in its humble way. Several pieces were missing entirely, creating jagged holes through which birds and filth had entered. Others hung precariously, threatening to fall at the slightest disturbance.

"I'll need a carpenter," she murmured, mentally adding it to her growing list of needs. "And glass. And someone who knows how to repair stained-glass."

The enormity of the task suddenly pressed down on her. She was alone in a strange town where she knew almost no one, with limited funds and little practical experience. For a moment, doubt crept in, cold and insidious.

The memory of her father's voice came to her then, clear as if he stood beside her: "When the task seems impossible, Abigail, that's when faith matters most."

She squared her shoulders and returned to the pulpit, retrieving her brush with renewed determination. The work would be done one task at a time, one day at a time.

Abigail had just begun scrubbing again when a sharp knock at the church door startled her. She turned to see a tall, slender woman with auburn hair pulled back in a practical bun standing in the doorway, a basket over one arm.

"Hello?" the woman called, peering into the dim interior. "Miss Whitaker?"

"Yes, that's me," Abigail replied, setting down her brush and wiping her hands ineffectively against her skirt. "Please, come in."

The woman stepped inside, her eyes widening as she took in the state of the church. "My goodness. It's worse than I imagined." Her gaze shifted to Abigail, taking in her disheveled appearance with evident surprise. "I'm Libby Martin, the schoolteacher. Margaret Hale mentioned you'd arrived and might need some assistance."

"It's a pleasure to meet you, Miss Martin," Abigail said, crossing to shake hands despite her dirty appearance. "And yes, any help would be most welcome."

Libby smiled, her green eyes warming. "Please, call me Libby. We're not much for formality in Clear Springs." She held up her basket. "I've brought some cleaning supplies and a bit of lunch. I thought you might be hungry after a morning's work."

"That's incredibly thoughtful. Thank you." Abigail gestured around the sanctuary. "As you can see, there's plenty of work to be done."

"So I see," Libby agreed, setting her basket on a pew. "Where would you like me to start?"

Before Abigail could answer, another figure appeared in the doorway, a stocky woman with weathered features and calloused hands that spoke of hard work. She carried a child of about two on her hip, her expression guarded as she surveyed the scene.

"Ah, Ruth!" Libby called. "You decided to come after all."

The woman stepped inside hesitantly. "Just came to see what all the fuss was about," she said, her tone noncommittal. "Heard the missionary's daughter was fixing up the church."

Abigail approached with a smile, extending her hand. "Abigail Whitaker. It's a pleasure to meet you."

Ruth shifted her child to her other hip and briefly clasped Abigail's hand. "Ruth Patterson. This here's my youngest, Emma." She glanced around the church, her expression unreadable. "You've got your work cut out for you."

"Yes," Abigail agreed. "But with help, it won't seem so daunting."

Ruth's eyes narrowed slightly. "Why're you doing this, anyway? This town hasn't had a proper church service in months. Most folks have gotten used to spending Sundays otherwise."

The blunt question caught Abigail off guard, but she recognized it as an honest one deserving an honest answer.

"Because every community needs a place to gather in faith," she said simply. "A place to find hope and strength beyond what we can provide for ourselves. My parents believed that, and so do I."

Ruth studied her for a long moment, then gave a small nod. "Well, I will help you clean. Emma can play in that corner while I help." She set the child down on a relatively clean patch of floor, handing her a small rag doll from her pocket. "Stay there, Emma. Mama's going to help clean."

Abigail felt a surge of gratitude. "Thank you, Mrs. Patterson."

"Ruth," the woman corrected, already rolling up her sleeves. "Just Ruth."

With three pairs of hands at work, the sanctuary began to transform more rapidly. Libby attacked the pews with a determination that matched Abigail's own, while Ruth, clearly accustomed to hard, practical work, tackled the floor with a broom and mop.

As they worked, the conversation flowed more easily than Abigail had dared hope.

"How long have you been teaching here, Libby?" she asked, moving on to clean the small table that would hold the communion elements.

"Two years now," Libby replied, wiping dust from a hymnal. "I came from Denver after finishing my education. The school here is small—just one room for all ages—but the children are eager to learn."

"Most of them, anyway," Ruth interjected with a snort. "My Jimmy's more eager to fish than to read, though he's coming around."

Abigail nodded. "Not to change the subject, but I'm curious. Is the mine the primary employer here?"

Both women exchanged glances.

"The only real employer," Ruth said flatly. "McGrant Silver Mine. If you're a man in Clear Springs, you either work for Silas McGrant or you leave town."

"Unless you have a specialized trade," Libby added. "Like Doc Carpenter or Jonah Brooks."

"The blacksmith?" Abigail asked.

Ruth's expression softened slightly. "Jonah's a good man. Keeps to himself mostly, but he's fair with his prices and does quality work. Fixed our stove last winter when we couldn't afford a new one."

"He's also the most stubborn man in three counties," Libby said with a small smile. "And about as talkative as a fence post."

"He has his reasons," Ruth said, in a tone that discouraged further discussion.

Abigail sensed a story there but knew better than to press. "I hope to meet him properly soon. I suspect I'll need his services for some of the church repairs."

"Speaking of repairs," Libby said, looking up at the damaged stained-glass window, "that's going to need a specialist. I'm not sure anyone in town has experience with stained-glass."

"Perhaps it could be boarded temporarily," Abigail suggested. "Until proper repairs can be arranged."

Ruth nodded. "Timothy Wells at the livery might help with that. He does carpentry on the side, and he knows many people in surrounding towns as well that may be able to help."

"And the pulpit needs to be secured," Libby added, examining the tilted structure. "It looks like someone knocked it askew."

"Probably those Jackson boys," Ruth muttered. "Always causing trouble. Broke into this church last spring on a dare, from what I heard."

"The reason for the padlock, I assume?" Abigail said. "Regardless, I'm truly grateful for both of your help today, both the physical assistance and the information."

"Don't thank me yet," Ruth said pragmatically. "Getting this church back in order is one thing. Getting folks to attend is another matter entirely."

"Why is that?" Abigail asked, though she suspected she knew part of the answer from her conversation with Reverend Blake.

Ruth's expression darkened. "Sundays are the only day most miners get to rest. And McGrant has been known to schedule 'essential' work on Sundays for anyone who shows too much interest in matters outside the mine."

"That can't be legal," Abigail protested.

"Legal doesn't matter much here," Ruth replied with a shrug that didn't quite hide her bitterness. "McGrant owns the mine, and the mine owns Clear Springs."

"Surely, not everyone feels that way," Abigail said, looking at Libby.

The schoolteacher hesitated. "It's... complicated. Mr. McGrant serves on the school board. He donated the funds for our new slate boards last year. He can be quite generous when it serves his interests."

"And quite the opposite when it doesn't," Ruth added darkly.

Abigail's mind raced with implications.

"Tell me about your families," Abigail said, deliberately shifting to a lighter topic. "You mentioned your son Jimmy, Ruth. Do you have other children?"

Ruth's face softened. "Two others. Penny's eight, and little Emma here is just turned two." She glanced fondly at the toddler, who was contentedly playing with her doll in the corner. "My husband Billy is a good man. Works hard in that mine six days a week."

"And you, Libby? Are you married?"

The schoolteacher shook her head with a smile. "No, though not for lack of my mother's prayers. She writes weekly from Denver, suggesting eligible men might be found there rather than in a 'rough mining town.'"

"But you stay," Abigail observed.

"I stay," Libby agreed simply. "These children need education, and I've grown fond of Clear Springs, despite its challenges."

Abigail understood completely. Already, despite having been in town less than a day, she felt drawn to this community and its struggles.

"What about you, Miss Whitaker?" Ruth asked, her tone softening slightly. "Leaving Boston society for our little town must have been quite a change."

"Please, call me Abigail," she replied. "And yes, it's different, but not in ways that matter. People are people, whether in Boston drawing rooms or Colorado mining towns. We all need the same things: purpose, community, and faith."

"And your family?" Libby inquired gently. "We heard about your parents, of course. I'm truly sorry for your loss."

Abigail swallowed against the sudden tightness in her throat. "Thank you. They were remarkable people. This church was very important to them. This was the first church they fully funded and helped build from the ground up." She paused, composing herself. "I have no siblings, and my only aunt lives in England, so there was little to keep me in Boston after they passed."

Ruth studied her with newfound respect. "Takes courage to travel across the country alone."

"Or foolishness," Abigail said with a small smile. "I'm not always sure which. This church was deeply meaningful to my parents and held a cherished place in their hearts. They had intended to come here to assist in rebuilding the church and restoring its operations, but the good Lord called them home before they had a chance. I made a solemn promise to myself and to God that I would fulfill this mission in their stead, as they no longer can."

The conversation continued as they worked, gradually shifting to the practicalities of church restoration. By midday, they had made significant progress. The pulpit and the altar gleamed, most of the pews had been dusted and wiped down, and the floor was considerably cleaner, though still showing the wear of neglect.

"We should eat," Libby suggested, retrieving her basket. "I've brought enough to share."

They settled on the front pew, and Libby unpacked her offerings—fresh bread, cheese, sliced apples, and a small jar of preserves. Ruth contributed a cloth-wrapped bundle of oatmeal cookies that she'd brought.

"This is wonderful," Abigail said gratefully, accepting a piece of bread spread with preserves. "I hadn't realized how hungry I'd become."

"Physical labor does that," Ruth said matter-of-factly, cutting a small piece of cheese for Emma, who had climbed into her lap. "You'll need to eat hearty if you're going to keep working like this."

"I intend to keep working as hard as I can manage," Abigail assured her. "The sooner the church is ready, the sooner we can hold services."

"And when might that be?" Libby asked, her tone curious rather than challenging.

Abigail considered. "With help, perhaps a few days... maybe a week... or two? The most urgent matters are the broken windows, securing the pulpit, fixing the doors, and ensuring the roof doesn't leak."

"Ambitious," Ruth commented, but there was a note of approval in her voice.

"Faith without works is dead," Abigail quoted softly. "My father always said that faith must be put into action to have meaning."

Ruth nodded slowly. "Your father sounds like a sensible man."

"He was," Abigail agreed, the past tense still painful to use. "Both my parents were practical in their faith. They believed in rolling up their sleeves alongside those they served."

Their quiet meal was interrupted by the sound of approaching footsteps, not the light tread of a woman or child, but the heavy, deliberate stride of a man. All three women turned to look as a shadow fell across the open doorway.

A tall, imposing figure filled the entrance. The man who stepped into the church was perhaps fifty, with iron-gray hair and a neatly trimmed beard. His clothing was of obvious quality. A tailored suit that would not have looked out of place in Boston's financial district, though it seemed incongruous in a frontier mining town. His eyes, sharp and assessing, took in the scene before him with calculated interest.

Abigail noticed both Ruth and Libby stiffen, their expressions becoming carefully neutral. Little Emma buried her face in her mother's shoulder.

"Ladies," the man said, his voice cultured and pleasant despite the tension his presence had created. "I heard we had a new arrival in town and thought I should introduce myself." His gaze settled on Abigail. "Silas McGrant, at your service. I own the silver mine that keeps Clear Springs on the map."

Abigail rose, smoothing her dusty skirt as best she could. "Abigail Whitaker. It's a pleasure to meet you, Mr. McGrant."

"Miss Whitaker," he acknowledged with a slight bow that seemed both courtly and somehow mocking. "Samuel Whitaker's daughter, I presume? News travels quickly in small towns."

"Yes, that's right."

McGrant's gaze swept the sanctuary, taking in the evidence of their work. "I see you've wasted no time in tackling this... project. Admirable enthusiasm, though perhaps misplaced."

"I don't understand," Abigail said, though a chill ran through her at his tone.

McGrant stepped further into the church, his polished boots echoing on the wooden floor. "Clear Springs is a working town, Miss Whitaker. These good people—" he gestured toward Ruth and Libby, who remained silent, "—labor hard six days a week. Sunday is their only respite. Burdening them with religious obligations seems... uncharitable."

The implication was clear, yet delivered with such smooth courtesy that it was difficult to directly challenge.

"I believe faith provides strength rather than burden, Mr. Mc-Grant," Abigail replied evenly. "And attendance at church services will, of course, be entirely voluntary."

A tight smile crossed his features. "Of course. Everything in Clear Springs is voluntary." He turned slightly toward Ruth. "Isn't that right, Mrs. Patterson? Your husband Billy understands the voluntary nature of our arrangements quite well."

Ruth's face paled slightly, but she nodded, her expression carefully blank.

McGrant returned his attention to Abigail. "I merely wished to welcome you to our community and offer any assistance my resources might provide. Clear Springs prospers through the mine, and I consider it my duty to support worthwhile endeavors."

The emphasis on "worthwhile" hung in the air between them.

"That's very generous," Abigail replied carefully. "Though at present, our needs are quite modest."

"Indeed." His gaze lingered on the broken windows. "Though I see repairs are needed. Perhaps my company carpenter could assist? He's quite skilled, though naturally, his primary obligations are to mine operations."

Before Abigail could respond, Libby spoke up, her tone deliberately light. "That's kind of you, Mr. McGrant, but I'm sure Mr. Wells will help with the carpentry."

McGrant's eyes narrowed almost imperceptibly. "I see. Well, the offer stands should you find Mr. Wells... unavailable." He turned back to Abigail. "I host a small gathering at my home each month for Clear Springs's leading citizens. As the daughter of Samuel Whitaker and our new... spiritual guide, you would be most welcome to attend this Friday evening."

The invitation caught Abigail off guard. "That's very kind, but I'm afraid I'll be quite busy with the church restoration."

"Surely, you can spare one evening?" McGrant pressed his tone remaining pleasant, though his eyes hardened slightly. "It would be an excellent opportunity to meet those who shape this community's future."

Abigail recognized the invitation for what it was, not merely social courtesy, but a chance for McGrant to assess her more thoroughly. Declining outright might establish unnecessary antagonism.

"I shall consider attending," she said with a smile that didn't quite reach her eyes.

McGrant nodded, satisfied. "Excellent. Eight o'clock, then. My home is just beyond the north end of town, the only three-story residence. You can't miss it." He glanced once more around the church. "I won't keep you ladies from your... charitable work. Good day."

With a slight bow, he turned and departed, his footsteps fading as he made his way down the path.

The silence that followed his exit was profound. Emma whimpered softly against Ruth's shoulder, and the woman gently patted her back, murmuring reassurances.

"Well," Libby said finally, her voice unnaturally bright, "that was unexpected."

Ruth's expression had darkened. "He never does anything without purpose. Coming here, inviting you to his home... he's measuring you, Miss Whitaker. Deciding whether you're a threat."

"A threat?" Abigail echoed, genuinely confused. "To what? I'm simply restoring a church."

"To his control," Libby explained quietly. "Silas McGrant doesn't merely own the mine, he owns the loyalty and dependence of nearly everyone in Clear Springs. Anything that might shift that loyalty elsewhere concerns him."

"Even a church?" Abigail asked, incredulous.

"Especially a church," Ruth replied grimly. "Faith gives people strength beyond what puts food on their tables. McGrant prefers to be the only source of strength folks rely on."

Abigail considered this. "Well, his concern is misplaced. I have no interest in challenging Mr. McGrant's business or influence. My only concern is providing spiritual guidance to the community."

"He won't see it that way," Ruth warned. "And that invitation... you should be careful. McGrant's gatherings are where he reinforces his position. Everyone who attends leaves either more firmly in his pocket or more aware of what crossing him might cost."

"I really prefer not to attend," Abigail pointed out.

"Just be prepared if you decide to go. Be pleasant but noncommittal. Observe more than you speak."

Abigail nodded, grateful for the advice. "I will. Thank you both for your candor."

Ruth stood, lifting Emma into her arms. "I should go. Dinner won't cook itself." She hesitated, then added, "I'll come again tomorrow if you'd like. Bring some proper cleaning supplies."

The offer, delivered in Ruth's matter-of-fact tone, warmed Abigail's heart. "I would appreciate that very much."

"I'll return as well," Libby added, gathering her now-empty basket. "School is out since it's summer and I have spare time."

"Thank you both," Abigail said sincerely. "Not just for the help, but for the welcome."

After they had gone, Abigail stood alone in the partially cleaned sanctuary, mulling over the encounter with Silas McGrant. His outward courtesy had barely masked an underlying warning. Or was it a threat? Either way, she had clearly stepped into a community with deeper tensions than she had initially realized.

# Chapter 4

The hammer struck the hot iron with precision, sending a shower of orange sparks dancing through the air. Jonah Brooks didn't flinch as they landed on his leather apron, too focused on the task before him. The rhythmic pounding filled the smithy with a familiar cadence—strike, turn, strike, turn—a metallic heartbeat.

Sweat trickled down his temple despite the cool spring morning. He paused only long enough to wipe his brow with his forearm before returning to the horseshoe taking shape beneath his hammer.

The forge's heat pressed against him like a living thing. He'd been at it since dawn, stoking the coals to glowing life, preparing for a day of work that would leave his muscles aching and his mind, mercifully, exhausted.

Jonah plunged the horseshoe into the water barrel, where it hissed and steamed in protest. The sudden sound, sharp and angry, made him stiffen momentarily, his jaw clenching against the unbidden image that flashed across his mind: the hiss of a bullet just before impact.

He shook his head as if to dislodge the memory physically.

Fishing out the horseshoe with tongs, he examined it with a critical eye before placing it with the others he'd completed that morning. Three down, one to go. Sheriff Holden's deputy had dropped off the request yesterday, new shoes for the sheriff's bay gelding. A straightforward job, the kind Jonah preferred.

"Mornin', Mr. Brooks," came a youthful voice.

Ethan Sheldon, gangly and earnest at eighteen, stood nearby with his weather-worn hat clutched in his hands. The boy had been hanging around the smithy for months, watching Jonah work with undisguised admiration.

"Ethan." Jonah's greeting was curt, but not unkind. He selected another iron bar for the next horseshoe.

"Thought maybe you could use some help today," the boy ventured, stepping further inside.

"Didn't ask for any."

"No, sir, you didn't." Ethan remained undeterred. "Pa said I could come if my chores were done, and they are."

Jonah glanced at the boy, noting the hopeful expression, the eagerness in his stance. Something in him softened almost imperceptibly.

"Pump the bellows," he said finally, nodding toward the forge. "Keep the fire hot, but not blazing. Think you remember how?"

Ethan's face broke into a grin. "Yes, sir, I remember." He hung his coat on a peg and rolled up his sleeves, moving to the bellows.

The pair worked in silence for a time, the only sounds the whoosh of the bellows, the clang of hammer on anvil, and the hiss of hot metal meeting water. Jonah found the boy's presence tolerable, a rare quality in this town of gossips and busybodies.

"Heard the new lady arrived yesterday," Ethan said eventually, his voice casual. "The missionary's daughter."

Jonah's rhythm didn't falter. "Is that so?"

"Stayed at Mrs. Hale's boardinghouse last night." Ethan worked the bellows with steady strokes. "Pa says she's come to fix up the church."

"Town's full of things that need fixing. Church is just one of them."

"She's from Boston. Never lived a day outside the city, from what they say."

"Then she won't last long." The words came out harder than Jonah intended. He felt Ethan's eyes on him, but didn't elaborate.

The eastern missionary woman wasn't his concern. Nothing in Clear Springs was his concern beyond his forge and anvil.

"Mr. Brooks?" Ethan's voice interrupted his thoughts.

"What."

"Do you think—" The boy hesitated. "Do you think it'll make a difference? Her being here, trying to bring the church back?"

Jonah paused, hammer suspended mid-stroke. "No," he said simply, then brought the hammer down with finality.

The conversation lapsed as they returned to their work. When the church bell suddenly tolled, a sound not heard in Clear Springs for months, both man and boy looked up in surprise.

"Well, I'll be," Ethan said, a smile spreading across his face. "Guess she's getting right to it."

Jonah made no comment, but his jaw tightened as the sound continued, clear and insistent, echoing through the town. Four years he'd lived in Clear Springs, and the church bell had fallen silent not long after his arrival. He'd grown accustomed to its absence, just as he'd grown accustomed to the absence of many things.

The bell fell silent after a minute. Jonah returned to his work with renewed intensity, as if trying to drive out the lingering echo with the sound of his hammer.

"Mr. Brooks?" Ethan asked again, his voice hesitant.

"What now?"

"When's the last time you went to church?"

The question hung in the smoky air between them. Jonah's hand tightened around the hammer handle until his knuckles whitened.

"Mind the bellows, boy," he said gruffly.

***

By midday, the smithy had grown uncomfortably hot. His shirt clung to his back, dark with sweat.

"Go get us some water," he told Ethan. "And see what Mrs. Tuttle has for lunch at the café."

The boy nodded eagerly and darted out, clearly pleased to be trusted with the errand.

Alone, Jonah set down his tools and rolled his shoulders, feeling the familiar ache that came from hours of repetitive motion. He moved to the small basin in the corner, splashing water on his face and on the back of his neck.

As he straightened, his gaze fell on a small wooden chest tucked beneath his workbench. He rarely allowed himself to look at it, though he was always aware of its presence. Like a splinter under the skin, painful but too deeply embedded to remove.

Jonah knelt and pulled out the chest. His fingers hovered over the simple iron latch for a moment before decisively flipping it open.

Inside lay the carefully preserved remnants of a life from long ago: a faded daguerreotype of a young woman with gentle eyes and a serious expression; a folded Confederate uniform jacket with sergeant's stripes, now bearing the musty scent of disuse; a small Bible with a cracked leather cover; a stack of letters tied with fraying ribbon; and a silver pocket watch that had stopped at 2:17 on an August afternoon nine years ago.

Jonah lifted the watch. He made no attempt to wind it. Let it remain frozen, like everything else from that time.

"Emily," he said, the name foreign on his lips after so long unspoken.

The daguerreotype stared back at him. Emily Brooks, his wife. Dead.

The church bell tolled again suddenly, startling him. His hands jerked, and the watch and daguerreotype slipped from his fingers, clattering against the wooden floor.

Jonah snatched them up, checking them for damage before returning them to the chest. He closed the lid firmly, shoving the box back under the workbench with more force than necessary.

He'd just stood up when Sheriff Holden stepped into the shop through the wide open doorway.

"Brooks," he nodded in greeting. "Got those shoes ready?"

Jonah gestured toward the finished horseshoes without speaking. The sheriff examined them, nodding in approval.

"Fine work, as always." He handed over the payment, which Jonah pocketed without counting. "Heard our new arrival got the church bell working."

"So it seems."

"Quite a feat, considering the state of that building," Holden said, clearly in no hurry to leave. "Stopped by this morning to check on her. Found her hard at work. Determined young woman."

Jonah grunted noncommittally as he returned to the plow blade he had been working on, making it clear he had no interest in town gossip.

The sheriff, however, seemed unusually talkative. "Deputy Mansfield just helped me load her trunk and belongings into the wagon. He's taking her things to the parsonage house. That place hasn't been lived in for months now? Not since that last circuit preacher moved on."

"Something like that." Jonah positioned the blade on the anvil.

"She asked about you, you know."

The hammer paused mid-swing. "What?"

Holden's expression remained neutral, but something like amusement flickered in his eyes. "Miss Whitaker. Asked who the blacksmith was. Seems she noticed your shop when she arrived yesterday."

"She need something fixed?" Jonah brought the hammer down harder than necessary.

"Didn't say. Just curious, I expect. Being new to town and all."

"Well, when she needs something fixed, she knows where to find me." Jonah struck the metal again, the sound effectively ending the conversation.

The sheriff took the hint. "I'll send Deputy Mansfield for the shoes later." He touched the brim of his hat and departed, leaving Jonah alone with the reverberating echo of metal on metal.

He worked with increased intensity, as if trying to drive away thoughts with physical exertion. The eastern woman, this Miss Whitaker, was nothing to him. Just another idealistic do-gooder who would discover soon enough that Clear Springs wasn't the sort of place that welcomed change or salvation.

The silver mines ground men down in this town until there was nothing left but exhaustion and despair. The saloon provided temporary oblivion. The church...well, the church had stood empty for good reason.

She'd learn. They all did eventually.

***

"Saw the missionary lady over at the church on my way over," Ed Thatcher said as Jonah worked on his broken pickaxe handle that needed a new fitting. "Got herself covered in dust and cobwebs, but she was smiling like she'd found gold instead of mouse droppings and rotted floorboards."

Jonah made no reply, focusing on securing the new fitting.

"Clair says we ought to help her," Thatcher continued. "Says it's not right, a young woman like that taking on such a task alone."

"Your wife's got a soft heart," Jonah said, testing the strength of the repair.

"That she does." Ed smiled briefly. "She's making a pie to take over later. Says it's the Christian thing to do."

Jonah handed over the repaired pickaxe. "That'll hold."

Ed tested the weight and balance, nodding in satisfaction. "Much obliged. What do I owe you?"

"Dollar fifty."

As Ed paid, he hesitated before asking, "You planning to stop by? The church, I mean."

"Got work to do."

"Sure, sure." Ed tucked the pickaxe under his arm. "Just thought, with your skills, you might—"

"I fix metal, Thatcher. Not churches." Jonah turned away, making it clear the conversation was over.

After Ed left, Jonah stood in the wide open doorway of his smithy, looking down the length of Main Street toward the small white church at the far end. From this distance, he could make out a figure moving around the building, occasionally disappearing inside, then emerging again, as if taking stock of what needed to be done.

He watched, telling himself he was merely taking a needed break from the heat of the forge. The figure, Miss Whitaker, presumably, moved with purpose despite what must have been overwhelming odds. The church had been neglected for some time.

"A fool's errand if I've ever seen one," he thought to himself.

The slam of the general store's door brought Jonah's attention back to his immediate surroundings. Silas McGrant emerged onto the boardwalk, his expensive suit and gold watch chain marking him immediately as different from the rest of Clear Springs' citizens. The mine owner paused on the steps, his gaze following Jonah's toward the church. A frown creased McGrant's face before he turned and strode purposefully in that direction.

Something cold settled in Jonah's stomach. McGrant rarely involved himself directly in town matters unless they affected his business interests. His sudden interest in the church—or, more likely, its new occupant—couldn't bode well.

Before Jonah could consider why he should care, Ethan returned, balancing a bucket of fresh water and a cloth-wrapped bundle that smelled enticingly of Anne Tuttle's meat pies.

"Sorry it took so long, Mr. Brooks," the boy apologized. "Everyone at the café was talking about Miss Whitaker and the church. Mrs. Tuttle sent an extra pie and said to tell you its payment for fixing her kitchen stove last month."

"Set it down there." Jonah nodded toward his workbench, deliberately turning his back on the view of the church and McGrant's figure.

Ethan laid out their lunch, chattering about town gossip as Jonah ate in silence. The pie was good. Anne Tuttle had a way with a crust that few could match, but it sat uneasily in his stomach.

"...and Doc Carpenter says he's going to donate some supplies for the parsonage house, seeing as how it's been sitting empty so long," Ethan was saying. "Mrs. Hale's organizing a group of ladies to help with the cleaning tomorrow after... Mr. Brooks? Are you listening?"

"No," Jonah replied honestly, tossing his napkin aside and standing. "Break's over. We've got Widow Johnson's plow to finish before sundown."

As they returned to work, Jonah found himself listening for the church bell, though it remained silent throughout the rest of the afternoon. Twice he caught himself glancing toward the door, as if expecting someone to enter, though who he might be expecting, he couldn't have said.

The day wore on, customers came and went, and gradually the unusual restlessness that had plagued him since morning began to fade, replaced by the familiar rhythm of work and the comfortable certainty of his solitude.

By the time dusk approached, Jonah had nearly convinced himself that the disturbance in his routine was temporary.

"That should do it for today," he told Ethan as they finished the last repair. "You did good work. Here." He pressed two coins into the boy's palm, more than he usually paid for a day's assistance.

Ethan's eyes widened. "Thank you, Mr. Brooks! Can I come again tomorrow?"

Jonah considered declining, but found himself nodding instead. "Be here at nine. Not before. And only if your chores at home are completed to your dad's liking."

The boy's face lit up. "Yes, sir! I'll be here." He grabbed his hat and coat, then paused at the door. "Mr. Brooks? You really think Miss Whitaker won't make a difference here?"

The question caught Jonah off guard. He frowned, considering his answer carefully.

"I think," he said finally, "that some things can't be fixed, no matter how much faith or determination you bring to them."

Ethan's expression fell slightly. "My ma says nothing's beyond God's power to restore."

"Your ma's entitled to her opinion." Jonah began cleaning his tools, signaling the end of the conversation.

# Chapter 5

Abigail wiped her dusty hands on her apron, surveying the disaster that was the church interior. Hours of cleaning had revealed problems far worse than she'd initially feared. Broken or weakened floorboards created treacherous issues in the church. Rat nests occupied several spaces. Water stains mapped the ceiling like strange continents on a faded atlas. And the hinges on nearly every door hung loose or broken entirely.

She'd made progress with the help of Ruth and Libby. Some of the dirt and debris inside the church conquered, and the pews were cleaned, but the structural repairs loomed impossibly large. Abigail tugged at the sagging front door, which hung precariously from a single functioning hinge.

"This simply won't do," she murmured, testing the wobbly door frame. Her limited carpentry skills would never be enough.

Abigail glanced at the setting sun. If she hurried, she might catch the blacksmith before he closed his shop for the day. Untying her apron, she hung it on a nail and brushed at her skirts, dislodging a small cloud of dust. Her appearance was hardly presentable. Her once-neat bun now had rebellious tendrils escaping in every direction, and her serviceable calico dress bore evidence of her day's labor.

Squaring her shoulders, Abigail made her way down main street, which was livelier than she expected for the evening hour. Miners fresh from their shifts filled the boardwalks, many heading toward the saloon. Some nodded politely as she passed; others averted their eyes when they noticed her looking their way.

The distinct rhythmic clanging grew louder as she approached the smithy near the center of town. The wide doorway stood open, revealing the silhouette of a large man moving within the dimly lit interior. Sparks erupted with each strike of his hammer against metal, briefly illuminating his features in orange flashes.

Abigail hesitated at the threshold, suddenly uncertain. The smithy's heat pressed against her face even from several feet away. The smell of hot metal, coal, and sweat hung heavy in the air. This was a man's domain in every sense, utterly foreign to her Boston upbringing.

Taking a steadying breath, she stepped inside the doorway. "Excuse me? Mr. Brooks?"

The hammering continued. Whether because he hadn't heard her or was choosing to ignore her, she couldn't tell.

Abigail cleared her throat and tried again, louder. "Mr. Brooks? Might I have a moment of your time?"

The hammering stopped abruptly. The blacksmith straightened to his full height, which was considerable. In the fading daylight, supplemented by the forge's glow, Abigail could now see him clearly for the first time.

He was taller than she'd realized, with shoulders broad enough to fill a typical doorway. His cotton shirt, darkened with sweat, clung to his muscular frame. Dark hair fell across his forehead. But what struck her most were his eyes, a startling gray-blue that regarded her with unmistakable wariness. A jagged scar ran along his jawline, disappearing beneath his collar.

"Shop's closing," he said, his voice deep and rough, like gravel underfoot.

Abigail lifted her chin. "I apologize for the late hour, but I have a need for your services."

He set the hammer down and wiped his hands on a nearby rag. "What services would those be, Miss...?"

"Whitaker. Abigail Whitaker." She stepped further into the smithy, fighting the urge to retreat from the oppressive heat. "I'm restoring the church, and I require several pairs of hinges, as well as other hardware for repairs."

Recognition flickered in his eyes. "The missionary's daughter."

"Yes." She met his gaze steadily. "My parents funded the church's construction years ago and helped build it. I've come to continue their work."

He assessed her with a slow, deliberate gaze that took in her dust-covered dress, disheveled hair, and the small scratches on her hands from the day's labor. Something that might have been amusement crossed his features.

"Continuing their work," he repeated, his tone making it clear what he thought of such an endeavor. "And how long do you plan to stay in Clear Springs, Miss Whitaker? A week? Perhaps two before heading back East?"

Heat that had nothing to do with the forge rose in Abigail's cheeks. "I'm not here temporarily, Mr. Brooks. I intend to reestablish the church as a permanent fixture in this community and live here."

He actually smiled at that, though there was no warmth in it. "Clear Springs has a way of crushing good intentions, Miss Whitaker.

Particularly, those brought by eastern ladies who've never known real hardship."

The dismissive assessment stung, but Abigail kept her composure. "You seem very certain about my character and capabilities despite our brief acquaintance."

"I've seen your kind before." He turned back to his workbench, clearly considering the conversation had finished. "Circuit preachers, missionaries, do-gooders. They come with grand visions and leave once they realize the West isn't something they can tame with pretty words and Sunday sermons."

Abigail remained where she stood, refusing to be dismissed. "I need six door hinges, Mr. Brooks. Along with nails, brackets for shelving, and, if possible, tools for basic carpentry. I'm prepared to pay a fair price."

He glanced back at her, a flicker of surprise crossing his face before his expression hardened again. "Can't help you today. Come back tomorrow."

"The front door of the church is hanging by a single hinge. I can't secure the building properly."

"Not my problem."

"Is there truly no possibility of assistance today?"

Brooks turned fully to face her, crossing his arms over his chest. "Why this rush? The church has been falling apart for a while now. Another day won't make a difference."

"It matters to me," Abigail said simply.

Something in her tone made him pause, studying her with narrowed eyes. The silence stretched between them, broken only by the occasional pop from the cooling forge.

"You met Silas McGrant yet?" he asked abruptly.

"Briefly. He stopped by the church this afternoon."

"And?"

"And... he's an interesting fellow."

Brooks let out a short, humorless laugh. "I'll bet he was. Did he mention he owns most of this town, including the land your church sits on?"

"He implied his... influence," Abigail acknowledged carefully. "The church itself and the parsonage were paid for by my parents. He does not own those."

"Make no mistake, Miss Whitaker. If Silas McGrant doesn't want a church in Clear Springs, there won't be one, no matter how many hinges I make for you."

"Are you attempting to discourage me, Mr. Brooks?" She met his gaze directly.

"I'm telling you how things are. This isn't Boston. There are no society rules here, no gentlemen looking out for a lady's interests. There's just survival and avoiding McGrant at all costs."

"And where do you fit into this community? Are you also under Mr. McGrant's thumb?"

His expression darkened dangerously. "I work for whoever pays me. I don't take sides."

"A convenient position."

"A practical one." He turned away again, placing tools methodically on their hooks. "Come back tomorrow if you still need those hinges."

Abigail stood her ground, though everything in her wanted to retreat from this intimidating man and his dismissive attitude. Her father had often told her that sometimes God's work required persistence in the face of rejection. This, she decided, was one of those times.

"Mr. Brooks," she began again, her voice softer, but no less determined. "I understand you have no reason to help me. I'm a stranger to you and to Clear Springs. But that church represents more than just a building to me. It was my parents' legacy. Their belief was that even in difficult places, people need spiritual comfort and community. The church meant something to them, and it means something to me."

He continued organizing his tools, his broad back to her, giving no indication he was listening.

"My father always said that true faith manifests in action," she continued. "I'm not here to preach empty words. I'm here to rebuild something tangible that can serve this community. The church and this town were very important to my parents. They intended to come here to repair the church and help rebuild this community, but they passed before being able to do so. I promised myself and God I would see to this church and the people here."

His movements slowed, though he didn't turn around.

"All I'm asking is for a few hinges and, possibly, your professional assistance with repairs. I'll pay whatever is fair." She took a deep breath. "If you truly believe my efforts are doomed to fail, what harm is there in taking my money before I learn that lesson?"

At this, Brooks turned, a strange expression on his face, something between irritation and reluctant respect. For a long moment, he simply looked at her, as if seeing her properly for the first time.

"You're either remarkably brave or remarkably foolish," he said finally.

"Perhaps a bit of both," Abigail admitted, offering a small smile.

He shook his head slightly, then moved to a workbench along the wall. "I've got some spare hinges. Not enough for all your doors, but enough for the front, at least."

Relief flooded through her. "Thank you, Mr. Brooks."

"Don't thank me. This is business, nothing more." He rummaged through a wooden box and extracted two iron hinges. "I'll need to see the church to determine what else you need."

"Of course. Could you come now or would tomorrow be convenient?"

He looked at her sharply. "I'm done for the day."

"Tomorrow then."

Brooks seemed to weigh his options, clearly unhappy with all of them. "Fine. I'll come by tomorrow." He gestured to the hinges he'd selected. "And we'll determine what else you need."

"Thank you." Abigail reached for her reticule. "How much do I owe you for today?"

He named a sum that seemed reasonable, and she counted out the coins carefully. As she handed over the payment, their fingers briefly touched. A strange, small shock ran through her at the contact—his calloused hand against her much smaller one.

Brooks seemed to feel it too, for he withdrew his hand quickly, pocketing the money with undue focus.

"Will there be anything else, Miss Whitaker?" His tone had returned to its original gruffness.

"No, thank you. I appreciate your assistance, despite your reservations."

"Don't make more of this than it is," he warned. "I'm a blacksmith. You need metal work. That's the beginning and end of our interaction."

"Of course," she replied smoothly, though something in his insistence struck her as defensive. "I'll see you tomorrow, Mr. Brooks."

As she turned to leave, she hesitated, then looked back at him. "May I ask you something?"

His expression suggested he'd rather she didn't, but he gave a curt nod.

"Why are you so certain nothing can change in Clear Springs? You speak as if it's a foregone conclusion."

The question seemed to catch him off guard. For a brief moment, something vulnerable flickered across his features before being quickly masked.

"Because I've been here long enough to see how things work," he said. "This town takes more than it gives, Miss Whitaker. The silver mine takes men's health and sometimes their lives. The saloon takes what's left of their dignity. And Silas McGrant takes everything else."

"And yet, you stay."

His jaw tightened. "We all have our reasons."

"Yes," she agreed. "We do."

Their eyes met across the shop's dim interior, and Abigail had the distinct sensation of standing at the edge of something significant.

"Good evening, Mr. Brooks," she said at last, breaking the tension.

"Miss Whitaker." He nodded once, then turned back to his forge, effectively dismissing her.

Abigail stepped back onto the boardwalk, the hinges clutched carefully against her chest. The exchange had left her feeling strangely unsettled. Jonah Brooks was unlike any man she'd encountered in Boston—raw, unapologetically blunt, carrying himself like he wore armor.

Yet beneath his gruff exterior, she'd glimpsed something else. Not kindness, exactly, but perhaps a begrudging fairness. He hadn't sent her away empty-handed, despite his clear skepticism about her mission. That, she decided, was something to build upon.

As she made her way back toward the church, she considered the challenge ahead. Jonah Brooks might believe Clear Springs was beyond redemption, but Abigail had been raised to see possibility where others saw only defeat. God's grace worked most powerfully in the most unlikely places. Her father had taught her that.

And if God could find His way into a mining town ruled by Silas McGrant, perhaps He could also find His way into the hardened heart of a certain blacksmith.

*Chapter 6*

The first pale light of dawn streaked across the eastern horizon as Abigail jerked awake, momentarily disoriented by the unfamiliar surroundings. The narrow bed creaked beneath her as she sat up, blinking sleep from her eyes. Rough wooden walls replaced the floral wallpaper of her Boston bedroom. A patchwork quilt, borrowed from Margaret's boardinghouse, covered her instead of the fine linens she'd grown up with.

The parsonage. Clear Springs. Her new home.

She had moved her belongings into the small house beside the church yesterday with Deputy Mansfield's help, though she'd barely had time to unpack essentials before exhaustion claimed her. Now, as consciousness fully returned, she became aware of the mustiness that permeated the small bedroom, evidence of months without habitation.

A clattering sound from outside drew her to the window. Pulling aside the threadbare curtain, Abigail peered out at the town coming to life in the early morning light. Men trudged in small groups toward the northern edge of town, their shoulders already slumped, despite the day having barely begun. The miners, heading for their daily shift at McGrant's silver mine.

One miner knelt briefly to hug a small boy who had run out to him, tousling the child's hair before continuing on his way. The child stood watching until his father disappeared from view.

"Lord, be with those men today," Abigail whispered, her breath fogging the cool glass. "Keep them safe in their dangerous work."

She dressed quickly in a practical brown skirt and cream-colored shirt waist, knowing today would bring more physical labor. Her hands already showed signs of hard work, reddened palms and a small blister forming at the base of her right thumb. She smiled ruefully as she pinned her hair into a simple knot at the nape of her neck.

The parsonage kitchen proved disappointingly bare when she ventured into it. A cast-iron stove stood cold against one wall, and a small table with two mismatched chairs occupied the center of the room. The pump at the sink produced a rusty stream after several attempts and then finally ran clear, splashing against the stained porcelain basin.

"First order of business—provisions," she murmured, making a mental list. She would need to visit the general store soon.

After a breakfast of bread and preserves from the small basket Margaret had insisted she take when leaving the boardinghouse, Abigail made her way to the church. The morning air held a crispness that invigorated her spirits despite the daunting tasks ahead.

The front door of the church hung slightly askew. Last night, she had to slam it just to get it to close properly. Her attempt to replace the broken hinge had been less successful than she'd hoped, leaving the heavy wooden door tilting at an awkward angle. The second hinge still lay inside the doorway, right where she'd left it, alongside the borrowed tools from Reverend Blake.

"Well, it's not getting fixed by staring at it," she told herself firmly.

For the next half hour, Abigail struggled with the recalcitrant door. The hinge refused to align properly, and the door's weight made it nearly impossible to hold in place while attempting to secure the metal plate.

"Of all the stubborn, difficult—" She bit back the rest of her frustrated exclamation as the hammer slipped, narrowly missing hitting her foot. Stepping back, she wiped perspiration from her forehead with her sleeve and assessed the situation.

"Perhaps there's a technique I'm missing," she mused aloud, studying the door.

"Several, actually."

The deep voice startled her so badly she nearly dropped the hammer again. Spinning around, Abigail found Jonah Brooks standing at the bottom of the church steps, arms crossed over his broad chest, watching her with an expression hovering between amusement and exasperation.

"Mr. Brooks! I didn't hear you approach."

"Evidently." His gaze moved from her flushed face to the hinge on the door. "Having some trouble?"

Heat crept up Abigail's neck. "Just a slight difficulty with alignment."

One dark eyebrow arched skeptically. "Is that what you call it?"

Before she could formulate a suitably dignified response, Brooks climbed the steps and examined her handiwork more closely. His proximity made her acutely aware of her disheveled appearance—hair already escaping its pins, sleeves rolled up past her elbows, and a smudge of dirt decorating her cheek.

"You've got the hinge upside down," he said after a moment, his tone matter-of-fact rather than mocking. "And these screws are too short for a door this weight."

"Oh." Abigail fought the urge to defend herself. "I see."

Brooks sighed, setting down a leather tool bag she hadn't noticed before. "Step aside."

"I beg your pardon?"

"Unless you want this door falling on someone's head the first time a strong wind blows, you'd better let me fix it." He removed his jacket and hung it on the porch railing, revealing a simple cotton shirt that stretched across his shoulders as he moved.

Abigail hesitated, torn between pride and practicality. "I did mention I would pay you for repairs."

"So you did." He rolled up his sleeves, exposing forearms corded with muscle and marked with small scars. "Consider this the assessment phase."

She stepped back, relinquishing the hammer. "Thank you."

Brooks grunted in acknowledgment, already focused on removing her failed hinge installation. With efficiency born of experience, he detached the door completely and laid it flat across the porch.

"These hinges are decent, but not right for this door," he commented, examining the hardware she'd purchased. "Too light."

"You didn't mention that yesterday," Abigail pointed out.

He rummaged in his tool bag and produced several larger, sturdier hinges. "These will hold better."

As he worked, Abigail observed the transformation in his demeanor. The wariness that had marked their previous interaction gave way to focused concentration. His hands, large and calloused, moved with surprising delicacy as he positioned the new hinges and drove screws with precise, powerful strokes.

"Were you a carpenter before becoming a blacksmith?" she asked, genuinely curious.

Brooks didn't look up from his work. "No."

When no further explanation seemed forthcoming, Abigail tried again. "You seem quite skilled at woodworking for someone who primarily works with metal."

A moment passed before he responded. "Man living alone in the West needs to know how to fix things." Another pause. "Or they break and stay broken."

There was something in his tone that suggested he meant more than just physical repairs, but Abigail knew better than to press. Instead, she watched in appreciative silence as he completed the hinge installation, then lifted the door with ease and aligned it perfectly with the frame.

"There." He tested the door, swinging it open and closed several times. "That'll hold."

"It's perfect," Abigail said honestly. "Thank you, Mr. Brooks."

He grunted, wiping his hands on a rag from his pocket. "Door's just the beginning of what needs fixing here."

"Yes, I'm discovering that." She gestured toward the church interior. "Would you... would you mind taking a look inside? To assess what else requires immediate attention?"

Brooks hesitated, and for a moment, Abigail thought he might refuse. Reluctance flickered across his features and, perhaps, a deep discomfort.

"Just an assessment," she added quickly. "I understand you have your own work to return to."

After a moment's consideration, he nodded curtly and followed her into the church.

Inside, morning light streamed through the damaged windows, illuminating dust motes dancing in the air despite yesterday's cleaning efforts. Brooks paused just inside the doorway, his gaze sweeping the sanctuary with a critical eye.

"The roof's leaking in at least three places," he noted, pointing to water stains on the ceiling. "Floor's got dry rot in several places. Pulpit's unstable. Window frames have warped." His eyes landed on the broken stained-glass window behind the altar. "And that's beyond my skills to fix."

Abigail's heart sank at the comprehensive list of problems, but she kept her expression determined. "What would you recommend addressing first?"

"Roof," he said without hesitation. "No point fixing anything else if rain keeps getting in."

"Can it be repaired, or does it need replacing entirely?"

Brooks moved further into the sanctuary, his boots echoing on the wooden floor. He studied the ceiling carefully. "Might be able to patch it if the damage isn't too extensive."

"And the floor?"

"Affected boards need replacing. Not difficult, but time-consuming."

Abigail nodded, making a mental note. "The pulpit?"

Instead of answering, Brooks crossed to the tilted pulpit and examined its base. With a sudden, powerful shove, he pushed it back into position. The wooden structure groaned in protest, but remained upright.

"Just knocked askew," he explained. "Needs to be secured to the floor properly."

As he continued his inspection, moving methodically around the sanctuary, Abigail studied him. There was something compelling about Jonah Brooks—not just his imposing physical presence, but the intensity with which he approached every task. Despite his obvious reluctance to be involved, he gave the church his full attention, missing nothing.

"The pews?" she asked when he paused to examine one with a broken back.

"Fixable." He ran a hand along the splintered wood. "Need glue, clamps, and patience."

"All of which I have," Abigail assured him.

Brooks glanced at her, skepticism in his gray-blue eyes. "You've done furniture repair before, Miss Whitaker?"

"No," she admitted. "But I'm a quick learner."

"Hmm." The sound conveyed volumes of doubt.

"Mr. Brooks," Abigail began carefully, "I realize this is presumptuous, but... would you consider undertaking some of these repairs? I would compensate you fairly, of course."

He straightened, wariness returning to his expression. "I told you yesterday—I'm a blacksmith, not a carpenter."

"Yet you clearly possess the skills needed," she countered. "And from what I've gathered, there isn't a dedicated carpenter in Clear Springs."

"Timothy Wells does carpentry."

"When he's not running the livery stable, yes, I've been told. But..." She gestured around the sanctuary.

Brooks shook his head. "I've got my own business to run. Can't be spending days fixing up a church that half the town doesn't even remember exists."

The blunt assessment stung, but Abigail refused to be deterred. "What if we started with just the most critical repairs? The roof, perhaps, and securing the pulpit? Mr. Wells might handle the floor later."

He studied her for a long moment, his expression unreadable. "Why is this so important to you?"

The question caught her off guard with its directness. "I told you yesterday—"

"About your parents' legacy, yes," he interrupted. "But there's more to it than that."

Abigail hesitated, considering how much to reveal to this man, who seemed determined to maintain his distance from her and everyone else in Clear Springs.

"My father once told me," she said finally, "that a church isn't just a building. It's a physical manifestation of God's presence in a community. A reminder that we're not alone, even in our darkest moments." She met Brooks's gaze directly. "This town needs that reminder, Mr. Brooks. These people need it."

Something shifted in his eyes, not softening, exactly, but a flicker of... recognition, perhaps. As if her words had touched a memory or a feeling he preferred to keep buried.

"And you think fixing a building will fix what's broken in Clear Springs?" His tone remained skeptical, but lacked its earlier dismissiveness.

"No," Abigail replied honestly. "Buildings are easier to repair than hearts or lives. But sometimes, having a place to gather, to seek comfort and community... it can be the beginning of healing."

Brooks turned away, running a hand through his dark hair in a gesture that seemed unconsciously revealing, like a crack in his carefully maintained composure.

"Two days," he snapped.

"I'm sorry?"

"I can spare two days to fix the roof and secure the worst of the structural problems." He turned back to face her, his expression once again controlled. "After that, you'll need to find someone else."

Joy and relief flooded through Abigail, though she carefully moderated her response, sensing that too much enthusiasm might cause him to reconsider.

"That's very generous, Mr. Brooks. Thank you."

"It's not generosity," he corrected sharply. "It's business. You'll pay my regular rates."

"Of course."

"And don't expect miracles. Two days of work won't transform this place."

"I understand."

Brooks nodded curtly, satisfied with their arrangement. "I'll need to get supplies. Lumber, tar paper for the roof, nails."

"Whatever you need," Abigail agreed. "When can you begin?"

"Tomorrow. I've got commitments at the smithy today." He hesitated, then added, "I'll bring my apprentice, Ethan. The boy needs to learn more than just metalwork."

"That would be wonderful. I'm sure he'll be a great help."

Brooks grunted, already moving toward the door. "Don't go trying to fix anything else until I get back. You're likely to bring the whole roof down on your head."

The comment might have been insulting from anyone else, but Abigail detected a hint of reluctant concern beneath the gruffness.

"I'll focus on cleaning until then," she promised.

At the doorway, Brooks paused, testing his hinge installation one more time. The door swung smoothly on its new hardware.

"Mr. Brooks," Abigail called as he started down the steps. "May I ask why you changed your mind?"

He stopped but didn't turn around immediately. When he finally looked back at her, his expression was guarded.

"Sometimes a broken thing deserves a chance to be fixed," he said quietly. "Even if it seems hopeless."

Before she could respond, he continued down the steps and strode away, his long legs carrying him quickly down the road through town.

Abigail watched him go, a curious sensation settling in her chest. Not quite hope, but perhaps its precursor. The man was an enigma, his gruff exterior at odds with the care he had shown in repairing the church door, the thoroughness of his inspection, and that final, cryptic statement.

"Thank you, Lord," she whispered. "For sending help, even from unexpected quarters."

Returning to the sanctuary, Abigail surveyed the space with renewed determination. Two days of Jonah Brooks' skilled assistance would make an enormous difference, but there remained plenty for her to do in the meantime.

# Chapter 7

Abigail had just retrieved her broom after Jonah left when voices outside caught her attention. Looking through the newly repaired door, she spotted Libby and Ruth approaching, each carrying baskets.

"Good morning!" Libby called cheerfully as they reached the steps. "We've come bearing supplies and willing hands."

"Was that Jonah Brooks we passed on the way here?" Ruth asked, shifting Emma to her other hip as they entered the church.

"Yes," Abigail confirmed. "He came to assess the repairs needed and fixed the front door."

Ruth's eyebrows rose in surprise. "Wonders never cease."

"He committed to two days of work," Abigail clarified. "For the most critical repairs."

"That's more involvement than he's shown in any community project since I've lived here. You must have made quite an impression," Libby said, setting her basket on a pew.

Abigail felt a flush creep into her cheeks. "I simply appealed to his professional expertise."

"Mmm-hmm," Ruth hummed skeptically, a knowing look in her eyes that Abigail chose to ignore.

"What have you brought?" she asked, changing the subject as she peered into Libby's basket.

"Cleaning supplies, rags, lye soap, and beeswax polish for the pews," the schoolteacher replied. "And Margaret sent along some fresh bread and preserves, knowing you likely haven't had an opportunity to stock your kitchen."

"This is all incredibly thoughtful."

Ruth set down her basket. "I've brought a stew for your dinner tonight, and some basic provisions: coffee, sugar, flour, and such. Enough to tide you over until you can get to the general store."

Touched by their kindness, Abigail felt a sudden thickness in her throat. "I don't know what to say. You've all been so welcoming."

"Nonsense," Ruth said briskly, though her eyes softened. "It's just being neighborly."

"Besides," Libby added with a smile, "we're excited about having the church restored. It's been too long since this community had a proper gathering place."

Little Emma squirmed in her mother's arms, reaching toward the sunlight streaming through the broken stained-glass window.

"Pretty," the toddler declared, pointing at the colorful patterns cast on the floor.

"Yes, it is pretty," Abigail agreed, smiling at the child. "And it will be even prettier when it's repaired."

"Speaking of repairs," Ruth said, setting Emma down on a clean section of floor with a small rag doll to keep her occupied, "what's the plan for today?"

Abigail gestured around the sanctuary. "Mr. Brooks advised against attempting any structural repairs until he returns tomorrow, so I thought we'd continue cleaning. The altar needs more attention, and there's a storage room behind the pulpit I haven't even explored fully yet."

"And what about the parsonage?" Libby asked. "Did you get settled in all right?"

"Not really," Abigail admitted. "It was so late by the time I finished up here for the evening, I barely had the energy to make up the bed before collapsing into it. The house needs a thorough cleaning before it will truly be habitable."

Ruth nodded decisively. "Then that's where we should focus today. No sense working on the church if you don't have a proper place to lay your head at night."

"But there's so much to do here," Abigail protested.

"The church has waited this long," Libby pointed out gently. "It can wait one more day while we make your living quarters comfortable."

Looking at their determined faces, Abigail realized resistance would be futile and, truthfully, the prospect of having help with the parsonage was deeply appealing.

"All right," she conceded. "The parsonage, it is. But first, let me show you what Mr. Brooks discovered during his inspection."

She led them around the sanctuary, pointing out the leaking roof, rotted floorboards, and other structural issues that would need addressing.

"He's agreed to fix the roof first," she explained.

"Smart," Ruth commented. "No point fixing the inside if rain's still getting in."

"That's precisely what he said."

Libby ran her hand along a water-stained pew. "It's going to take a lot of work, but I can already imagine how beautiful this place will be when it's restored. The light through that stained-glass window, when it's repaired... it will be magnificent."

"Yes," Abigail agreed, her heart lifting at Libby's vision. "It will be."

After completing their walk through of the church, the three women made their way to the parsonage. The small house sat about a hundred yards beside the church, connected by a well-worn path now overgrown with weeds and wildflowers.

"This was quite nice in its day," Ruth observed as they approached the weathered structure. "Just needs some care."

The parsonage was modest by any standard. A simple one-story building with a small covered porch. Its white paint had faded to a dingy gray, and several shutters hung at odd angles or were missing entirely. But the roof appeared sound, and the foundation showed no obvious signs of settling or damage.

"How long has it been since anyone has lived here? I can't quite remember," Libby said as Abigail unlocked the front door.

"Reverend Blake mentioned the last visiting preacher only stayed here for a short time. Before that, the house stood empty for quite some time, as I understand it." Abigail pushed the door open, revealing the small sitting room beyond.

Ruth wrinkled her nose at the musty odor that greeted them. "First order of business—air this place out."

Together, they moved through the house, opening windows and assessing what needed to be done. The parsonage consisted of four rooms: the sitting room with its faded settee and single armchair; a kitchen with a cast-iron stove, a small table, and a sink with a hand pump; a bedroom barely large enough for the narrow bed and dresser it contained and a small study lined with empty bookshelves.

"It's perfect," Abigail declared, despite the dust covering every surface and the cobwebs festooning the corners. "Just the right size for one person."

"It needs a woman's touch," Libby observed, running her finger through the dust on a windowsill. "But the bones are good."

They set to work with the energy of women accustomed to household labor. Ruth tackled the bedroom, stripping the bedding and replacing it with the fresh linens she had thought to bring with her. Libby attacked the kitchen, scrubbing the sink and stove until they gleamed. Abigail focused on the sitting room, dusting the sparse furniture, washing the walls, and sweeping the wooden floor.

As they worked, conversation flowed easily among them, punctuated by little Emma's occasional commentary as she toddled from room to room, "helping" in her own way.

"How long have you lived in Clear Springs, Ruth?" Abigail asked as they paused for a cup of tea, using supplies from Ruth's basket.

"Going on six years now," the miner's wife replied, settling Emma on her lap. "The mine was just opening then, before McGrant took it over. Times were hard, but there was hope, you know? People looked out for each other."

"And now?" Abigail prompted gently.

Ruth's expression darkened. "Now it's different. McGrant changed things. Made it so the mine's the only way to make a living."

"Surely, there are other opportunities in town," Abigail suggested. "Mr. Brooks seems to have established an independent business."

"Jonah is different," Ruth said. "He arrived with skills the town needed desperately. And he keeps to himself, doesn't challenge McGrant directly."

"Even so," Libby added, "I've seen the way McGrant watches him. Like he's waiting for Jonah to step out of line."

Abigail considered this. "Mr. Brooks mentioned that McGrant owns the land the church, and this house sits on. Is that true?"

The two women exchanged glances.

"Yes and no," Libby answered carefully. "McGrant owns much of the land in and around Clear Springs. The land beneath the church and this home... it's complicated. There was an arrangement with the town before McGrant pushed his influence here. The town owned this land."

"I see." Abigail filed this information away for further consideration. "And now?"

Ruth snorted. "Who's to say who owns this land now? The town council is firmly in McGrant's pocket. Mayor Jenkins does whatever Silas wants, and most of the councilmen work for the mine in some capacity."

"Not all," Libby corrected. "Doc Carpenter maintains his independence, and Sheriff Holden and Deputy Mansfield both try to keep the peace."

"For all the good it does them," Ruth muttered.

Abigail sipped her tea thoughtfully. "Tell me more about Mr. Brooks. How long has he been in Clear Springs?"

"About four years," Ruth replied. "Just appeared one day, set up his smithy, and started working. Barely spoke to anyone beyond what was necessary for business."

"He's a good man," Libby said. "Gruff as a bear with a thorn in its paw, but decent underneath."

"He fixed our stove last winter when we couldn't afford a new one. Wouldn't take payment, though Billy left a brace of rabbits on his doorstep anyway," Ruth added.

"Has he always been so... reserved?" Abigail asked, choosing her words carefully.

Ruth shrugged. "Far as I know. Some say he fought in the war, the Confederate side. Has the look of a man who's seen too much."

"That scar along his jaw," Libby added softly. "Battle wound, they say."

"Does he have family?" Abigail found herself curious about the taciturn blacksmith, despite her better judgment.

"None that anyone knows of," Ruth replied. "Never speaks of his past. Ethan Sheldon's the only person in town he seems to tolerate for any length of time, and that's just because the boy's determined to learn smithing."

Abigail thought of Brooks's cryptic parting words: Sometimes a broken thing deserves a chance to be fixed, even if it seems hopeless. Had he been speaking of the church or something else entirely?

"Enough about Jonah," Ruth declared, setting down her teacup. "We've got work to finish."

They returned to their cleaning with renewed vigor. By mid-afternoon, the parsonage had undergone a remarkable transformation. The floors gleamed from Ruth's vigorous scrubbing. The windows sparkled in the afternoon sunlight. Even the faded furniture looked more inviting after Abigail had beaten the dust from the cushions and applied beeswax polish to the wooden frames.

"This is wonderful," Abigail exclaimed, surveying the sitting room with satisfaction. "I can hardly believe it's the same place."

"Amazing what soap and elbow grease can accomplish," Ruth said with a smile, watching Emma play contentedly with her doll.

"The kitchen still needs organizing," Libby pointed out, "but at least it's clean now. And I've put your provisions away."

"I don't know how to thank you both," Abigail said sincerely. "You've turned this house into a home in just one afternoon."

"That's what neighbors do," Ruth replied matter-of-factly. "Besides, it's nice having another woman in town who isn't afraid to speak her mind, especially to the likes of Jonah Brooks."

Abigail laughed. "I wouldn't say I wasn't afraid. He's rather intimidating."

"But you stood your ground," Libby observed. "And somehow convinced him to help with the church repairs. That's no small feat."

"I simply appealed to his professional pride," Abigail explained modestly. "And perhaps a bit to his better nature."

Ruth snorted. "Jonah keeps that part of himself well hidden. You must have seen something the rest of us missed."

A knock at the front door interrupted their conversation. Libby, being nearest, went to answer it.

"Reverend Blake!" she exclaimed. "Please, come in."

The elderly minister entered, leaning heavily on his cane. His bushy white eyebrows rose in surprise as he took in the transformed sitting room.

"My, my," he said, his voice warm with approval. "What a difference a day makes, and the touch of capable hands."

"Ruth and Libby have been wonderfully helpful," Abigail said, rising to greet him. "Would you like some tea?"

"That would be most welcome." Reverend Blake lowered himself carefully into the armchair Libby offered. "These old bones feel every change in the weather, and there's rain coming."

Abigail busied herself preparing fresh tea while the others chatted. As she worked, she found herself reflecting on the day's events. From Brooks's unexpected assistance to Ruth and Libby's generous help with the parsonage, she had experienced more kindness than resistance in her short time in Clear Springs. Perhaps the town wasn't as hardened as Jonah believed, or as controlled by McGrant as everyone feared.

Returning with the tea tray, she found Reverend Blake regaling the others with stories of Clear Springs's earlier days.

"—and when the first church was built out by the creek, before this one, it was little more than a shack with a cross nailed to the door," he was saying. "But folks gathered there every Sunday, rain or shine. Had to, in those days. Life on the frontier was hard enough without the comfort of faith and community."

"What happened to that first church?" Abigail asked, pouring tea for the elderly minister.

"Burned down during a lightning storm," he replied, accepting the cup with a nod of thanks. "We held services in the schoolhouse for a while thereafter until your parents' generosity made this new church possible."

"And then what changed?" Abigail pressed gently. "Why did attendance dwindle?"

Reverend Blake's eyes grew distant. "Many things, my dear. McGrant's influence grew. The mine expanded, demanding more hours from the men. Sunday work became common. And then..." He hesitated. "There were accidents. Deaths. Some lost their faith in the face of such tragedy."

A somber silence fell over the room. Even little Emma seemed to sense the change in mood, cuddling closer to her mother.

"I understand Mr. Brooks has agreed to help with repairs," Reverend Blake said after a moment, changing the subject. "That's quite unexpected."

"Yes," Abigail confirmed. "He'll begin tomorrow, focusing on the roof and structural issues."

The minister nodded thoughtfully. "Interesting. Jonah has kept his distance from church matters since arriving in Clear Springs. Never attended a service, to my knowledge."

"Do you know why?" Abigail couldn't help asking.

"Some men carry burdens that make faith difficult," Reverend Blake replied carefully. "I've never pressed him. The Lord works in His own time."

The conversation shifted to practical matters of church restoration, with Reverend Blake offering suggestions based on his years of experience. As they talked, Abigail found her thoughts returning to Jonah. What burdens did he carry? What had shaped him into the guarded, solitary man she had encountered?

And why, despite his obvious reluctance, had he agreed to help with the church?

As the afternoon waned toward evening, Ruth gathered Emma and prepared to leave. "Billy will be home from the mine soon, and I need to have supper ready."

"I should go as well," Libby added. "I promised to help Margaret with some mending this evening."

"Will you both return tomorrow?" Abigail asked hopefully. "Mr. Brooks is bringing his apprentice, Ethan, to begin work on the church roof."

"I'll come after my morning chores," Ruth promised. "I'll bring lunch for the workers."

"And I'll join you in the afternoon," Libby said. "School may be out for summer, but I still have some lessons to prepare for when classes resume."

Reverend Blake also rose to leave, moving slowly with the stiffness of age. "I'll stop by to check on progress. And perhaps..." he smiled gently, "to observe how our taciturn blacksmith fares with church repairs."

After they had gone, Abigail stood in the doorway of the parsonage, watching the sun begin its descent toward the western mountains. Clear Springs stretched before her, bathed in a golden evening light that softened its rough edges and weathered buildings.

In just two days, she had begun to see beyond the town's surface, glimpsing both its struggles and its resilience. McGrant's shadow might loom large, but it hadn't extinguished the community's spirit entirely. There was Ruth's practical kindness, Libby's quiet determination, Reverend Blake's enduring faith.

And then there was Jonah Brooks, with his gruff exterior and hidden depths. A man who claimed to believe nothing could change in Clear Springs, yet had agreed to help restore its church.

"Guide my steps, Lord," Abigail prayed softly. "Show me how to rebuild not just this church, but the faith and community it represents."

# Chapter 8

Abigail lingered on the porch of the parsonage, savoring the stillness of the evening. The distant mountains stood purple against the darkening sky, and the first stars had begun to appear above them. She took a deep breath of the cooling air, grateful for the progress of the day and the kindness of her new friends.

Her moment of peace shattered at the sound of raised voices from the direction of the saloon. A man's angry shout cut through the evening quiet, followed by what sounded like something or someone hitting the ground hard.

Abigail stepped off the porch, straining to see through the gathering dusk. The commotion continued, drawing her down the path toward Main Street.

A small crowd had gathered outside the Silver Strike Saloon. At its center stood Silas McGrant, his expensive suit gleaming in the light spilling from the saloon windows. Before him on the ground knelt a miner, his clothes filthy with dust and sweat from a day's labor. Blood trickled from the man's split lip, and he clutched his side as if in pain.

"Please, Mr. McGrant," the miner was saying, his voice strained. "I've got three children at home. I just need another week to pay what I owe."

McGrant adjusted his cuff links with deliberate slowness. "Mr. Dawson, your financial difficulties are of no interest to me. When you borrowed against your wages, the terms were quite clear."

"The cave-in wasn't my fault," Dawson protested. "I lost two weeks of work because of it!"

"Safety protocols exist for a reason," McGrant replied coldly. "If you'd followed them properly, perhaps the accident wouldn't have occurred."

Abigail's breath caught. From the murmurs in the crowd, she gathered this was Gerald Dawson, who'd been injured in a recent mine collapse.

"That section was unsafe," another miner called from the crowd. "We reported it three times!"

McGrant's head snapped toward the speaker, who immediately fell silent and stepped back. "As I was saying, Mr. Dawson," he continued smoothly, "the company store requires payment. Your debt has grown quite substantial."

"I'll work extra shifts," Dawson pleaded.

"That won't be necessary," McGrant smiled thinly. "I've already arranged for your family's eviction from company housing tomorrow morning."

A collective gasp rose from the onlookers. Dawson's face crumpled in despair.

"You can't do that!" he cried. "Where will my children sleep?"

"That, Mr. Dawson, is not my concern." McGrant turned to leave, then paused. "Oh, and consider your employment terminated, effec-

tive immediately. We can't have workers who disregard safety proce-
dures."

The blatant injustice of it all hit Abigail like a physical blow. Before
she could consider the wisdom of her actions, she pushed through the
crowd.

"Mr. McGrant!" Her voice rang out clear and strong in the evening
air.

The crowd parted, faces turning toward her in surprise. Mc-
Grant himself seemed momentarily taken aback before his features
smoothed into practiced pleasantness.

"Miss Whitaker," he acknowledged with a slight bow. "This is
hardly a suitable environment for a lady of your standing."

"And this is hardly suitable treatment for a man who's been injured
in your mine," Abigail countered, stepping forward to stand between
McGrant and the kneeling miner. "Mr. Dawson was hurt through no
fault of his own, from what I understand."

McGrant's eyes narrowed, though his smile remained fixed. "I
wasn't aware you had expertise in mining operations, Miss Whitaker.
Or that you were privy to the details of this situation."

"I don't need mining expertise to recognize injustice," Abigail
replied, helping Dawson to his feet. The man swayed slightly, and
she steadied him with a hand on his arm. "This man needs medical
attention, not eviction."

McGrant studied her for a long moment, his expression shifting from surprise to calculation. "Your concern for my employees
is touching, if misplaced." He addressed the crowd without taking
his eyes from Abigail. "It seems our new spiritual guide believes she
understands business better than those who conduct it."

Several onlookers shuffled uncomfortably. Others watched with
undisguised interest.

"I understand that Christian principles include compassion and fair treatment of those in need," Abigail said firmly. "Punishing a man for an injury sustained in your mine hardly seems fair or compassionate."

McGrant stepped closer, lowering his voice so only Abigail and those nearest could hear. "Miss Whitaker, while I admire your... enthusiasm, I must caution you against involving yourself in matters beyond your comprehension. Clear Springs operates according to certain realities. Your interference, however well-intentioned, may have consequences you haven't considered."

The threat was unmistakable despite his pleasant tone. Abigail felt a flicker of fear but forced herself to stand her ground.

"Are you threatening me, Mr. McGrant?"

He laughed, the sound lacking any genuine mirth. "My dear Miss Whitaker, I'm merely offering friendly advice. You're new here. There are... complexities you don't yet understand."

"I understand right from wrong," Abigail insisted. She turned to Dawson, who was watching the exchange with wide eyes. "Mr. Dawson, have you seen a doctor about your injuries?"

The miner shook his head. "Can't afford it," he mumbled.

McGrant sighed theatrically. "If you're so concerned, perhaps your church fund could cover his medical expenses? Oh, but I forget, your church can barely cover its own repairs." He glanced meaningfully at the church building visible down the street.

Heat rose in Abigail's cheeks, but she kept her voice steady. "The church will be restored, Mr. McGrant. As will a sense of community and justice in Clear Springs." She turned to the crowd. "Would someone please help Mr. Dawson to the doctor's office? Tell the doctor I'll personally ensure his fee is paid."

Two miners stepped forward immediately, supporting Dawson between them.

"Thank you, miss," Dawson said, his voice choked with emotion. "God bless you."

McGrant watched this development with cold calculation. "How touching. Though I wonder where you'll find the resources for such generosity, given the... modest state of your affairs."

"The Lord provides," Abigail replied simply.

"Indeed?" McGrant raised an eyebrow. "Well, we shall see what the Lord provides for the Dawson family." He adjusted his jacket with a precise motion. "As for your church, Miss Whitaker... I admire your determination, truly I do. But Clear Springs has managed quite well without spiritual guidance. Perhaps your energies would be better directed elsewhere."

"The church will reopen," Abigail stated firmly. "And all will be welcome there... even you, Mr. McGrant."

A ripple of surprised murmurs ran through the crowd. McGrant's face hardened momentarily before resuming its mask of civility.

"How generous," he said with a thin smile. "Now, if you'll excuse me, I have business to attend to." He turned to the crowd. "I believe this... entertainment has concluded. Good evening."

As McGrant strode away, the crowd began to disperse, many casting curious or concerned glances at Abigail. She stood her ground until McGrant disappeared into the darkness, ignoring the trembling in her legs that threatened to betray her outward composure.

"That was either very brave or very foolish," a deep voice said behind her.

Abigail turned to find Jonah standing a few feet away, arms crossed over his broad chest. In the dim light from the saloon windows, his expression was unreadable, but his posture radiated tension.

"Perhaps both," she admitted, suddenly aware of how public her confrontation had been.

"McGrant doesn't forget slights," Brooks said, his voice low. "And he certainly doesn't forgive them."

"I couldn't stand by and watch that display of..... oh... that just made me so mad!."

Brooks's jaw tightened. "Noble. Won't help Dawson much when he and his family are homeless tomorrow, though."

The harsh reality of his words hit Abigail like cold water. "Surely, there's something that can be done."

"Like what? You planning to house a family of five in your parsonage?" When she didn't immediately respond, Brooks's eyes narrowed. "You are, aren't you?"

"I hadn't thought that far ahead," Abigail admitted. "But I can't simply abandon them to the streets."

Brooks ran a hand through his dark hair in evident frustration. "This is exactly what I meant about Clear Springs. McGrant owns everything... the mine, the company store, most of the housing. Cross him, and you've nowhere to go."

"Then something needs to change," Abigail insisted.

"And you think you're the one to change it?" There was no mockery in his tone, only weary skepticism.

Before she could answer, Deputy Mansfield approached, his expression concerned. "Miss Whitaker, are you alright?"

"I'm fine, Deputy, thank you." She forced a smile. "Though I fear Mr. Dawson and his family are not."

Mansfield nodded grimly. "I heard what happened. Not much the law can do, I'm afraid. McGrant's within his rights as property owner."

"Legal doesn't always mean right," Abigail said quietly.

"No, ma'am, it doesn't." The deputy glanced between her and Jonah. "You heading back to the parsonage? It's getting dark."

"Yes, I was just—"

"I'll see her there," Jonah interrupted, surprising both Abigail and the deputy.

Mansfield raised an eyebrow, but nodded. "Good evening, then."

As the deputy walked away, Abigail turned to Jonah. "That's not necessary. I can find my way."

"It's dark, and you just made an enemy of the most powerful man in town," he replied bluntly. "Use some common sense."

The rebuke stung, but Abigail recognized the truth in it. "Very well. Thank you."

They walked in silence for several moments, the sounds of the saloon fading behind them. The night had grown cooler, and Abigail wrapped her arms around herself, wishing she'd thought to bring a shawl.

"Here." Jonah shrugged out of his jacket and held it out to her.

"Oh, I couldn't—"

"Just take it," he said gruffly. "Night air gets cold in the mountains, even in summer."

Abigail accepted the jacket, draping it around her shoulders. It was still warm from his body and smelled of smoke, metal, and something indefinably masculine. "Thank you."

They continued walking, the silence between them growing uncomfortable. Abigail searched for something to say that wouldn't provoke his evident irritation.

"I meant to ask," she began carefully, "what supplies will you need for tomorrow's repairs? I should have funds ready to pay for them."

Jonah seemed relieved at the practical topic. "Lumber, tar paper, nails. I've already ordered them from Paulson's store. They'll be delivered in the morning."

"I'll reimburse you, of course."

He grunted in acknowledgment. "Ethan and I will start at first light. Roof first. Then the structural supports inside."

"I appreciate your help," Abigail said sincerely. "Especially after seeing how... complicated the situation in Clear Springs can be."

He cast her a sideways glance. "What you did back there... standing up to McGrant in public... it's going to make things harder. Not just for you, but for anyone who supports you."

"I couldn't remain silent," Abigail said quietly. "Not when faced with such injustice."

"Noble sentiments don't feed hungry children or keep the rain off their heads," Jonah replied, though his tone held more resignation than censure.

They had reached the path leading to the parsonage. Abigail stopped, turning to face him fully in the gathering darkness. "Mr. Brooks, I understand your skepticism. But sometimes standing against injustice is necessary, even when the cost is high."

"And who pays that cost, Miss Whitaker? The Dawson family? The miners who might lose their jobs for supporting you? The town that depends on the mine for survival?" His voice had grown intense, though he kept it low. "There are no simple solutions here."

"I never said it would be simple," Abigail countered. "But doing nothing guarantees nothing will change."

Jonah fell silent, his expression hidden in the shadows. Finally, he spoke, his voice quieter. "You should be careful. McGrant doesn't make idle threats."

"Are you concerned for my welfare, Mr. Brooks?"

He shifted uncomfortably. "I'm concerned about anyone who underestimates Silas McGrant. He's ruined men for less than what you did tonight."

"Then I shall have to be vigilant," Abigail replied, trying to keep her tone light despite the genuine worry his words provoked.

Jonah studied her for a long moment. "I'll keep an eye on things," he said finally. "While I'm working on the church. Make sure there's no... trouble."

The offer surprised her. "That's very kind."

"It's not kindness," he corrected sharply. "It's practicality. I've already committed to the repairs. Can't have McGrant's men interfering with my work."

"Of course." Abigail bit back a smile at his insistence on practical motivations. "Purely a business consideration."

Jonah narrowed his eyes, as if suspecting she was mocking him, but said nothing more on the subject. "Lock your doors tonight," he advised instead. "And stay inside until morning."

"Do you truly think Mr. McGrant would resort to physical intimidation?"

"I think McGrant will do whatever serves his interests," he replied grimly. "And right now, you're standing in the way of those interests."

The seriousness of his tone sent a chill through Abigail that had nothing to do with the night air. "I'll be careful," she promised.

He nodded once, apparently satisfied. "I'll be here at first light. Have coffee ready, if you can manage it."

"I believe I can handle that much," Abigail said, a hint of dry humor creeping into her voice despite the circumstances.

A barely perceptible softening appeared around his eyes. "Good night, Miss Whitaker."

"Good night, Mr. Brooks." She slipped his jacket from her shoulders and handed it back to him. "And thank you for the escort."

He took the jacket and turned without another word, striding back toward town with long, purposeful steps. Abigail watched until his figure disappeared into the darkness before making her way to the parsonage door.

# Chapter 9

The insistent rapping on her front door jolted Abigail from sleep. Disoriented, she blinked at the early morning light filtering through her curtains. The knocking came again, more forcefully this time.

"Miss Whitaker?" a woman's voice called. "Are you awake?"

Abigail scrambled out of bed, hastily pulling a shawl over her nightdress. She moved the chair from in front of her bedroom door and hurried to the front of the house.

"Who is it?" she called, one hand on the door latch.

"Ruth Patterson. I've got news you need to hear."

Abigail opened the door to find Ruth standing on her porch, a sleeping Emma balanced on her hip. The miner's wife looked as if she hadn't slept, dark circles shadowing her eyes.

"Ruth, what's happened? Is everything all right?"

"No, it's not," Ruth replied grimly, stepping inside when Abigail moved back. "Word's all over town about your confrontation with

McGrant last night. The Dawson's were evicted at first light. Mc-Grant's men didn't even wait until a decent hour."

Abigail's hand flew to her mouth. "Already? But he said they had until morning."

"This is morning in McGrant's book," Ruth said bitterly. "They're over at the livery stable now. Timothy Wells is letting them stay temporarily in the hayloft, but it's no place for children."

Guilt and dismay washed over Abigail. "This is my fault. If I hadn't interfered—"

"Don't," Ruth cut her off sharply. "McGrant was going to evict them, anyway. You just gave him an excuse to do it sooner and more cruel." She shifted Emma to her other hip. "The question is, what happens now?"

Abigail's mind raced. "They need shelter, proper shelter. The parsonage—"

"Is barely big enough for you, let alone a family of five," Ruth pointed out. "And putting them here would only confirm in McGrant's mind that you're directly challenging him."

"I can't leave them in a hayloft!"

"No one's suggesting that," Ruth assured her. "But we need a solution that doesn't make things worse."

Abigail paced the small sitting room, thinking furiously. "There must be empty houses or rooms somewhere in town that aren't owned by McGrant."

Ruth's expression brightened slightly. "There might be. Old Man Jenkins—the mayor's father, not the mayor himself—has a cabin on the edge of town. He passed last winter, and the place has stood empty since. It's small and needs work, but it's not on McGrant property."

"Would the mayor allow the Dawson's to use it?"

Ruth hesitated. "Mayor Jenkins isn't as firmly under McGrant's thumb as some. He tries to play both sides. If approached correctly…"

"Then we'll approach him correctly," Abigail decided. "But first, I need to see the Dawsons. Assess their immediate needs."

"There's something else," Ruth said, her expression grave. "Billy heard talk at the mine. McGrant's been asking questions about you… your background, your finances, how long you plan to stay."

A chill ran down Abigail's spine. "Why would he care about such things?"

"Knowledge is power for men like McGrant. He's looking for leverage." Ruth adjusted the sleeping child on her shoulder. "Be careful what you share, even with those who seem friendly."

Abigail nodded slowly, absorbing this warning. "Thank you for telling me. And for coming so early."

"Figured you should know before Jonah and his apprentice arrive. Speaking of which…" Ruth glanced out the window. "They're coming up the road now."

Sure enough, Jonah Brooks and young Ethan Sheldon were approaching, each carrying tools and supplies. Jonah's expression was characteristically stern, while Ethan looked around eagerly, clearly excited about the day's work.

"I need to dress," Abigail said, suddenly acutely aware of her nightclothes. "Would you mind…"

"I'll keep them occupied," Ruth assured her with a knowing smile. "Take your time."

Abigail hurried to her bedroom, her mind whirling with the morning's developments. As she quickly dressed in a practical work dress and pinned up her hair, she tried to formulate a plan. The Dawsons needed immediate help, but Ruth was right. Any solution would have to be carefully considered to avoid making their situation worse.

By the time she emerged, Jonah and Ethan had deposited their tools on the church steps and were speaking with Ruth on the parsonage porch. Jonah looked up as Abigail appeared, his expression unreadable.

"Morning," he said simply. "Lumber's being delivered within the hour."

"Good morning, Mr. Brooks, Ethan." Abigail nodded to each in turn. "Thank you for coming. I... I've just heard about the Dawsons."

Jonah's jaw tightened. "Word travels fast."

"Miss Whitaker," Ethan burst out, unable to contain his excitement despite the somber topic, "everyone's talking about how you stood up to Mr. McGrant! Nobody ever does that, not in public!"

"Ethan," Jonah warned, silencing the boy with a look.

"It's all right," Abigail assured them. "Though I fear my intervention may have made things worse for the Dawsons."

"McGrant was going to evict them regardless," Jonah said, echoing Ruth's earlier assessment. "He just moved up the timeline to make a point."

"And the point is...?"

"That crossing him has consequences," he replied bluntly. "For everyone involved."

Abigail straightened her shoulders, refusing to be intimidated. "Well, I plan to visit the Dawson's this morning, to see what assistance they require."

His frown deepened. "The church repairs—"

"Can proceed without my constant supervision," Abigail finished for him. "I trust your judgment completely, Mr. Brooks."

Something flickered in his eyes. Surprise, perhaps, or discomfort at her expressed trust. "It's your money," he said finally. "Spend it how you like."

"I promised coffee," Abigail remembered suddenly. "Please, come inside the parsonage while I prepare it. We can discuss the day's plan."

Jonah hesitated, then nodded curtly. "Ethan, get the tools organized. I'll bring you a cup when it's ready."

The boy looked disappointed at being excluded, but nodded obediently. "Yes, sir."

Inside the parsonage, Abigail busied herself with the coffeepot, grateful that Ruth had shown her how to operate the unfamiliar stove the previous day. Jonah stood awkwardly in the center of the small kitchen, seeming too large for the space, while Ruth settled at the table, Emma still sleeping against her shoulder.

"You shouldn't go to the livery alone," Jonah said abruptly.

Abigail looked up from measuring coffee grounds. "I beg your pardon?"

"To see the Dawsons," he clarified. "After last night, walking around town alone isn't wise."

"I'll be perfectly fine in broad daylight," Abigail assured him.

He exchanged a glance with Ruth, who nodded slightly as if confirming something. "McGrant doesn't limit his influence to the shadows, Miss Whitaker. His men are everywhere, and they follow his lead."

"Are you suggesting I might be physically harmed?" Abigail couldn't keep the disbelief from her voice. "Surely, even Mr. McGrant wouldn't resort to such tactics against a woman."

"Not direct harm," Ruth interjected softly. "But intimidation takes many forms. Hostile words, blocked paths, accidental collisions. Especially for a woman alone."

Abigail absorbed this, her hands stilling on the coffee pot. "I see."

"I'll accompany you," Jonah said, the words seeming to surprise even himself. "After I get the roof work started."

"That's not necessary," Abigail began, but he cut her off.

"It is." His tone left no room for argument. "I told you last night I'd keep an eye on things. That includes making sure you don't walk into trouble needlessly."

The coffee pot began to boil, saving Abigail from having to respond immediately. She busied herself with pouring the strong, dark liquid into cups, using the moment to gather her thoughts.

"I appreciate your concern," she said finally, handing him a steaming cup. "But I don't want to disrupt your work schedule."

"Ethan can continue working while I'm gone," he replied, accepting the coffee. "Boy needs to learn to work independently, anyway."

Ruth watched this exchange with undisguised interest, a knowing look in her tired eyes. "Seems like a sensible arrangement to me," she offered.

Abigail looked between them, sensing she was being managed, but unable to find a reasonable objection. "Very well," she conceded. "We'll go to the livery after you've started the roof repairs."

Jonah nodded, satisfied, and took a sip of his coffee. His eyebrows rose slightly. "This is good."

"You sound surprised," Abigail noted, unable to keep a hint of amusement from her voice.

"Most easterners can't make decent coffee," he replied with a shrug. "Too weak."

"My father insisted on strong coffee," Abigail explained. "Said it was the only proper way to start a day of the Lord's work."

Something indefinable crossed his face at the mention of the Lord's work, but he merely nodded and continued drinking.

Ruth rose carefully, adjusting Emma without waking her. "I should get back home." She turned to Abigail. "I'll spread word about the

Dawson's situation discreetly. See if we can gather some provisions for them."

"Thank you, Ruth," Abigail said sincerely. "For everything."

After Ruth departed, an awkward silence fell between Abigail and Jonah. He finished his coffee quickly, setting the cup down with a decisive movement.

"I should get to work," he said, moving toward the door. "Ethan will be wondering where I am."

"Of course." Abigail followed him to the porch. "I'll bring coffee for Ethan as well."

Jonah paused at the top of the steps, turning back to face her. The morning sunlight caught in his dark hair and illuminated the sharp angles of his face, softening them slightly. For a moment, he seemed to struggle with something he wanted to say.

"What happened last night," he began, his voice low and serious, "standing up to McGrant like that? It was foolish."

Abigail stiffened, preparing to defend her actions again.

"But," he continued before she could speak, "it was also one of the bravest things I've ever seen from a woman in Clear Springs." He looked away, as if uncomfortable with his own admission. "Just... be more careful going forward. Courage without caution is just another form of recklessness."

With that, he descended the steps and strode toward the church, leaving Abigail staring after him in surprise. Had that been a compliment buried within the criticism? From Jonah Brooks, it certainly seemed so.

Shaking her head slightly, Abigail returned to the kitchen to prepare Ethan's coffee and gather her thoughts. The day ahead promised to be challenging on multiple fronts, helping the Dawsons, navigating McGrant's apparent interest in her background, and now managing the unexpected complexity of her interactions with the taciturn blacksmith.

"One step at a time," she murmured to herself, a phrase her mother had often used when tasks seemed overwhelming. "First, coffee for Ethan. Then we face the rest as it comes."

# Chapter 10

Abigail followed Jonah through the wide doors of the livery stable, blinking as her eyes adjusted to the dimmer interior after the bright morning sunlight. The stable smelled of hay, horses, and leather. Not unpleasant, but certainly not ideal for housing a family.

Timothy Wells, a lean man with weathered features, approached them, wiping his hands on a rag. "Morning, Jonah," he greeted, then turned to Abigail with a respectful nod. "Miss Whitaker. Heard you'd be coming by."

"Mr. Wells, it's a pleasure to meet you. Thank you for providing shelter to the Dawsons," Abigail said warmly. "It was very kind of you."

Wells shrugged uncomfortably. "Couldn't leave 'em on the street. Not with those little ones." He jerked his head toward a ladder leading to the hayloft. "They're up there. Been keeping to themselves mostly."

Jonahs stepped forward. "We'd like to see them, if that's all right."

"Course," Wells agreed readily. "Gerald is a good man. Doesn't deserve what's happened to him." He lowered his voice. "McGrant's men were rough with the eviction. They threw their belongings into the street. Some things broke. The missus was crying, and the children were scared half to death."

Anger flashed through Abigail at this description, but she kept her expression composed. "All the more reason to find them proper accommodations quickly."

Wells nodded approvingly. "The ladder's sturdy, but mind your skirts, miss. I'll keep watch down here, make sure you're not disturbed."

The implication that they might need such protection sent a chill through Abigail, but she thanked him and followed Jonah to the ladder. The blacksmith ascended first, his movements surprisingly agile for a man of his size. At the top, he turned and extended a hand to assist her onto the hayloft floor.

Abigail hesitated only briefly before accepting his help, feeling the strength in his calloused grip as he pulled her up the final steps with ease. For a moment, they stood close enough that she could see the flecks of blue in his gray eyes and the faint stubble darkening his jaw. Then he released her hand and stepped back, clearing his throat.

The hayloft was spacious, but clearly not intended for human habitation. Bales of hay had been arranged to create makeshift walls, providing some semblance of privacy. In the far corner, a woman sat on a blanket spread over the hay, cradling an infant, while two young children played quietly nearby. Gerald stood as they approached, his face showing the bruises from the previous night's confrontation.

"Miss Whitaker," he said, his voice rough with emotion. "I don't know how to thank you for what you tried to do."

"Please, don't thank me," Abigail replied, distressed by the visible evidence of his family's circumstances. "I fear my intervention only hastened your eviction."

"McGrant was going to throw us out anyway," Gerald said, echoing what seemed to be the consensus. "At least someone finally stood up to him." He nodded respectfully to Jonah. "Mr. Brooks."

Jonah returned the nod but remained silent, his posture tense as he surveyed the family's situation.

Mrs. Dawson rose carefully, the infant still in her arms. She was a slight woman with tired eyes and prematurely graying hair, but her gaze held a quiet dignity despite their circumstances.

"Natalie Dawson, ma'am," she introduced herself. "These are our children—Ester, who's just six months old, Byron, who's five, and Lucy, who's eight." The older children looked up briefly before returning to their quiet game with what appeared to be carved wooden animals.

"I'm very pleased to meet you all," Abigail said sincerely. "Though I wish it were under better circumstances."

"We're grateful for any help," Natalie said simply. "Mr. Wells has been kind, but..." She glanced around the hayloft, her meaning clear.

"That's why I'm here," Abigail assured her. "To find a more suitable arrangement for your family."

Hope flickered in Natalie's eyes, though she quickly tempered it. "McGrant owns most of the housing in town," she said. "And no one will risk crossing him by taking us in."

"Not all housing," Abigail replied. "Ruth Patterson mentioned a cabin belonging to Old Man Jenkins that stands empty."

Gerald and Natalie exchanged glances. "The Jenkins place is rough," Gerald said cautiously. "Been abandoned since the old man died. The roof probably leaks, and there are likely critters inside by now."

"But it has walls and a door," Jonah spoke up unexpectedly. "Better than a hayloft for the little ones."

Abigail glanced at him, surprised by his contribution. "Exactly. And any deficiencies can be addressed once you're settled."

"Mayor Jenkins would have to agree," Gerald pointed out. "And he's cautious about crossing McGrant."

"Leave Mayor Jenkins to me," Abigail said with more confidence than she felt. "Meanwhile, what do you need most urgently? Food? Clothing?"

Natalie hesitated, pride warring with necessity. "The children need proper meals," she admitted finally. "We lost most of our supplies in the... eviction. They didn't give us time to grab everything."

"And Gerald needs his injuries tended," Abigail observed, noting how he winced when he shifted position. "Did you see a doctor as I suggested?"

Gerald looked down, embarrassed.

Abigail's heart ached. "Mr. Dawson, please see the doctor today. I'll speak with him personally about payment."

"That's very generous, miss, but—"

"No arguments," Abigail said firmly. "You can't work and support your family if you're injured."

"Dawson, you've done carpentry work before, haven't you?" Jonah asked.

Gerald looked surprised at the question. "Yes, sir. Before the mine opened. Not much call for it once McGrant took over."

Jonah nodded thoughtfully. "Church needs a lot of work beyond what Ethan and I can manage in two days. The floors need sanding in spots, pews need repaired, window frames need attention, the yard needs to be tended to, the church and parsonage need painted... just to name a few things." He glanced at Abigail. "If Miss Whitaker is agreeable, there might be paid work for you there once you're healed up."

Abigail caught his meaning immediately and smiled gratefully. "Of course. We'll need a skilled carpenter. It would be a fair wage for honest labor, Mr. Dawson."

Hope kindled in Gerald's eyes. "I'd be much obliged for the opportunity, miss. I can still work despite the ribs. Done it before."

"Not until the doctor says you're fit," Abigail insisted. "In the meantime, let me speak with Mayor Jenkins about the cabin."

As they prepared to leave, Lucy approached Abigail shyly, holding out one of the wooden animals, a carefully carved horse.

"Papa made this," she said softly. "He makes the best horses."

Abigail knelt at the child's level, admiring the carving. "It's beautiful, Lucy. Your father is very talented."

"He made lots of them before," Byron piped up, joining his sister. "But then the bad man said he couldn't sell them anymore."

Natalie made a small, distressed sound. "Byron, hush now."

"The bad man?" Abigail asked gently.

"Mr. McGrant," Lucy explained with a child's directness. "He said Papa had to work in the mine, not make toys."

Jonah's jaw tightened visibly at this revelation. "We should go," he said to Abigail, his voice controlled but with an undercurrent of anger. "Let the Dawson's rest."

Abigail nodded, rising to her feet. "I'll return soon with news about the cabin," she promised. "And I'll bring food and supplies this afternoon."

Gerald clasped her hand earnestly. "God bless you, Miss Whitaker. The church has been empty for a long time, but the Lord sent you to fill it again."

Touched by his faith despite his circumstances, Abigail squeezed his hand. "I believe He has a purpose for all of us in Clear Springs, Mr. Dawson."

As they descended the ladder, Abigail's mind whirled with plans and concerns. The Dawson's' situation was even more dire than she'd realized, and McGrant's control over the town was more pervasive. Yet, she'd also glimpsed possibilities. Gerald's carpentry skills, the empty Jenkins cabin, and most surprisingly, Jonah's unexpected suggestion of employment.

Outside the livery, he walked beside her in silence for several moments, his expression thoughtful.

"That was a kind offer," Abigail said. "Suggesting work for Mr. Dawson."

Jonah shrugged. "Just practical. The church needs the work, and he needs the income. Simple solution."

"I've noticed your simple solutions often happen to be kind ones as well," Abigail observed with a small smile.

He frowned at her. "Don't go making me into something I'm not, Miss Whitaker."

"And what is that?"

"A good man," he replied bluntly.

Abigail studied him as they walked, noting the tension in his shoulders and the careful way he scanned their surroundings... always alert, always watchful. "I think you might be wrong about that, Mr. Brooks."

A commotion from the direction of the church caught their attention. Ethan was running toward them, his young face flushed with exertion.

"Mr. Brooks!" he called, skidding to a stop before them. "You need to come quick!"

"What's happened?" Jonah demanded, instantly alert.

"Someone's been at the lumber delivery," Ethan explained breathlessly. "Cut the ropes and scattered the boards all over. I just left for a few moments to get a drink from the well behind the cafe... and there's something written on the church door as well."

Abigail's heart sank. "Written? What does it say?"

Ethan glanced between them nervously. "It... it's not fit for a lady's ears, Miss Whitaker."

Jonah's expression darkened dangerously. "McGrant didn't waste any time." He turned to Abigail. "Stay here with the boy. I'll go see."

"No," Abigail said firmly, already moving forward. "This is my church. I'm coming with you."

For a moment, it seemed he might argue, but instead, he fell into step beside her, his stride lengthening to match her hurried pace. "Stay close," he instructed tersely.

As they approached the church, the damage became visible. Lumber lay scattered across the churchyard, some boards broken, others simply thrown about. But what drew Abigail's gaze was the crude message painted across the front door in dripping red paint:

"GOD HAS NO PLACE WHERE SILVER RULES. GO HOME, MISSIONARY WOMAN."

Abigail stopped short, a mixture of shock, anger, and determination washing over her. "Well," she said after a moment, her voice steadier than she felt, "it seems Mr. McGrant has made his position quite clear."

Jonah studied her face carefully. "This doesn't frighten you?"

"Oh, it does," she admitted. "But it also tells me something important."

"What's that?"

Abigail met his gaze directly. "That I'm right to be here. If restoring this church threatens Silas McGrant's control so much that he resorts to vandalism and intimidation, then Clear Springs needs it more than I realized."

"You're either the bravest or the most foolhardy woman I've ever met, Abigail Whitaker."

It was the first time he had used her given name, and the unexpected intimacy of it momentarily distracted her from the vandalism before them. "Perhaps a bit of both," she replied.

Jonah held her gaze for a moment longer, then turned to Ethan. "Get water and rags. We'll clean the door first, then sort the lumber."

"Yes, sir," the boy replied.

"McGrant's men will be watching," he warned Abigail in a low voice. "To see if this scares you off."

Abigail straightened her shoulders. "Then let's give them something to see." She moved purposefully toward the scattered lumber and began gathering the nearest boards. "We have a church to rebuild, Mr. Brooks. Vandalism won't change that."

After a brief hesitation, Jonah joined her, his muscular hands making quick work of the heavier pieces. As they worked side by side in the morning sunlight, Abigail felt a curious sense of rightness despite the circumstances. Threats and intimidation would come, perhaps worse than this, but she would not be deterred.

Clear Springs needed healing, not just its church building, but its people. And somewhere deep inside, she suspected Jonah Brooks might need that healing too, though he'd likely be the last to admit it.

# Chapter 11

Abigail hefted another broken board, wincing as a splinter dug into her palm. She paused only long enough to extract it before continuing her work, refusing to show weakness. Sweat beaded on her forehead despite the morning's mild temperature, her hair escaping its pins as she labored alongside Jonah to restore order to the scattered lumber.

"That's the last of it," Jonah announced, stacking a final board onto the neat pile they'd reconstructed. His shirt clung to his broad shoulders, dampened by exertion. He studied the red paint still visible on the church door despite Ethan's scrubbing efforts. "The door will need repainting. That paint won't come off completely."

"Then I'll repaint it," Abigail said firmly, straightening her back and brushing dirt and debris from her skirts. "A fresh coat will cover the message and brighten the entrance."

Jonah regarded her with that now-familiar mixture of skepticism and reluctant admiration. "McGrant could just have his men vandalize it again."

"And I will clean it again," she replied without hesitation. "However many times necessary."

Ethan approached, his young face troubled as he carried a bucket of now-reddish water. "Miss Whitaker, I'm sorry I didn't see who did this. I was only gone a few minutes to get water."

"It's not your fault, Ethan," Abigail assured him gently. "Whoever did this was watching and just waiting for an opportunity."

"McGrant's men know how to work quickly and disappear." Jonah surveyed the lumber pile with a critical eye. "Some boards are damaged beyond use. We'll need replacements."

Abigail nodded. "I'll speak with Mr. Paulson at the general store. But first, I need to see Mayor Jenkins about the cabin for the Dawsons. And I should visit Doc Carpenter about Gerald's injuries and the bill for his visit."

Jonah frowned, crossing his arms. "That's a lot of ground to cover, and McGrant's men will be watching your every move."

"All the more reason to proceed as planned. I won't hide away in fear."

"I didn't suggest hiding," Jonah said, his tone clipped. "Just caution."

Abigail softened her expression. "I appreciate your concern, Mr. Brooks. Truly. But these matters can't wait." She glanced at the church with its defaced door and then back to him. "Can you and Ethan continue with the roof repairs while I'm gone?"

A muscle worked in Jonah's jaw as he visibly struggled with his response. "I don't like the idea of you walking around town alone after this," he finally said, gesturing toward the vandalism.

"I'll be careful. And I'll stay in public places."

Jonah studied her for a long moment, then abruptly turned to Ethan. "Go and tell Deputy Mansfield what happened here. He should know about the vandalism, even if there's little he can do."

"Yes, sir," Ethan nodded, setting down his bucket and hurrying off toward town.

When the boy was out of earshot, Jonah stepped closer to Abigail, his voice lowering. "McGrant doesn't play fair, Miss Whitaker. This—" he gestured at the vandalism "—is just the beginning. He's testing your resolve."

"Then he'll find it stronger than he anticipated," Abigail replied, though she couldn't entirely suppress a shiver at the warning in Jonah's eyes.

"At least wait until Ethan returns," he insisted. "I'll continue to work on the roof, and I'd feel better knowing you had someone with you in town."

Abigail considered protesting further but recognized the genuine concern beneath his gruff manner. "Very well," she conceded. "I'll prepare a list of what I need from the general store while I wait."

Relief flickered briefly across Jonah's face before his expression returned to its usual stoic mask. "Good. I'll get started on the roof." He hesitated, then added awkwardly, "Be... careful whenever you do go out and about by yourself in the future."

"I will," she promised, touched by his concern despite his attempts to disguise it.

As Jonah gathered his tools and headed toward the rear of the church, Abigail returned to the parsonage to compose her list and gather her thoughts. The morning's events had left her shaken, though she'd done her best not to show it. The crude message on the church door revealed not just McGrant's opposition, but the depth of his concern about her presence in Clear Springs.

*"Lord, give me wisdom and courage,"* she prayed silently as she sat at her small desk. *"Show me how to help these people without bringing more hardship upon them."*

Abigail had composed herself and prepared a detailed list of supplies needed for herself, the church repairs, and the Dawson family by the time Ethan appeared at her door, slightly breathless from his errand.

"Deputy Mansfield says he'll come by to take a formal report," Ethan informed her. "And he said to tell you he'd keep an eye out while you're in town today."

"That's very kind of him," Abigail replied, gathering her reticule and a small parasol. "Did you tell Mr. Brooks you've returned?"

Ethan nodded. "He's up on the roof, pulling off the damaged shingles. Said I should stick with you until you're done in town, then come back to help him." The boy looked pleased with this assignment, though he tried to maintain a serious expression. "I'll make sure nobody bothers you, Miss Whitaker."

Abigail smiled at his earnest declaration. Though Ethan couldn't be more than eighteen, his sturdy build and determined expression made him a reassuring companion. "Thank you, Ethan. I appreciate your escort."

As they walked toward town, Abigail noticed how Ethan positioned himself slightly ahead of her at crossings and carefully scanned each street before they proceeded. The boy was clearly taking his protective duties seriously.

"You've worked with Mr. Brooks for some time?" she asked, partly to ease the tension she felt walking through town after the morning's incident.

"Going on two years now," Ethan replied proudly. "Started when I was sixteen. My pa wanted me to work the mine like most boys do when they're old enough, but Ma worried after the accidents. Mr. Brooks needed help, and I've always been good with my hands."

"He seems like a demanding teacher," Abigail observed.

Ethan grinned. "Oh, he is! He accepts nothing less than your best work. But he's fair, and he knows more about metal than anyone I've ever met. The way he can look at a piece and know exactly how to shape it, how hot the fire needs to be..." The boy's admiration was evident in his voice.

"He's fortunate to have such a dedicated apprentice," Abigail said sincerely.

Ethan shrugged, though he looked pleased. "I'm the fortunate one. Few options for a man in Clear Springs besides the mine."

They reached the mayor's office, a modest building near the center of town. Ethan positioned himself outside the door. "I'll wait here, Miss Whitaker."

"Thank you, Ethan. I shouldn't be long."

Inside, a clerk looked up from his desk with mild surprise. "May I help you, miss?"

"I'd like to speak with Mayor Jenkins, please. It's regarding his family property."

The clerk's eyebrows rose slightly. "Do you have an appointment?"

"No, but the matter is relatively urgent. Please tell him Miss Abigail Whitaker would appreciate a few moments of his time."

The clerk hesitated, then nodded and disappeared through a door behind his desk. When he returned moments later, his manner had shifted to one of deference.

"The mayor will see you now, Miss Whitaker."

Mayor Harold Jenkins was a portly man in his fifties with thinning gray hair and an air of perpetual caution. He rose from behind his desk as Abigail entered, offering a practiced smile.

"Miss Whitaker, what a pleasure. I've been meaning to officially welcome you to Clear Springs." His eyes betrayed a wariness that belied his cordial tone.

"Thank you, Mayor Jenkins. I appreciate you seeing me without an appointment."

"Of course, of course." He gestured to a chair across from his desk. "Please, sit. How may I assist you?"

Abigail settled into the chair, arranging her skirts carefully. "I'll come straight to the point, Mayor. I understand your father's cabin on the edge of town has stood empty since his passing."

Jenkins's smile faltered slightly. "Yes, that's correct. A modest place. I've had little time to address the property with my mayoral duties."

"I'd like to propose a solution that might benefit everyone involved," Abigail continued. "The Dawson family, as you may know, was evicted from their company housing this morning. They need shelter."

The mayor's expression grew guarded. "Ah, yes. Unfortunate situation. I heard there was some... disagreement between Mr. Dawson and Mr. McGrant regarding payment terms."

"The disagreement," Abigail said carefully, "stemmed from Mr. Dawson's injury in a mine accident. An accident that occurred after safety concerns were reportedly ignored. He was unable to work and thus unable to pay."

Jenkins shifted uncomfortably in his chair. "Mining is dangerous work, Miss Whitaker. Accidents happen despite the best precautions."

"Indeed," Abigail agreed, choosing not to press that point for now. "What matters at present is that a family with three young children needs shelter. Your father's cabin, while perhaps not in perfect condition, would provide them with basic protection and dignity."

"I see." Jenkins steepled his fingers, his expression calculating. "And what would the arrangement be? Rental terms? Duration?"

"I would propose a low monthly rent, if any fee at all, for the first few months," Abigail replied. "The Dawson family residing in your father's former home will not cost you a dime nor put you in any jeopardy. During that time, Mr. Dawson could make necessary repairs to the property in exchange for the rent. He's a skilled carpenter from my understanding, currently unable to return to mining due to his injuries."

Interest flickered in the mayor's eyes. "The cabin does need work. Father was... not one for maintenance in his later years."

"Then this arrangement would benefit both parties," Abigail pressed gently. "The property would be improved, and a worthy family would have shelter."

Jenkins leaned back in his chair, studying her. "You realize, Miss Whitaker, that Mr. McGrant might view this as... interference."

"I realize that Mr. McGrant has a significant influence in Clear Springs," Abigail acknowledged. "But surely, he doesn't dictate how you manage your family's private property?"

After a long moment, the mayor sighed. "Three months, with repairs in lieu of rent. I'll want to inspect the improvements regularly."

Relief washed through Abigail, though she kept her expression composed. "That seems entirely reasonable. When might the Dawson's take occupancy?"

"I suppose they could move in today," Jenkins conceded. "I'll have the clerk draw up a simple agreement. I have the key here." He pulled open a drawer and extracted a large iron key. "The cabin is at the eastern edge of town, just past the creek crossing. Small place, one room with a loft. It's... basic."

"I'm sure it will seem like a palace compared to a hayloft where the family is currently staying," Abigail said, accepting the key. "Thank you, Mayor Jenkins. This is truly Christian charity."

Jenkins cleared his throat awkwardly. "Yes, well. I try to look after the town's interests. All of its interests." He rose, signaling the end of their meeting. "I'll have the paperwork ready by tomorrow. Have Gerald stop by to sign it when convenient."

"I will," Abigail promised, standing. "And I believe you'll find this arrangement beneficial for everyone involved."

Outside, Ethan straightened from where he'd been leaning against the building. "How'd it go?"

Abigail held up the key with a smile. "The Dawsons will have a roof over their heads again soon."

"That's wonderful!" Ethan exclaimed, then lowered his voice, glancing around. "Mr. McGrant won't be happy, though."

"Perhaps not," Abigail agreed as they started walking toward Doc Carpenter's office. "But Mayor Jenkins made a decision about his own property. Even Mr. McGrant can't reasonably object to that."

Ethan looked skeptical, but said nothing more as they continued down the street. Abigail noticed several townspeople watching her with undisguised curiosity, some nodding respectfully, while others quickly averted their gaze when she looked their way. Word of her confrontation with McGrant, and likely the morning's vandalism at the church, had clearly spread throughout Clear Springs.

Doc Carpenter's office was a small building near the edge of town, distinguished by a weathered sign proclaiming "Medical Services" hanging above the door. As they approached, the door opened, and a woman emerged with a small child in her arms, nodding gratefully to someone inside.

Abigail and Ethan waited for the woman to descend the steps before approaching. Inside, they found a sparse but meticulously clean waiting area with a few wooden chairs against one wall. A door to an inner room stood open, and a man's voice called out, "Be with you in a moment!"

Dr. Elijah Carpenter appeared moments later, wiping his hands on a clean cloth. He was a man of about fifty, with kind eyes behind wire-rimmed spectacles and a full beard streaked with gray. His shirtsleeves were rolled up, revealing forearms corded with unexpected strength for a medical man.

"Miss Whitaker, I presume?" he said, offering his hand. "I've been hoping to meet you soon."

"It's a pleasure to meet you, Doctor." Abigail replied with a smile, shaking his hand.

"Elijah, please. Or Doc, as most folks call me." His gaze shifted to Ethan. "Young Mr. Sheldon. No injuries from blacksmith work today, I hope?"

"No, sir," Ethan replied. "I'm just escorting Miss Whitaker."

Something in the boy's tone made Doc's expression sharpen. "I see. Well, come in, both of you." He gestured toward the inner room. "What brings you to my humble practice?"

Once they were seated in his office, a room lined with bookshelves and medical equipment, Abigail explained Gerald Dawson's situation and her promise to cover his medical expenses.

Doc listened without interruption, his expression growing increasingly grim. When she finished, he removed his spectacles and pinched the bridge of his nose.

"I've been trying to get Gerald in here for days," he said, frustration evident in his voice. "Those ribs need proper binding, and I'm concerned about possible internal injuries from the mine collapse."

"He mentioned not being able to afford treatment," Abigail said carefully.

Doc snorted. "The man has three young children and a mountain of debt at the company store. Of course, he couldn't afford it." He replaced his spectacles and leaned forward. "Miss Whitaker, I appreciate your offer to cover his expenses, but you should know what you're getting into. McGrant has made it clear he considers Gerald responsible for the accident."

"And what do you think, Doctor?" Abigail asked quietly.

Doc's expression hardened. "I think the northwest shaft of that mine has been dangerous for months. I reported concerns to McGrant twice after treating miners for injuries sustained there. Nothing was done."

Ethan shifted uncomfortably in his chair. "My cousin works in that section. Says the support beams were old, some of them rotting."

"Precisely," Doc agreed grimly. "But McGrant's more concerned with production than safety. When the collapse happened, he needed someone to blame. Gerald was the crew leader that day."

Abigail absorbed this information with growing dismay. "So not only was Mr. Dawson injured in an accident that wasn't his fault, but he's being scapegoated for conditions Mr. McGrant refused to address?"

"Welcome to Clear Springs, Miss Whitaker," Doc said with a humorless smile. "Where silver matters more than men's lives."

"That's unconscionable," Abigail declared, anger rising within her. "Surely, there's some authority that oversees mine safety? Someone beyond Mr. McGrant's influence?"

"The territory mining inspector comes through once a year," Doc replied. "Usually stays at McGrant's house, enjoys his hospitality, signs whatever papers are put in front of him, and leaves."

Abigail's hands were clenched in her lap. "Then changes must come from within Clear Springs itself."

Doc studied her thoughtfully. "You remind me of your parents, you know. Same fire, same determination to stand against injustice." His voice softened. "They were good people. This town was better for their presence, brief though it was."

"You knew them well?" Abigail asked, surprised.

"As well as anyone here did. Your father came to me for supplies and advice. Your mother helped deliver some of the children in this very town." Doc smiled at the memory. "They envisioned a real loving community here in Clear Springs."

Emotion tightened Abigail's throat. "That's what I want too," she admitted. "To continue their work. To help build and strengthen this community."

"Then you've already made one ally," Doc said firmly. "I'll see to Gerald today and don't worry about the cost. We'll work something out that doesn't strain your resources."

"Thank you," Abigail said sincerely. "And if you could give me a list of medical supplies, the Dawsons might need for ongoing care, I'll ensure they have them."

Doc nodded. "I'll put something together." He rose from his chair. "Now, if you'll excuse me, I think I'll head over to the livery and check on my patient immediately."

As they prepared to leave, Doc paused, his expression growing serious. "Miss Whitaker, a word of caution. McGrant doesn't respond well to challenges. What happened at the church this morning... that's his way of testing boundaries."

Abigail's eyes widened. "You know about that already?"

Doc's gaze was sympathetic but grave. "Be careful. McGrant has ways of making life difficult that go beyond simple vandalism."

"I won't be intimidated," Abigail said firmly.

"I didn't expect you would be," Doc replied with a small smile. "Just... watch your back. And maybe consider who your real friends are in this town. Appearances can be deceiving."

With that cryptic warning, he saw them to the door, promising again to visit Gerald Dawson immediately.

Outside, Ethan looked at Abigail with newfound respect. "You really aren't afraid of McGrant, are you?"

"I wouldn't say that," Abigail admitted as they started toward the general store. "I'm certainly aware of the danger he represents. But fear can't be allowed to dictate one's actions when people's well-being is at stake."

Ethan considered this as they walked. "Mr. Brooks says sometimes fear keeps us alive. Makes us cautious when we need to be."

"Mr. Brooks is a wise man," Abigail acknowledged. "There's a difference between healthy caution and paralyzing fear. The former can protect us; the latter prevents us from doing what's right."

# Chapter 12

Abigail and Ethan reached Paulson's General Store, a large establishment that occupied a prominent position on Main Street. The bell above the door jingled cheerfully as they entered, announcing their arrival to the handful of customers inside. Conversations faltered briefly as heads turned toward them, then resumed in hushed tones.

Sid Paulson, a thin man with a shopkeeper's perpetually attentive expression, looked up from where he was measuring fabric for a customer. His eyebrows rose slightly at the sight of Abigail.

"Be with you in just a moment, Miss Whitaker," he called, his tone neutral.

Abigail nodded acknowledgment and began examining the shelves while she waited. Ethan stayed close beside her, his young face serious as he surveyed the other customers with barely disguised suspicion.

When Sid finally approached, his manner was polite but cautious. "What can I help you with today?"

"Several things, Mr. Paulson," Abigail replied, matching his businesslike tone. "First, we need additional lumber to replace some damaged boards from this morning's delivery."

Paulson's expression tightened almost imperceptibly. "Yes, I... heard about that unfortunate incident. I can arrange another delivery this afternoon."

"Thank you." Abigail handed him her list. "We'll also need these items for the church and myself, plus some basic provisions for a family in need."

The shopkeeper scanned the list, his eyebrows rising steadily. "This is... quite extensive, Miss Whitaker."

"Is there a problem fulfilling it?" Abigail asked, her tone pleasant but firm.

Sid hesitated, glancing around the store. The remaining customers were watching the exchange with undisguised interest. "No, no problem," he said finally. "It will take some time to gather everything, however."

"I understand. Perhaps Ethan could help you while I complete one more errand?" Abigail suggested.

Ethan looked alarmed at the prospect of leaving her side. "Mr. Brooks said—"

"I'm just going to speak with Mrs. Tuttle at the café across the street," Abigail assured him. "I'll be perfectly safe there. You can see the door from here."

The boy still looked dubious, but nodded reluctantly. "All right, but please don't go anywhere else without me."

"I promise," Abigail said solemnly, touched by his protective instinct.

Leaving Ethan to assist Sid, Abigail crossed to the café. The establishment was busy with the midday meal crowd, tables filled with miners on their break and townspeople conducting business over coffee and pie.

Anne Tuttle, a plump woman with a perpetually flushed face from working near the stove, spotted Abigail immediately and bustled over, wiping her hands on her apron.

"Miss Whitaker! What a pleasure! It's so nice to finally meet you! Please come sit. You must be famished after all the excitement this morning."

Abigail allowed herself to be led to a small table in the corner, aware of the many eyes following her progress through the room. "Thank you, Mrs. Tuttle, and it's a pleasure to meet you as well. I could use a cup of tea, if you have it."

"Tea, of course. And you must try my shoo fly pie. Best in the territory, if I do say so myself." Mrs. Tuttle leaned closer, lowering her voice. "I want you to know, miss, that not everyone in town agrees with what happened at the church. Some of us are right pleased to see it being restored."

"That's very kind of you to say," Abigail replied, warmed by the woman's support.

"The Dawsons," Mrs. Tuttle continued, straightening a fork on the table. "Terrible business, throwing a family with little ones out like that. My husband, Luther took some breakfast over to them this morning. Not much, mind you, but enough to fill the children's bellies at least."

"That was very generous," Abigail said sincerely. "I've just secured housing for them—Mayor Jenkins's father's cabin. They will be able to move in today."

Mrs. Tuttle's eyes widened. "Well now, that's something! Old Jenkins's place has been sitting empty for some time now. Perfect for them, once it's cleaned up a bit." She glanced around and lowered her voice again. "I'll put together some supper for them. Nothing fancy, but hot and filling. My boy Andy can deliver it once they're settled."

"You're very kind, Mrs. Tuttle. That is precisely why I came, to have food brought to them while they get situated in their new living space. Thank you for your generosity."

The café owner waved away the compliment. "It's just being neighborly. Something this town used to know more about before..." she trailed off, glancing toward the door.

Abigail followed her gaze to see Silas McGrant himself entering the café, accompanied by two men whose hard expressions and watchful eyes marked them as his personal guards rather than business associates. The room quieted noticeably as McGrant surveyed the patrons, his gaze finally landing on Abigail.

He made his way directly to her table, his men hanging back just far enough to give the appearance of privacy while remaining within earshot.

"Miss Whitaker," McGrant greeted her, his voice carrying into the now-silent café. "What a delightful coincidence. I was just thinking about our conversation last night."

Abigail maintained her composure, though her heart hammered in her chest. "Mr. McGrant. Good afternoon."

"May I join you?" Without waiting for a response, he pulled out the chair opposite her and sat down, signaling to Mrs. Tuttle. "Coffee, please. And whatever pastry is freshest."

Mrs. Tuttle nodded stiffly and hurried away, casting a concerned glance at Abigail as she went.

McGrant turned his attention back to Abigail, studying her with calculated interest. "I understand there was some... unpleasantness at the church this morning. Vandalism, I believe?"

"You seem remarkably well-informed," Abigail replied evenly.

"Clear Springs is a small town, Miss Whitaker. Little occurs here without my knowledge." He leaned forward slightly. "I want to assure you that I had nothing to do with such childish behavior. Completely beneath me."

"I'm relieved to hear it," Abigail said, meeting his gaze steadily. "Then I can count on your support in finding those responsible?"

McGrant's smile tightened almost imperceptibly. "Of course. Though I doubt the culprits will be identified. Probably just young boys with too much idle time. Youth today lack proper discipline."

Mrs. Tuttle returned with Abigail's tea and a generous slice of pie, followed by a young girl bringing McGrant's coffee and a pastry. The café owner hovered anxiously for a moment before McGrant dismissed her with a flick of his fingers.

"I understand you've been quite busy today," McGrant continued once they were relatively alone again. "Visiting the mayor, the doctor, arranging housing for the Dawson family..." He took a sip of his coffee.

"I'm simply trying to help those in need," Abigail replied. "As any Christian would."

"Ah, yes. Christian charity." McGrant's tone made the words sound almost vulgar. "A noble sentiment, certainly. Though perhaps misplaced in this instance. Gerald Dawson's situation is of his own making. The man was negligent, causing injury to himself and others."

"That's not how some people describe the incident," Abigail said, unable to let the falsehood stand unchallenged.

McGrant's eyes hardened, though his smile remained fixed. "The safety of my mine is my highest priority, Miss Whitaker. I would never knowingly endanger my workers."

The blatant lie hung between them. Abigail took a sip of her tea to compose herself before responding. "I'm pleased to hear that, Mr.

McGrant. Then perhaps you'll reconsider Mr. Dawson's termination once his injuries have healed."

"Unfortunately, I cannot reward negligence with continued employment," McGrant replied smoothly. "It would send the wrong message to the other workers. However..." He paused, studying her. "I am not without compassion. I could be persuaded to forgive the Dawson's debt at the company store as a gesture of goodwill."

Abigail's eyes narrowed slightly. "In exchange for what, Mr. Mc-Grant?"

"Your cooperation, Miss Whitaker." His voice lowered, becoming almost intimate. "Clear Springs has operated quite smoothly under my guidance. The church, while a charming addition to our community, represents certain... complications. Religious fervor can distract workers from their duties, encourage unrealistic expectations of charity rather than honest labor."

"I believe faith encourages diligence and integrity in all aspects of life," Abigail countered. "Including fair treatment of workers and honest business practices."

McGrant's smile vanished entirely. "Let me be direct, Miss Whitaker. Your presence in Clear Springs is becoming disruptive. The Dawson situation, the church renovation—these activities challenge the natural order I've established here. For the good of the community, I suggest you reconsider your mission. Perhaps another town would benefit more from your... particular brand of ministry."

Before Abigail could respond, the café door burst open, and Jonah strode in, his expression thunderous. His gaze swept the room until it landed on Abigail and McGrant, and he moved toward them with purposeful strides.

"Miss Whitaker," he said, his voice tight with controlled anger. "Ethan was concerned when you didn't return." His eyes shifted to McGrant. "I see why."

McGrant leaned back in his chair, his composure returning. "Mr. Brooks. Taking an interest in church affairs now, are we? How unexpected, given your... history."

A muscle twitched in Jonah's jaw, but he kept his attention on Abigail. "If you've finished here, I believe we have matters to attend to at the church."

Abigail recognized the barely contained fury in his expression and decided that a strategic retreat was wisest. She quickly removed a coin from her pocket and left it on the table to cover her bill. "Yes, of course." She rose from her chair, nodding politely to McGrant. "Thank you for the conversation, Mr. McGrant. I'll consider what you've said."

"Please do," McGrant replied, remaining seated as he watched them with calculating eyes. "For everyone's benefit."

Jonah placed a protective hand at the small of Abigail's back as they moved toward the door. The gesture was not lost on anyone in the café who watched the tableau with avid interest.

Outside, Jonah maintained his silence until they had walked several paces from the café entrance. Then he stopped abruptly, turning to face her with barely suppressed anger.

"What were you thinking, you foolish woman?" he demanded in a low, intense voice. "Sitting with McGrant after everything that's happened?"

"I didn't invite him to join me, Mr. Brooks, and I am not a foolish woman," Abigail replied, matching his quiet tone. "He arrived after I was already seated."

"You should have left immediately."

"And show fear? Give him that satisfaction?" Abigail shook her head. "No, Mr. Brooks. That would only confirm his belief that intimidation works."

Jonah ran a hand through his hair in frustration. "This isn't some polite society disagreement, Miss Whitaker. McGrant is dangerous. Those men with him? Hired guns. Former outlaws. They don't threaten with words; they use fists and weapons."

"I was in a public place," Abigail pointed out. "He would hardly have harmed me in front of the entire cafe."

"You don't understand how this works," Jonah insisted, his voice rough with concern. "Today it's a chance meeting in the cafe. Tomorrow it could be an accident on a deserted street."

A chill ran through Abigail at his words, but she maintained her composure. "What would you have me do, Mr. Brooks? Hide in the parsonage? Abandon the church restoration? Leave the Dawson's to their fate?"

Jonah's expression shifted, frustration giving way to something more complex. Respect mingled with exasperation. "No," he admitted. "But at least don't face him alone. That's all I'm asking."

The genuine concern in his voice touched something in Abigail. "I'll be more careful," she promised. "But I won't stop doing what's right just because it's difficult or dangerous."

Jonah studied her face for a long moment, then nodded once, seemingly satisfied with her compromise. "Ethan's still at the store. Let's collect him and your supplies."

As they walked toward the general store, Abigail glanced at him. "Weren't you supposed to be working on the roof?"

"I was," he replied gruffly. "Until Ethan came running back, saying you'd disappeared into the cafe and McGrant had followed you in."

"So you abandoned your work to... what? Rescue me?" There was a hint of amusement in her voice, despite the seriousness of the situation.

Jonah shot her a dark look. "To prevent a confrontation that could have escalated. McGrant doesn't like being challenged, especially by a woman."

"And yet, that's precisely what I intend to continue doing," Abigail said firmly. "Challenging him. Not for the sake of opposition itself, but for the people of Clear Springs, who deserve better than his tyranny."

Jonah was silent for several steps. "You sound like your father," he said finally, his voice so low she almost didn't hear it.

Abigail stopped short, staring at him in surprise. "You knew my father?"

Jonah continued walking for a few paces before realizing she had stopped. He turned back, his expression guarded. "Not well, but I remember him. He had... similar ideas about standing up to people."

"And you disagreed with him?" Abigail asked, hurrying to catch up.

"I thought he was idealistic," Jonah admitted. "Underestimating what he was up against. But..." He hesitated, seeming to choose his words carefully. "He made an impression. Had a way of making you believe change was possible, even in a place like Clear Springs."

Emotion tightened Abigail's throat at this unexpected glimpse of her father through Jonah's eyes. "Thank you for telling me that," she said.

Jonah nodded once, clearly uncomfortable with the personal turn of the conversation. "You will be the death of me, woman. Now, we should get those supplies," he said, gesturing toward the store. "Daylight's wasting, and that roof won't fix itself."

Ethan was helping load the wagon with lumber and supplies outside the back door of the store. The boy's face lit up with relief when he realized Abigail was safe.

"Miss Whitaker! I was worried when you didn't come back!"

"I'm fine, Ethan," she assured him. "Just a longer conversation than anticipated."

Sid approached, wiping his hands on his apron. "Everything on your list is accounted for, Miss Whitaker. The wagon's nearly loaded. Timothy Wells lent us his smaller one for the delivery."

"Thank you, Mr. Paulson," Abigail said, reaching for her reticule. "What do I owe you?"

Sid named a sum that made Abigail blink in surprise. It was considerably more than she had anticipated.

"That seems... rather high," she said carefully.

The shopkeeper shifted uncomfortably, not quite meeting her eyes. "Prices have gone up recently. Freight costs from Denver, you understand."

Jonah stepped forward, his expression darkening as he examined the invoice. "These prices are nearly double what you charged the Thorton family last week for similar supplies."

Sid's face flushed. "Different quality. Better grade lumber for the church work."

"Sid," Jonah said flatly.

An uncomfortable silence fell as Sid's gaze darted nervously toward the street. Abigail understood immediately.

"Mr. McGrant suggested you increase your prices for me specifically, didn't he?" she asked quietly.

The shopkeeper's silence was answer enough.

"I see," Abigail said, her voice steady despite her dismay. Refusing to pay would only hurt Sid, who was clearly caught between McGrant's pressure and his own conscience.

"I'll pay the fair price, Mr. Paulson," she said firmly. "The same amount you would charge anyone else in Clear Springs. No more, no less."

Paulson looked torn, glancing again toward the street, as if expecting McGrant to materialize at any moment.

"Sid," Jonah said, his voice low but carrying authority, "you know what's right here."

The shopkeeper hesitated, then sighed heavily and scratched out the original figure on the invoice, writing a new, substantially lower amount. "This is the regular price," he admitted, handing the revised bill to Abigail.

"Thank you for your honesty," she said, counting out the money and handing it to him.

"McGrant won't be pleased if he finds out," Sid muttered.

"Let me worry about McGrant," Jonah said, clapping the man on the shoulder. "You just keep treating folks fairly."

As they climbed onto the wagon, Jonah taking the reins with Abigail and Ethan beside him, Abigail felt a growing unease. McGrant's reach extended further than she had anticipated, influencing even everyday transactions in Clear Springs.

"It will only get worse," Jonah said, seeming to read her thoughts as they pulled away from the store. "McGrant doesn't accept defeat gracefully."

"Then I must be prepared," Abigail replied, her resolve strengthening despite her concerns. "And I must show the people of Clear Springs they have choices... that one man's influence, however pervasive, can be countered by a community standing together."

Jonah gave her a sidelong glance. "You really aren't going to back down, are you?"

"No, Mr. Brooks," Abigail said, meeting his gaze steadily. "I am not."

A ghost of a smile touched his lips before he turned his attention back to the horses. "Then God help us all," he murmured, but there was no mockery in his tone, only a grudging respect that warmed Abigail more than she cared to admit.

As they approached the church, Abigail noticed several people gathered near the steps. Ruth and her sister Clair Thatcher, along with Doc Carpenter and Deputy Mansfield. They appeared to be examining the vandalized door, their expressions troubled.

"Word seems to have spread pretty quick," Ethan observed.

"In Clear Springs, gossip is the most reliable form of communication," Jonah replied dryly, pulling the wagon to a stop.

Deputy Mansfield approached as they climbed down. "Miss Whitaker, I came by to take that report and found these good folks already here, ready to lend a hand. Seems they were concerned after hearing about this morning's incident."

"We brought some food," Ruth added, gesturing to a basket at her feet. "Figured you wouldn't have time for cooking with all this chaos."

"That's incredibly kind of you," Abigail said.

"It's the least we could do," Clair said, shifting her youngest child to her other hip. "After what you're doing for the Dawsons. The whole town's talking about it."

Doc Carpenter stepped forward. "I've seen to Gerald. His ribs are properly bound now, and I've given him something for the pain. They'll be moving to the Jenkins's cabin this afternoon."

"With help," Deputy Mansfield added. "I've arranged for a couple of men to assist with their belongings."

Abigail looked from face to face, momentarily overwhelmed by this spontaneous rallying of support. "I... don't know what to say."

"Don't need to say anything," Ruth replied matter-of-factly. "This is what neighbors do. Or used to do, before McGrant got everyone too scared to breathe without his permission."

"Well, I'm breathing just fine," Doc Carpenter said with a wry smile. "And I suspect Miss Whitaker here has reminded a few others how to do the same."

Jonah, who had been unloading supplies from the wagon with Ethan, paused to survey the small gathering. His expression was unreadable before he turned back to his task.

"Now," Ruth said, rolling up her sleeves, "let's get this mess cleaned up. I brought a good scrubbing brush with me, and Clair here makes a paste that'll take paint off anything."

As the small group set to work, Doc and Deputy Mansfield helping Jonah unload the wagon while Ruth and Clair attacked the red streaks on the door with determined energy, Abigail smiled.

# Chapter 13

The hammer slipped from Jonah's grip, narrowly missing his boot before clattering against the church roof with a sound that echoed across the yard. He mumbled under his breath, wiping sweat from his brow with his forearm. The afternoon sun beat down mercilessly, turning the air above the newly laid shingles into a shimmering haze.

"Need some water, Mr. Brooks?" Ethan called from below, holding up a ladle and bucket.

"Might as well," Jonah grunted, making his way to the ladder.

His gaze drifted to the parsonage as he descended. Abigail stood on the porch with Ruth, their heads bent together over a basket of linens destined for the Dawson's new home. Abigail's golden hair caught the light as she gestured animatedly, a gentle smile illuminating her face. His chest pounded, an unwelcome feeling he'd been fighting with increasing difficulty.

"You're staring," Ethan said as he handed over the water ladle.

Jonah scowled. "I'm not staring. I'm making sure she's not running off to confront McGrant single-handedly."

"Of course," Ethan replied.

"Don't you have shingles to carry up?" Jonah growled, thrusting the empty ladle back at the boy.

Ethan's grin widened. "Yes, sir. Right away, sir."

Jonah watched the boy bound away, wondering when his apprentice had grown so perceptive and so bold. Or perhaps the question was when he himself had grown so transparent. The thought unsettled him.

Movement caught his eye as Abigail descended the parsonage steps and walked toward him, a small package in her hands. He straightened unconsciously, suddenly aware of the sweat staining his shirt and the dirt coating his trousers.

"Progress looks impressive from down here," Abigail called as she approached, shielding her eyes to look up at the church's roof. "You and Ethan work quickly."

"Need to finish before the rain comes," Jonah replied, striving for a neutral tone. "Weather's changing. Can smell it in the air."

Abigail nodded, taking a deep breath. "I thought I noticed a difference. Is that why your shoulder's troubling you?"

Jonah blinked in surprise. "What makes you think my shoulder's troubled?"

"You've been favoring your left arm all morning," she said. "And you winced when you picked up a beam earlier."

The observation startled him. Few people noticed such details about him or cared enough to mention them if they did.

"Old injury. Acts up sometimes when the weather shifts."

"I thought so." Abigail held out the small package. "I've made a salve that might help. My mother taught me the recipe. It's comfrey root, arnica, and a few other herbs. It reduces inflammation."

Jonah stared at the package, making no move to take it. "I don't need—"

"Please," Abigail interrupted gently. "Consider it a gift."

Jonah accepted the package awkwardly, unused to such concern. "Thank you," he managed to say.

"You're welcome." She smiled, then glanced toward the road where Deputy Mansfield was approaching on horseback. "I wonder what brings the deputy here again."

Jonah turned, grateful for the distraction. Mansfield dismounted, tying his horse on the hitching post before walking toward them with purposeful strides.

"Miss Whitaker, Jonah," he greeted them, removing his hat. "Thought you should know... Gerald Dawson and his family are settled in at the old Jenkins cabin. I finished helping them move in about an hour ago."

"That's wonderful news," Abigail said warmly. "How are they faring?"

"Cabin's rough, but dry. Better than the livery by far." Mansfield shifted his weight, his expression turning serious. "There's something else, though. McGrant's men were watching the move. They didn't interfere, just... observed. Taking notes seemed like."

Jonah's jaw tightened. "Taking inventory of who helped them, most likely."

"That's my thinking too," Mansfield agreed grimly.

Abigail's brow furrowed. "He's keeping a list of people who support the Dawson's? For what purpose?"

"Information is power, Miss Whitaker," Mansfield explained. "Mr. McGrant controls most jobs in town, directly or indirectly. Those who cross him often find themselves without work, or facing other... difficulties."

"People helping the Dawson's publicly... it's the first time in quite some time that folks have stood against McGrant openly," Jonah added.

"That's why Doc Carpenter said McGrant doesn't forgive slights. He punishes them."

"Systematically," Mansfield confirmed. "Though he's careful to maintain plausible deniability."

Jonah watched the emotions play across Abigail's face—concern, anger, and finally, determination.

"Then we must ensure those who've shown courage aren't left vulnerable," she declared. "Starting with the Dawson's. Mr. Brooks suggested Gerald could work on the church once he's healed enough. We'll need to provide more opportunities for others who might face McGrant's retaliation."

"The church needs plenty of work. Pews need rebuilding, windows need re-glazing. Could keep several men busy," Jonah said.

"And we'll need regular services soon as well," Abigail continued, warming to the idea. "Cleaning, arrangement of flowers, music... tasks that could provide income for women in need."

Mansfield looked between them with interest. "You might actually pull this off, Miss Whitaker," he mused. "Creating alternatives to McGrant's employment."

"Not alternatives," Abigail corrected. "Just... options. Breathing room."

Jonah felt an unwelcome surge of admiration. She wasn't just standing against McGrant; she was thinking strategically, planning moves ahead like a chess player.

Mansfield nodded thoughtfully. "Well, I'd best get back to my rounds. Wanted to update you on the Dawson's... and McGrant's men."

As the deputy rode away, Jonah became acutely aware of Abigail standing close beside him, her presence both comforting and disquieting. She smelled faintly of lavender and soap—clean, simple scents that somehow suited her perfectly.

"I should check on the Dawson's myself," she said after a moment. "See what else they might need?"

"I'll go with you," Jonah said. At her surprised look, he added gruffly, "Gerald might need help with some repairs."

"Of course. Shall we go after you and Ethan finish for the day? I could prepare a basket to take along."

"I'll tell the boy to just continue working while I'm gone," Jonah decided.

As he turned to call Ethan down from the roof, Jonah wondered at his own eagerness. He'd spent years in Clear Springs keeping to himself, avoiding entanglements. Yet here he was, volunteering his services, all because of a stubborn missionary woman with compelling blue eyes.

Dangerous territory, Brooks, he warned himself. The very kind of emotional quicksand he'd sworn to avoid.

# *Chapter 14*

The old Jenkins cabin stood at the eastern edge of town, a small structure nestled among scraggly pines. Smoke curled from its stone chimney as Jonah guided the wagon along the rutted path, Abigail bracing herself beside him against the jolting motion.

"It's more remote than I realized," she observed, taking in the cabin's isolation.

"Old Man Jenkins liked his privacy," Jonah explained. "Said town was getting too crowded for his liking, even twenty years ago."

As they approached, the cabin door opened, and Gerald Dawson stepped out, his face lighting with surprise and pleasure. "Miss Whitaker! Mr. Brooks! Hello, what brings you out this way?"

Jonah pulled the wagon to a stop, noting the cabin's condition. The roof appeared sound, though the porch sagged alarmingly on one side. Windows were intact but would offer little protection against winter winds without proper sealing.

"We wanted to see how you're settling in," Abigail explained as Jonah helped her down from the wagon. "And I've brought a few things that might make the cabin more comfortable."

Natalie appeared in the doorway, baby Esther in her arms, with Lucy and Byron peering around her skirts. Her face showed signs of recent tears, but her smile was genuine. "Please, come in. It's not much, but it's—"

"It's a home," Abigail completed gently. "And a fine one."

Jonah followed Abigail inside, ducking slightly to clear the low door frame. The cabin's interior was spare but clean, with a single main room serving as kitchen, dining area, and living space. A ladder led to a small loft where the children would presumably sleep. A few pieces of hastily gathered furniture, a rough-hewn table, three mismatched chairs, and an old rocking chair constituted the entirety of their possessions.

"The community has been kind," Gerald explained, gesturing to a small pile of blankets in the corner. "Ruth Patterson brought those. And Doc Carpenter left medicine for my ribs."

"Mrs. Tuttle from the café sent over a stew," Natalie added.

Abigail began unpacking the basket she'd brought, revealing homemade bread, preserves, a small sack of coffee, some clean linens, and various other supplies. "Just a few essentials to help you get established."

"Miss Whitaker, you've already done so much," Gerald protested weakly.

"Nonsense, Mr. Dawson," Abigail replied firmly. "Helping one another in times of need is a blessing."

As Abigail continued unpacking, Jonah moved around the cabin's perimeter, examining the construction with a critical eye. "The floor's solid," he noted. "Walls need chinked before winter, though. And that porch won't last another month without new supports."

Gerald nodded, following him. "I noticed the same. Once my ribs heal up a bit more, I can tackle all of it. Mayor Jenkins said repairs could count toward the rent."

Jonah glanced at the man's bandaged torso, visible beneath his partially buttoned shirt. "Ribs take time. I might be able to help with the urgent repairs myself."

"That's very generous, but—"

"Not generous," Jonah cut him off. "Practical. Winter comes early in the mountains. The cabin needs to be sound before the first snow. The children need to be kept warm."

Abigail kneeled beside little Lucy, admiring the child's wooden animals with genuine interest. The girl had initially hidden behind her mother, but now chattered animatedly, showing Abigail each carved creature in turn.

"Papa made this one for my birthday," Lucy explained, holding up a delicately carved deer. "Before the bad man made him stop."

Natalie made a small sound of distress. "Lucy, we don't talk about—"

"It's all right," Abigail assured her gently. "These are beautiful, Lucy. Your father is very talented."

Gerald shifted uncomfortably. "Just whittling, really. Passes the time."

Jonah picked up one of the figures, a bear standing on its hind legs, its features detailed despite its small size. "This isn't just whittling, Dawson. This is some fine craftsmanship."

"McGrant thought differently," Gerald said. "Said it was a waste of time better spent in the mine."

Jonah exchanged a glance with Abigail.

"Mr. Dawson," she began carefully, "have you ever considered selling these carvings? They would make wonderful gifts, especially with Christmas not so many months away."

Gerald shook his head. "McGrant has a say in everything in this town, said they wouldn't sell. Told me to not even try getting Sid Paulson to stock them in the General Store."

"The general store isn't the only market," Jonah said. "Stagecoaches bring passengers through regularly. Tourists like souvenirs."

Hope flickered briefly in Gerald's eyes before doubt extinguished it. "McGrant wouldn't allow it."

"McGrant doesn't own the entire town," Abigail said firmly. "And he certainly doesn't control what Mrs. Tuttle might display at her café counter, or what Mrs. Hale might put on display for sale in her boarding house."

Understanding dawned on Gerald's face. "You mean... sell them through others?"

"Precisely," Abigail confirmed. "A small commission to those willing to display your work, with the profits coming back to your family."

Natalie stepped forward, clutching baby Esther tighter. "McGrant would find out."

"Eventually, perhaps," Abigail said. "But by then, you'd have established customers and created demand."

The tension in the small cabin was palpable as Gerald and Natalie exchanged a long look, years of fear battling against the first fragile shoots of hope.

"I have wood," Gerald said finally. "Scraps, mostly. Enough for a dozen more carvings, maybe."

"I can bring more," Jonah offered. "Off-cuts from the church repairs. Good hardwood that would otherwise go to waste."

"And I can speak with Mrs. Hale and Anne Tuttle tomorrow," Abigail added. "Discreetly, of course."

A tentative smile spread across Natalie's tired face, the first real smile Abigail had seen from her. "Gerald always said these carvings would feed us someday. I didn't believe him."

"It might be time to start believing, Mrs. Dawson," Abigail said quietly.

As they prepared to leave, with promises to return with wood and news of selling arrangements, Lucy pressed the little carved deer into Abigail's hands.

"For you," the child insisted. "Because you're nice."

Abigail knelt, bringing herself to the girl's level. "Are you certain? This is one of your special treasures."

Lucy nodded solemnly. "Papa can make another. He makes the best animals in the whole territory."

Visibly moved, Abigail carefully tucked the small deer into her pocket. "Then I'll treasure it always, Lucy. Thank you."

Outside, as Jonah helped Abigail back onto the wagon, she paused, her hand lingering on his arm. "You surprise me sometimes, Mr. Brooks."

"How so?" he asked, uncomfortable under her scrutiny.

"You present yourself as a man concerned only with practical matters," she said thoughtfully. "Yet your practical solutions often align perfectly with what's right and compassionate."

Jonah looked away, unnerved by how easily she seemed to see through his carefully constructed façade. "Don't make me into someone I'm not, Miss Whitaker."

"I'm not making you into anyone," she replied. "I'm simply observing who you already are. A good man, Jonah Brooks."

Before he could formulate a response, she climbed onto the wagon seat, effectively ending the conversation. Jonah took his place beside her, aware of a peculiar warmth spreading through his chest despite the evening's growing chill.

They rode in silence for several minutes, the wagon's wheels creating a rhythmic creak against the rutted path. The setting sun cast long shadows across the landscape, painting the distant mountains in hues of purple and gold.

"It's beautiful here," Abigail said, her voice quiet with wonder. "Despite everything, there's a raw majesty to this land that touches the soul."

Jonah followed her gaze to the mountains. "It grows on you," he admitted. "When I first arrived, I only saw the harshness. The dangers. Now..."

"Now you see the beauty as well," she completed when he trailed off.

"Something like that."

Abigail turned to look at him directly. "What brought you to Clear Springs, Mr. Brooks? If you don't mind my asking."

For a moment, he considered deflecting with his usual gruff evasion. Instead, he found himself answering truthfully.

"Needed somewhere remote. Somewhere I could... start fresh, I suppose. After the war, I couldn't go home. Too many memories. Too many ghosts."

Abigail nodded, not pressing for details he wasn't ready to give. "And you found what you were looking for here?"

"Found peace of a sort," Jonah replied, choosing his words carefully. "A measure of quiet. Purpose in my work. It's enough."

"Is it?" The gentle question held no judgment, only genuine curiosity.

Jonah considered this as they crested a small rise, bringing Clear Springs back into view. Until recently, he would have answered without hesitation. His solitary existence, his carefully maintained distance from the town's emotional entanglements—these had been his safety net, his sanctuary. But lately...

"It was," he said finally. "Before you arrived and started stirring things up."

Instead of taking offense, Abigail laughed, a clear, genuine sound that seemed to lighten the very air around them. "I do seem to have a talent for disruption, don't I?"

Jonah felt the corner of his mouth twitch upward. "That's one word for it."

"And what is another word you would use to describe me, Mr. Brooks?" she asked, still smiling.

"Stubborn," he replied promptly. "Determined. Fearless to the point of foolishness."

"Those are three words," Abigail pointed out, her eyes twinkling.

"You inspire verbosity," Jonah retorted dryly.

Her laughter rang out again, and Jonah found himself inexplicably warmed by the sound. When had anyone last laughed in his presence? When had he last made someone smile rather than scowl or shrink away?

As they approached the church, the steeple silhouetted against the darkening sky, Jonah was struck by how much had changed in just a few days. Not just in Clear Springs, with its tentative stirrings of resistance against McGrant's control, but within himself as well.

Dangerous territory, he thought. Yet somehow, with Abigail Whitaker beside him, the danger seemed increasingly worth the risk.

# *Chapter 15*

The following morning dawned with the metallic scent of approaching rain hanging heavy in the air. Jonah had applied Abigail's salve the night before, surprised at the relief it provided in his shoulder—enough that he'd slept better than he had in quite some time, and it only throbbed mildly this morning.

Ethan was already waiting at the church, organizing tools with efficient movements that spoke of growing skill. The boy straightened when he spotted Jonah approaching.

"Morning, Mr. Brooks! Thought you might not come with the weather threatening."

"All the more reason to finish the roof today," Jonah replied, eyeing the gray clouds gathering on the horizon. "We'll have four, maybe five, hours before the rain hits."

"Miss Whitaker's inside," Ethan said. "Cleaning the church some more. Said she wanted it ready for Sunday."

Jonah raised an eyebrow. "Sunday?"

"Yes, sir. She's planning some kind of service. Simple one, she said. Just hymns and prayers, since Reverend Blake's not feeling up to preaching, and she hasn't found us a preacher yet."

The news gave Jonah pause. A service meant people gathering, publicly supporting the church's reopening.

"Did she mention this to many people?"

Ethan shrugged. "Not sure. But Mrs. Patterson was here earlier, and they were talking about it. Mrs. Patterson seemed excited."

Of course, she was proceeding with services already. Abigail Whitaker didn't waste time once she'd set her mind to something. Jonah sighed, already anticipating McGrant's response.

"Better get to work, then," he said, picking up his hammer. "That roof won't finish itself."

As they prepared to ascend, the church door opened, and Abigail emerged, a broom in one hand and a determined expression that shifted to a warm smile when she spotted him.

"Good morning," she called, setting the broom aside. "I was hoping you'd come, despite the weather."

"Roof's still the priority," Jonah replied, nodding toward the threatening sky. "Won't hold against a downpour."

"Then I won't keep you," Abigail said. "Though I was hoping to discuss something when you have a moment."

"The Sunday service?" Jonah asked. "Ambitious, considering the church's condition."

"Faith doesn't require perfect surroundings, Mr. Brooks," Abigail replied with a gentle smile. "Just willing hearts. And I believe there are many such hearts in Clear Springs, waiting for a chance to worship together again."

Jonah studied her for a moment, noting the quiet certainty in her eyes. She truly believed what she was saying, believed in the people of

Clear Springs, despite all the evidence that they had long ago surrendered to McGrant's control.

"McGrant won't like it."

"I'm counting on that," Abigail replied, surprising him. At his raised eyebrow, she continued, "Every time McGrant reacts, he reveals himself more clearly to the townspeople. Each threat, each act of intimidation, weakens his moral authority."

"You're deliberately provoking him?"

"Not provoking," Abigail corrected. "Simply refusing to be controlled by fear of his reaction. There's a difference."

"A subtle one."

"Perhaps," she conceded. "But an important distinction, nonetheless. I'm not seeking confrontation, Mr. Brooks. I'm simply doing what I came here to do: restore this church and serve this community."

Put that way, her actions seemed not just reasonable, but admirable. "Fair enough. But at least consider some precautions for Sunday. Have Mansfield present, at a minimum."

"Already arranged. The deputy offered without my asking. Sheriff Holden is coming as well. And Doc Carpenter has promised to attend with his wife."

"Good," Jonah said, relieved she wasn't being entirely reckless. "That's... good thinking."

Abigail tilted her head slightly, studying him with those perceptive blue eyes. "Will you attend, Mr. Brooks?"

"I'm not much for church services."

"I understand. The invitation remains open. Should you change your mind?"

Abigail turned and walked back into the church to continue her work, Jonah watching her disappear through the doorway.

***

Abigail knelt beside a stack of water-damaged hymnals, carefully separating those beyond salvation from those that might still serve with a bit of care. The musty scent of damp paper filled the air as she worked, her fingers gently turning fragile pages, assessing each book with careful consideration.

"Twenty-three salvageable, seventeen beyond repair," she thought to herself, adding another hymnal to the smaller pile. Despite the disheartening numbers, she hummed "Amazing Grace" softly as she worked, the familiar melody providing comfort.

The creak of the back door interrupted her cataloging. Abigail looked up to see Margaret Hale's sturdy figure silhouetted in the doorway, a covered basket over one arm.

"Mrs. Hale! What a pleasant surprise," Abigail said, rising to her feet and brushing dust from her skirt.

"Thought you might need something to keep your strength up," Margaret said, approaching with a warm smile. "And I wanted to see this church coming to life again." She surveyed the interior, her gaze taking in the progress and remaining challenges. "My, you have been busy. This place already looks twice as welcoming as it did."

"There's still so much to do," Abigail sighed, gesturing toward the damaged ceiling where sunlight still streamed through in narrow beams. "But Mr. Brooks and Ethan are making excellent progress on the roof."

Margaret set her basket on a pew and began unpacking its contents: a jar of fresh lemonade, sandwiches wrapped in cloth, and slices of apple pie. "Jonah Brooks working on a church," she mused, shaking her head. "Never thought I'd see the day."

"He's been invaluable," Abigail admitted, accepting the sandwich Margaret offered.

"That man," Margaret chuckled. "Spent four years in this town, keeping his distance from anything resembling faith or community. Now look at him, up on a church roof, and defending a missionary's daughter against Silas McGrant. Wonders never cease."

Abigail paused mid-bite. "You've known him long?"

"Since he first arrived," Margaret confirmed, sitting down on the pew and patting the space beside her. "Come, sit with me a moment. You're working too hard."

Abigail obeyed, realizing how tired her she was after cleaning so much.

"Jonah came to Clear Springs about four years ago," Margaret continued once Abigail was seated. "During a terrible winter when the passes were snowed in for months. Showed up half-frozen with nothing but his tools, a mule, and those haunted eyes." She sighed. "Didn't talk much about where he'd been or what he'd seen, but it was written all over him. A man running from something."

"The war?" Abigail asked.

Margaret nodded. "That, and more personal ghosts, I suspect. He took over the abandoned smithy, worked day and night, getting it operational. We needed a blacksmith desperately, so folks were grateful. But whenever anyone tried to get close to him..." She made a pushing-away gesture with her hands. "Like trying to befriend a wounded wolf."

Abigail thought of the man on the roof above them, stern, capable, and reluctantly kind despite his attempts to hide it. "He keeps people at a distance."

"Self-preservation," Margaret said sadly. "When a person's been hurt badly enough, they build walls around themselves. People like that tend to have this shield up and resist everything and everyone. Jonah's walls are fortress-thick." She poured lemonade into two cups she'd brought. "Which is why it's so remarkable to see him helping you like this."

"He's only doing it because of the practical need—"

"Oh, child," Margaret interrupted with a knowing smile. "If that were true, he would have sent Ethan alone with instructions. Jonah Brooks doesn't do anything he doesn't want to do, not for anyone." She handed Abigail a cup. "No, there's something about you that's gotten past those walls of his, just a crack. And that's no small thing."

Abigail felt heat rise to her cheeks. "Mrs. Hale, I assure you—"

"Margaret... Mrs. Hale makes me sound so old. Now... I'm not suggesting anything improper," Margaret said with a gentle laugh. "Just making an observation. That man has been alone too long with his grief and guilt. It does my heart good to see him engaged with something meaningful, whatever his reasons. God had a purpose for sending you here, and it's probably more than just restoring this here church."

They sat in silence for a moment, sipping lemonade and listening to the rhythmic pounding of hammers on the roof above.

"Your mother would be proud of you," Margaret said suddenly, her voice softening. "Eleanor had such hopes for this place."

Abigail's throat tightened with unexpected emotion. "You knew my mother well?"

"As well as anyone here did. I considered her a good friend. She would visit my boardinghouse often when they were here building this church. She planned community suppers and charity efforts." Margaret's eyes grew distant with memory. "You have her determination, gentle but unshakable. When your mother believed in something, wild horses couldn't drag her from it."

"I miss her," Abigail admitted quietly. "Both of my parents... I miss them so very much. There are moments when I wonder if I'm doing what they would have wanted, if I'm approaching things the right way."

Margaret reached over and patted Abigail's hand. "You're your own person, dear. They wouldn't expect you to be their carbon copy. But the heart of what you're doing... bringing hope to a place that sorely needs it. That's precisely what they dreamed of."

Footsteps on the roof paused, followed by Jonah's voice calling for Ethan to bring up more nails. The domestic sound contrasted sharply with the sacredness of the space, yet somehow felt perfectly appropriate.

"Will you be ready for Sunday?" Margaret asked, glancing around at the still-considerable work remaining.

"Ready enough," Abigail replied, her conviction returning. "It won't be perfect, but it will be a beginning." She hesitated. "Do you think people will come?"

Margaret smiled, her weathered face warming with certainty. "More than you might expect. People are hungry for community, hope, and purpose." She squeezed Abigail's hand.

The roof above them creaked as Jonah moved across it, his solid presence a reminder of both challenges and unexpected allies.

"Well," Margaret said, rising and gathering her basket, "I should let you get back to your hymnals. But promise me you'll eat everything I brought. You're too thin already, and Clear Springs weather is unforgiving to those without meat on their bones."

Abigail smiled, touched by the motherly concern. "I promise. And thank you, not just for the food, but for the encouragement. It means more than you know."

As Margaret made her way toward the door, she paused and turned back. "One more thing about Jonah Brooks," she said, her expression thoughtful. "That man measures everyone against their word. If you say you'll do something, he expects you'll move heaven and earth to do it. If you make a promise, he'll hold you to it absolutely."

"That seems reasonable," Abigail replied, slightly confused by this parting advice.

"It is," Margaret nodded. "But it works both ways. If Jonah Brooks gives you his word on something, you can stake your life on it. He doesn't promise easily, but when he does..." She smiled. "Well, let's just say there's no more reliable ally in all of Colorado Territory."

With that, she departed, leaving Abigail to ponder her words as she returned to her stack of damaged hymnals, the rhythmic sound of hammering above a strangely comforting accompaniment to her work.

# Chapter 16

The morning sunlight illuminated the freshly swept steps of Clear Springs Church as Abigail arranged a small vase of wildflowers by the entrance. Her hands trembled slightly, not from fear, but from the solemn anticipation of what this day represented. After all the cleaning, a few repairs, and preparation, the moment had finally arrived.

"Will they come?" she wondered silently, smoothing her best dress, a modest navy blue with a white collar. The doubt crept in despite her prayers and preparations. McGrant's influence ran deep in Clear Springs, and publicly attending this service represented a choice many might be afraid to make.

The sound of approaching footsteps pulled her from her thoughts. Ruth and her sister Clair appeared around the corner, with all of their children in tow.

"Good morning!" Abigail called, genuine joy warming her voice as she moved to greet them. "You're the first to arrive."

"Wouldn't miss it," Ruth declared, climbing the steps with a determined stride. "Been waiting far too long for these doors to open again." She carried a small bunch of wildflowers, similar to those Abigail had gathered. "Thought the altar might need these."

"They're perfect," Abigail said, accepting them gratefully.

More footsteps approached, and Abigail turned to see Doc Carpenter and his wife, a slender woman with kind eyes and graying hair secured in a neat bun. Behind them came Margaret, accompanied by two of her boarders, a young woman and an elderly gentleman Abigail hadn't met before.

"Miss Whitaker," Doc called warmly, "may I present my wife, Bonnie?"

"I'm delighted to meet you," Abigail said, clasping the woman's outstretched hands. "Dr. Carpenter speaks of you often and with such fondness."

"All lies, I assure you," Bonnie replied with a twinkle in her eye. "But kind ones, I hope." She glanced at the church behind Abigail. "It does my heart good to see these doors open again."

Margaret stepped forward. "Miss Whitaker, I'd like you to meet Mr. Felix Templeton, a guest at my boardinghouse, and Miss Silvia Cunningham, our town's new postmaster."

Mr. Templeton, stooped but dignified with a magnificent white mustache, bowed slightly. "A pleasure, Miss Whitaker. I'm a traveling book merchant, in town only until Tuesday, but I wouldn't miss a chance for worship."

Miss Cunningham, a petite woman perhaps a few years older than Abigail, smiled shyly. "I've been eagerly awaiting to meet you."

Abigail welcomed them warmly, feeling a growing sense of hope as more townspeople emerged from various directions. The Dawson family arrived, Gerald moving carefully with his bandaged ribs, but his face bright with determination. Natalie held baby Esther while Lucy guided Byron by the hand, the little boy clutching a wooden toy.

Deputy Mansfield appeared, looking uncomfortable in his Sunday best, but nodding respectfully to Abigail as he mounted the steps. He was accompanied by Sheriff Holden, whom Abigail had only briefly met.

"Sheriff Holden," Abigail greeted him, "thank you for coming."

"Figured it was time to dust off my Sunday manners, Miss Whitaker," he replied. "Besides, I like to keep an eye on gatherings, especially ones that might ruffle certain feathers."

She understood his meaning perfectly. The sheriff's presence, like Deputy Mansfield's, served dual purposes—both as worshipers and as a statement that this gathering had the law's protection.

Others continued to arrive, Anne Tuttle and her husband Luther from the café, Sid Paulson from the general store, looking nervous but determined, and several miners Abigail didn't recognize. They were accompanied by women and children who eyed the church with cautious hope.

Each person who mounted those steps represented an act of quiet courage, a choice to stand against the unspoken rule that Clear Springs' spiritual life belonged under McGrant's control. Abigail greeted each one personally, learning names, shaking hands, looking into eyes that ranged from eager to apprehensive.

Among the last to arrive was Mayor Jenkins, who approached with visible discomfort, glancing repeatedly over his shoulder.

"Miss Whitaker, good to see you," he said, his voice lowered as if fearing eavesdroppers.

Abigail smiled warmly. "Good to see you as well, Mayor Jenkins. Your support means a great deal to this community."

"Yes, well... the church is an important institution. Historically speaking."

"Indeed it is," she agreed. "And I hope you'll find today's service uplifting."

As the mayor slipped past her, Abigail scanned the street once more. No sign of McGrant or his men, though she had little doubt they were observing from somewhere. And no sign of Jonah, which disappointed her more than she cared to admit. Ethan had arrived earlier to help with the final preparations, but his mentor had remained conspicuously absent.

"Time to begin, I think," Abigail murmured to herself, taking a deep breath. She gave the town one last sweeping glance.

It was then that she noticed a lone figure in the distance, standing in the wide-open doorway of the blacksmith's shop. Even from this distance, she recognized Jonah's broad shoulders and watchful stance. He wasn't approaching, wasn't making any move to join them, but he was there—observing, witnessing what was unfolding.

Abigail offered a small nod in his direction before turning to enter the church, her heart inexplicably lighter knowing he was watching, even from afar.

Inside the church, the transformation was remarkable, considering how little time she'd had. The debris had been cleared, floors swept, and pews arranged in orderly rows, though many still showed water damage or missing sections. Jonah and Ethan's work on the roof had sealed out the elements, and the wooden boards covering the broken stained-glass window had been carefully positioned to allow light to filter through in a pleasing pattern.

The altar was simple, a sturdy table covered with a clean white cloth that Margaret had contributed. The hymnals had been distributed among the pews, their damaged pages carefully pressed and repaired where possible.

Abigail made her way to the front as the congregation settled, their voices a low murmur of anticipation. Nearly thirty people had gathered, not a large number by eastern standards, but significant for a town where attendance represented a choice with potential consequences.

"Good morning," Abigail began, her voice clear and steady despite the butterflies in her stomach. "I cannot express how deeply moved I am to see you all here today. Thank you for coming, for your courage and faith."

She glanced around at the faces watching her, some familiar now, others still new, but all part of the community she was growing to love.

"My name is Abigail Whitaker, for those I haven't had the pleasure of meeting yet. As many of you know, I've come to Clear Springs to restore this church, which my parents helped establish years ago."

Murmurs of recognition rippled through the gathering. Several of the older townspeople nodded knowingly.

"I'm not a minister," Abigail continued with a self-deprecating smile, "and I make no pretense of having theological training. But I believe that worship doesn't require fancy sermons or elaborate buildings, just sincere hearts gathered together in faith."

She gestured to the simple surroundings. "As you can see, we're still very much in the restoration process. But perhaps that's fitting. Because a church isn't primarily a building, it's a community of believers. And communities, like buildings, sometimes need restoration too."

Several people nodded in agreement, and Ruth released an audible "Amen" from her seat in the second row.

"Today, we'll share in song and prayer together," Abigail explained. "I've marked some familiar hymns in the hymnals. Let's begin with, 'Come, Thou Fount of Every Blessing.'"

As the congregation fumbled for the page, Abigail took a moment to step to the back doors again and push them both wide open, securing them with wooden wedges.

"So that music might reach those who couldn't join us today," she explained, returning to the front.

Abigail began the hymn, her clear soprano voice leading confidently despite the absence of an organ or piano. For a moment, only a few uncertain voices joined her, but by the second line, more gained courage. By the first chorus, the small congregation was singing with growing conviction, their voices blending and rising.

"Come, Thou Fount of every blessing,
Tune my heart to sing Thy grace;
Streams of mercy, never ceasing,
Call for songs of loudest praise..."

The words seemed to take on new meaning. Abigail felt tears prick her eyes as she led the singing, watching faces transform with the simple act of singing, tension easing, joy emerging, a sense of community visibly strengthening with each shared verse.

When the hymn concluded, Abigail offered a simple prayer of thanksgiving, followed by a reading from the Psalms. She then invited the congregation to share their own prayer requests or thoughts.

A brief silence followed, the kind that often occurs when people are unaccustomed to speaking in such settings. Then Gerald Dawson slowly rose from his seat, one hand pressed carefully against his bandaged ribs.

"I'd like to thank God," he said, his voice rough with emotion, "for this church being open again. For my family, having a roof over our heads. And for Miss Whitaker's kindness when we needed it most."

"Amen," several voices responded.

His words seemed to break a dam. Ruth Patterson stood next, sharing her joy at singing hymns in the church again after so long. Doc Carpenter offered thanks for the community spirit he was witnessing. One of the miners spoke simply but powerfully about finding hope again after months of despair.

Abigail listened, deeply moved, as person after person found their voice. Some offered traditional prayers, others simply shared experiences or gratitude, but each contribution wove another thread into the fabric of the community being restored before her eyes.

When everyone who wished to speak had done so, Abigail suggested they sing "Amazing Grace." As the familiar verses filled the church, she noticed a few figures pausing on the street outside, drawn by the music flowing through the open doors. Some continued on their way, but others lingered, listening.

One such figure, a young girl of perhaps fifteen or sixteen, caught Abigail's attention. She stood at a distance, partially hidden behind the corner of a building, her face a strange mixture of longing and defiance. Dressed in a faded but once-fine dress that suggested better times, she seemed torn between drawing closer and running away.

Abigail kept singing while maintaining gentle eye contact with the girl, offering a small smile of invitation. The girl didn't approach, but neither did she leave, remaining in her half-hidden position until the hymn concluded.

After a final prayer and the announcement that they would continue meeting each Sunday with a proper preacher as soon as one could be found, Abigail added with a smile. The service concluded. People lingered, however, reluctant to leave the warmth of the community they had experienced.

Conversations bloomed throughout the church as Abigail moved among the congregants, thanking them for coming, learning more about their lives and needs, and answering their questions about her plans for the church.

"Will there be a Sunday school for the children?" Elizabeth Morris asked. "I taught the little ones before the church closed."

"I would love that," Abigail replied enthusiastically. "Would you consider taking it up again?"

Elizabeth's face brightened. "I'd be delighted! I've missed it terribly."

Similar conversations unfolded throughout the building, offers to help with the restoration, questions about future services, suggestions for community outreach. The energy was palpable, a sense of possibility that had been dormant in Clear Springs for too long.

As the gathering finally began to disperse, Abigail stepped outside onto the church steps, watching as people made their way down the street in small groups, many still engaged in animated conversation.

Her gaze was drawn inevitably toward the blacksmith shop in the distance. Jonah was no longer standing in the doorway—had he left, or simply moved inside? She felt a curious disappointment at his absence, which she quickly tried to dismiss.

"Quite a turnout," Sheriff Holden commented, joining her on the steps. "More than I expected, to be honest."

"A good beginning," Abigail agreed. "Though I hope more will feel comfortable joining us as time goes on."

The sheriff nodded thoughtfully. "McGrant will have noticed. It might be wise to expect some response from his men."

"I'm prepared for that possibility," Abigail said calmly. "But I won't let fear of his reaction dictate what I do here."

"Didn't figure you would," Holden replied with a hint of approval. "Just saying, keep your eyes open." He touched his hat brim in farewell. "Good service, Miss Whitaker. Reminded me of simpler times."

As the sheriff departed, Abigail noticed the young girl she'd seen during the hymn singing, now hovering uncertainly nearby. Up close, Abigail could see that her dress, though worn, was of fine quality, and her dark hair was styled more elaborately than was common in Clear Springs.

Abigail approached her with a warm smile. "Hello there. I noticed you listening earlier. I'm Abigail Whitaker."

The girl eyed her warily. "Hannah McCallum," she replied after a moment's hesitation. The name immediately registered, McCallum was McGrant's business partner, one of the wealthiest men in town after McGrant himself.

"It's lovely to meet you, Hannah," Abigail said, giving no sign that she recognized the family connection. "Would you like to come inside and see the church?"

Hannah glanced toward the open door, clearly tempted, then shook her head. "My father doesn't approve of church activities. Says they're a waste of time that could be spent on practical matters."

"I see," Abigail said gently. "Well, perhaps another time. The doors are always open to you."

Something flickered in the girl's eyes, longing, perhaps, or simple curiosity. "The singing was nice," she admitted.

"We'll be singing again next Sunday," Abigail told her. "And you're welcome to listen from wherever you feel comfortable."

Hannah studied Abigail for a moment, her expression guarded yet hopeful. "My mother used to sing hymns," she said suddenly. "Before she died. Father forbade it afterward, said it showed weakness."

Abigail's heart ached at the girl's matter-of-fact tone. "Grief takes many forms," she said carefully. "But finding comfort in music isn't weakness. It's a gift that helps heal the soul."

Hannah seemed to consider this before her expression closed again. "I should go."

"Of course. But please know you're welcome here anytime, Hannah."

The girl nodded once, then turned and hurried away, her posture straight and dignified despite the evident conflict within her.

Abigail watched her go, adding another silent prayer to the many she'd offered that morning—this one for a lonely girl caught between her father's expectations and her own heart's yearnings.

With a sigh, she turned back to the church. There was still much to do, hymnals to reorganize, flowers to refresh, plans to make for the coming week. Yet, she felt a deep satisfaction in what had been accomplished today. Seeds had been planted, connections formed, hope kindled.

# *Chapter 17*

Abigail was so absorbed in her thoughts as she cleaned and organized after the church service that she didn't notice the figure approaching from the direction of the blacksmith's shop. When she glanced up, Jonah Brooks was striding toward her, his expression unreadable as always, but his purposeful gait suggesting he had something specific to say.

"Mr. Brooks," she called to him, unable to keep the pleasure from her voice. "I didn't expect to see you today."

He stopped at the foot of the steps, looking up at her with those penetrating eyes. "Heard the singing," he said simply. "Carried all the way to the shop."

"That was the intention," Abigail admitted with a small smile as she walked toward him. "I hoped the open doors would allow the music to reach beyond our walls."

"Effective strategy," he acknowledged, the ghost of a smile touching his lips before vanishing again. "You had a good turnout. No trouble?"

"None. The sheriff and deputy's presence likely helped with that." She tilted her head slightly. "Were you expecting trouble?"

"With McGrant, it's wise to expect it, even when it doesn't come." He shifted his weight, his hands going to his pockets in an uncharacteristically uncertain gesture. "Wanted to check the roof, too. Make sure it's holding properly."

Abigail recognized the excuse for what it was, but graciously accepted it. "Of course. Would you like to inspect it now?"

Jonah nodded, following her into the church. Inside, only Ruth remained, arranging the altar flowers more artfully than Abigail had managed.

"Mr. Brooks," Ruth greeted him with clear surprise.

"Just checking my workmanship," he replied gruffly.

Ruth exchanged a knowing glance with Abigail. "Of course," Ruth said. "Well, I'll leave you to it. Need to get home and start Sunday dinner." She squeezed Abigail's hand in passing. "Wonderful service, dear. Just what this town needed."

Left alone with Jonah, Abigail watched as he surveyed the ceiling with a critical eye, examining the repairs he and Ethan had completed.

"No leaks or signs of weakness," he pronounced after a moment. "Should hold against tonight's rain."

"There's more rain coming?" Abigail asked, looking toward the window, where a blue sky was still visible.

"By evening," Jonah confirmed. "Can smell it in the air. Feel it."

"Well, I'm grateful for your thorough work," she said sincerely.

Jonah nodded, his gaze moving from the ceiling to take in the rest of the church's interior. "The Place looks different," he observed. "More... alive."

"A church should feel alive, not just be a building."

He studied her for a moment, that intense gaze that always made her feel he was seeing more than she intended to reveal. "You believe that? That it's more than just a building?"

"With all my heart," she answered without hesitation. "A church building is just a shell. What makes it a church is the people who gather inside, the community it creates, the hope it fosters."

"And you still think Clear Springs needs that?" His tone wasn't challenging exactly, more genuinely curious.

"I know it does," Abigail said, moving to stand beside him as they both gazed toward the altar. "Every community needs a place where people can find meaning beyond daily survival, where they can re-member they're more than just workers or customers or... subjects of someone's control."

Jonah was silent for a long moment, absorbing her words. "Saw McCallum's daughter outside," he said, changing the subject abrupt-ly. "The girl doesn't usually venture far from home."

"Hannah," Abigail supplied. "Yes, she seemed... conflicted. Drawn to the music but afraid to enter."

"Her father's McGrant's right hand," Jonah said grimly. "The Man's as cold as a January morning. Enforces McGrant's will almost more zealously than McGrant himself."

"She mentioned her mother used to sing hymns," Abigail said. "Before she passed away. Said her father forbade it afterward."

Something dark passed across Jonah's face. "Sounds like McCal-lum. Man believes grieving is weakness, faith is foolishness, and control is strength." He shook his head. "The Girl's been under his thumb since her mother died three years ago. She's not allowed to have friends, and no outside activities beyond what benefits the family's position."

"How terrible for her," Abigail murmured, her heart aching anew for the lonely girl.

"McGrant nor her father will approve of her showing interest in the church," Jonah warned. "Could make things difficult for her."

"I'm not going to turn her away," Abigail said firmly. "If she finds comfort in the hymns, in being near this place, she deserves that much at least."

Jonah studied her with that enigmatic expression. "You really don't back down, do you?"

"Not when it matters," she replied.

A rare smile touched his lips, there and gone in an instant but unmistakable.

They stood in companionable silence for a moment, the quiet of the church enveloping them. Sunlight filtered through the boards covering the broken window, creating patterns across the floor that shifted with the passing clouds.

"I should go," Jonah said finally.

"Of course," Abigail nodded, strangely reluctant to see him leave. "Thank you for checking the roof... and for watching from a distance earlier."

"Just being prudent," he said, the gruffness returning to his voice. "Making sure McGrant's men didn't cause trouble."

"Well, I appreciate it, nonetheless," Abigail replied, choosing not to challenge his explanation.

They walked together to the door, stepping out into the bright midday sunshine. The streets of Clear Springs were relatively quiet now, most residents having returned home for Sunday meals.

"Next Sunday?" Jonah asked unexpectedly as they paused at the top of the steps.

Abigail blinked in surprise. "Yes, same time. Will you... attend?"

He hesitated, clearly uncomfortable. "No," he finally said. "But might listen from somewhere nearby."

"The door will be open," Abigail told him, unable to keep a note of warmth from her voice. "And your seat will be waiting if you decide to come inside."

Jonah nodded once, a sharp, decisive motion, then descended the steps without another word. Abigail watched him stride away, his shoulders squared, his pace steady. A complex man, so determined to present himself as detached and practical, yet revealing unexpected depths of thoughtfulness and concern.

Abigail turned back to the church, her mind already cataloging tasks for the coming week. But her thoughts kept returning to two encounters, one with a lonely girl seeking connection, another with a solitary man who preferred his isolation yet continued to orbit closer to the community forming around her.

Both represented challenges that went beyond the physical restoration of the church, wounded souls whose healing might prove far more complicated than replacing rotten boards or fixing broken windows. Yet, Abigail felt a sense of purpose stronger than any she'd experienced before. The church was coming alive again, not just as a building, but as a gathering place for those seeking something McGrant's control couldn't touch.

She closed her eyes briefly, offering a silent prayer of gratitude for this day, for the small victories it represented, and for the courage of those who had chosen to attend.

# Chapter 18

Jonah Brooks was not a man given to self-deception. He prided himself on a clear-eyed assessment of situations, unsentimental practicality, and a distinct lack of the wishful thinking that so often led others astray. So the fact that he found himself sitting in his workshop on Sunday afternoon, staring at his tools while hymns replayed in his mind, was a source of considerable irritation.

He hadn't planned to observe the church service, hadn't intended to position himself in his doorway with a clear view of the proceedings. Yet when the bell rang out across town that morning, he'd found himself drawn to that vantage point, watching as people gathered. People he knew well enough to be surprised by their attendance.

Jenkins, the spineless mayor who typically aligned himself with whichever way the wind blew. Paulson from the general store, whose livelihood depended on McGrant's goodwill. Several miners who risked their jobs by attending. And of course, Abigail Whitaker was at the center of it all, greeting each arrival with that genuine warmth that somehow never seemed performative or false.

The singing had reached him clearly, not just the melodies, but the growing confidence in the voices as the service progressed. Despite himself, he'd found the music stirring memories long buried, his mother's gentle voice singing those same hymns as she worked, his father's deep bass joining in from his workshop. Family gatherings where faith had been a simple, unquestioned foundation of daily life.

Before the war. Before, everything changed.

Jonah rose abruptly, moving to the workbench where several projects awaited his attention. A set of hinges for the Thompson's new barn door. Horseshoes for the stage line. A repaired plow blade for one of the small farms outside town. Practical work, useful work, the kind that anchored him in reality rather than sentiment or memory.

Yet, his mind kept drifting back to the church. To Abigail standing on those steps, her face alight with purpose. To the gathered townspeople, finding something there that had been missing from Clear Springs for so long. To the strange, unwelcome feeling in his own chest, a yearning he'd thought long extinguished.

The sound of approaching footsteps interrupted his thoughts. Jonah looked up to see Ethan entering the workshop, his Sunday clothes replaced by his work apron.

"It's Sunday. Day of rest," Jonah remarked.

"Wanted to get ahead on the Johnson order," Ethan replied, moving to his own workstation. "Those wagon wheel rims need to be ready by Tuesday."

Jonah watched him work for several minutes.

"Service was nice," Ethan ventured finally. "Lots of people came. Even Mayor Jenkins showed up for a while."

Jonah grunted noncommittally.

"Miss Whitaker has a really nice singing voice," the boy continued, undeterred by his mentor's lack of response. "And she knows how to make people feel welcome, even when the church isn't all fixed up yet."

"The roof's sound," Jonah said. "That's what matters with rain coming."

Ethan smiled slightly, recognizing the deflection. "Sure is." He paused, then added casually, "Miss Whitaker asked about you afterward. Wanted to know if you might come next Sunday."

"Did she now."

"Yes, sir. Told her I didn't know your church habits, but I'd pass along the invitation."

"Consider it passed."

Ethan worked quietly for another moment before trying again. "She's really changing things, isn't she? People talking more openly. Standing up to McGrant in little ways."

"For now," Jonah replied, his voice neutral. "McGrant won't tolerate it for long."

"You think he'll cause trouble?"

"McGrant's not a man to accept challenges to his authority. Miss Whitaker represents exactly that, not by direct confrontation, but by offering people something his control can't touch."

"Faith, you mean?"

"Community," Jonah corrected. "Purpose beyond the mine and the company script. McGrant rules through isolation as much as intimidation, keeping people separate, suspicious, focused on their own survival. What happened today undermines that strategy."

"So what will he do?"

"Hard to say. McGrant's careful. He works indirectly when possible. Might pressure Mayor Jenkins to find some regulation the church violates. Or force Sid Paulson to raise prices for supplies. Or the miners' foreman to schedule Sunday work regularly." Jonah's eyes narrowed. "But if those tactics don't work…"

He didn't need to finish the thought. They both knew McGrant's reputation for escalating when subtler methods failed.

"Miss Whitaker's not afraid of him," Ethan said, a note of admiration in his voice.

"She should be."

Ethan studied his mentor with unusual perceptiveness. "You're worried about her."

It wasn't a question, and Jonah didn't treat it as one.

"Just being practical. The town doesn't need another martyr."

"She's stronger than she looks," Ethan said. "And smarter too. Plus, she's got people on her side now. Not just you and me, but Doc Carpenter, the sheriff, the Dawsons, the Patterson's…" He shrugged. "That's more allies than anyone's had against McGrant in a long time."

Jonah grunted, neither agreeing nor disagreeing. He wanted to dismiss the boy's optimism as youthful naivety, but Ethan had a point. Something was shifting in Clear Springs, subtle but unmistakable, like the first hint of thaw after a long winter.

"Guess we'll see," was all he said.

Outside, clouds began to gather on the horizon, confirming Jonah's prediction of evening rain.

Ethan completed his tasks and hung up his apron. "Heading home for supper," he announced. "Ma's making her rabbit stew tonight."

Jonah nodded. "Good work today. Those rims are coming along well."

The boy beamed at the rare praise. "Thanks, Mr. Brooks." He hesitated at the door. "You know, if you ever wanted to attend church, I'd be happy to save you a seat. No one would think anything of it."

Jonah raised an eyebrow. "That right?"

"Yes, sir," Ethan replied earnestly. "No one would judge you."

The simple statement struck Jonah more deeply than the boy could know.

"I'll keep that in mind," he said, his voice rougher than he intended.

After Ethan left, Jonah continued sitting in his shop until the light became too poor to see clearly. Only then did he step outside into the gathering dusk.

The first fat drops of rain were just beginning to fall as he secured the workshop door. He tilted his face upward, letting the cool moisture strike his skin.

On impulse, he turned and looked toward the church, barely visible in the fading light. A single lamp burned in the parsonage window, casting a warm light that contrasted with the deepening gray of the storm clouds.

Abigail would be in there now, perhaps reading by that lamp, or writing letters, or planning for the week ahead. Alone but not lonely, sustained by the faith that had brought her.

The rain began to fall more heavily; the drops drumming against the dirt packed street in an accelerating rhythm. Jonah pulled his collar up against the weather.

He stood watching that distant parsonage lamp, a strange mixture of emotions churning within him. Concern for what might come. Admiration for Abigail's courage. And something else, something he wasn't ready to name, a feeling that both surprised him and terrified him.

"Fool's errand," he muttered to himself, finally turning away. "This town will break her heart."

But even as he spoke the words, he recognized their hollowness. Because what he'd witnessed today wasn't just Abigail's stubborn idealism at work. It was something more, the first fragile signs of a community remembering its own strength, rediscovering connections that McGrant had systematically weakened over years of control.

And Jonah Brooks, for all his determined isolation, found himself unwillingly drawn toward that awakening. Like iron to a magnet.

# *Chapter 19*

Abigail's fork clinked against her plate as she set it down, laughing at the story Margaret was telling about her most eccentric boarder. The Tuesday lunch crowd at Tuttle's Café buzzed around them.

"He insists on sleeping with the window open, even in a thunderstorm!" Margaret exclaimed, shaking her head. "He claimed it helps him breathe better."

"Some people have the strangest habits," Abigail replied, taking a sip of her tea. She welcomed this midday respite after having spent the morning cleaning and repairing things at the church.

Margaret's expression shifted, her earlier mirth fading. She leaned forward, lowering her voice. "I had three miners come in looking for rooms yesterday at the boardinghouse. They'd been let go from the mine after speaking up about safety concerns."

Abigail's brow furrowed. "What kind of concerns?"

Margaret glanced around before continuing. "There was an accident early yesterday. A support beam collapsed in one of the tunnels. Two men injured, one badly. These fellows suggested maybe the timber wasn't properly cured or had been tampered with." She shook her head. "By afternoon, all three were dismissed, told to clear out of company housing by nightfall."

"That's terrible," Abigail murmured. "Are the injured men receiving proper care?"

"Doc Carpenter's looking after them, but..." Margaret trailed off as Anne Tuttle approached their table with a coffeepot.

"More coffee, ladies?" Anne asked, her usually cheerful face drawn with worry.

"Please," Margaret replied, pushing her cup forward.

Anne filled both cups, then hesitated. "Your church service on Sunday was a blessing, Miss Whitaker. Sorry I couldn't stay long afterward." She lowered her voice. "Luther and I were glad to be there. It's been too long since this town had proper worship."

"Thank you, Mrs. Tuttle. You're both welcome anytime," Abigail replied warmly.

Anne nodded, glancing over her shoulder before adding, "Just... be careful. Mr. McGrant was in here for breakfast this morning, asking who attended. Seemed particularly interested in which miners were there."

A chill ran through Abigail despite the café's warmth. "Was he? And what did you tell him?"

"Said I was too busy to notice much," Anne replied with a tight smile.

After Anne moved to another table, Margaret sighed heavily. "McGrant's keeping tabs, making connections between the church attendance and who speaks up at the mine. That man's got his fingers in every aspect of town life."

Abigail considered this, remembering Jonah's warnings about Mc-Grant's methods. "The miners who lost their jobs, are they staying with you now?"

Margaret nodded. "Gave them reduced rates until they find new work, though that won't be easy. McGrant's influence extends to most businesses around here." She took a sip of her coffee. "One of them, a young fellow named Ellis, mentioned something else that troubled me. Said the support beams that failed looked like they'd been tampered with, not just poorly installed."

"Tampered with?" Abigail repeated, shocked. "Surely McGrant wouldn't risk his own mine operations?"

"Ellis thinks McGrant's cutting corners, using substandard materials." Margaret's voice dropped even lower. "Or worse, creating accidents to justify dismissing workers who ask too many questions."

The bell above the café door jingled, drawing their attention. Dr. Carpenter entered, removing his hat and scanning the room. When his gaze landed on their table, he made his way over, nodding to several patrons as he passed.

"Miss Whitaker, Mrs. Hale," he greeted them, his usually cheerful demeanor subdued. "Mind if I join you ladies for a moment?"

"Please do," Abigail replied, gesturing to an empty chair.

The doctor settled heavily into the seat, looking exhausted. Anne appeared almost immediately with a cup of coffee, which he accepted gratefully.

"Been up most of the night," he explained after taking a long sip. "Tending to Axel Frazier. He was caught in that mine collapse yesterday."

"How is he?" Margaret asked, concern etching her features.

"Stable, but it was touch and go. Broken leg, three cracked ribs, internal bleeding." He shook his head. "Could have been much worse. Would have been, if his partner hadn't pulled him out so quickly."

"Thank God for that," Abigail murmured.

Dr. Carpenter studied her for a moment. "Miss Whitaker, I was hoping to speak with you. Privately, if possible."

Margaret immediately began gathering her things. "I should be getting back to the boardinghouse, anyway. Those rooms won't clean themselves."

After Margaret departed with a meaningful glance at Abigail, Dr. Carpenter moved to her vacated seat, positioning himself with his back to most of the café.

"Sunday service was wonderful, Miss Whitaker," he began without preamble. "First time I've seen this town show any collective spirit in some time. It was... refreshing."

"Thank you," Abigail replied. "It meant a great deal to have you there."

He nodded, turning his coffee cup slowly between his hands. "I've been in Clear Springs for some time. Came when the mine was just beginning operations, full of optimism about building a practice in a growing community. This was before McGrant took control." A bitter smile crossed his face. "Things changed after he came. Gradually at first, then more rapidly after the previous owner died under questionable circumstances."

Abigail leaned forward, intrigued by this piece of history she hadn't heard before. "Questionable?"

"Fall from a horse. Convenient timing." The doctor shrugged. "Nothing provable, of course. Never is with McGrant."

"Why are you telling me this?" Abigail asked quietly.

Dr. Carpenter met her gaze directly. "Because I'm concerned about patterns I'm seeing. The accident yesterday wasn't isolated. Over the past several months, I've treated more serious mining injuries than in the previous two years combined."

"Margaret mentioned the miners thought the supports might have been tampered with."

"It's not just that," the doctor continued, his voice barely above a whisper. "It's the pattern of who gets hurt. Men who speak up about safety concerns. Workers who question wage reductions. Miners who don't show proper loyalty to McGrant's leadership."

A chill ran down Abigail's spine. "Are you suggesting these accidents are... deliberate?"

Dr. Carpenter glanced around before answering. "I have no proof. Just observations and suspicions. And the fact that Axel Frazier had recently been vocal about the need for better ventilation in the lower tunnels."

"Have you spoken to Sheriff Holden about this?"

"What can he do without evidence? Besides, Holden's jurisdiction is limited when it comes to the mine. McGrant has his own security force, answers to no one locally." The doctor sighed heavily. "I'm telling you this because your church is becoming a gathering place for people seeking something beyond McGrant's influence. That makes you both important and vulnerable."

"What would you have me do, Doctor? Abandon the church? Stop the services?"

"No," he replied firmly. "Quite the opposite. This town needs what you're bringing back to it. But you should be aware of the forces aligned against you." He hesitated, then added, "And perhaps consider who your allies are."

"Like yourself?" Abigail ventured.

"Like myself. Like Sheriff Holden, though, his official capacity limits him. Like Margaret Hale and others who remember what Clear Springs was before McGrant's shadow fell across it." He finished his coffee and set the cup down decisively. "And like Jonah Brooks, whether he admits it openly or not."

Abigail felt her cheeks warm slightly at the mention of Jonah. "Mr. Brooks has been very helpful to me."

Dr. Carpenter's expression softened with something like amusement. "Jonah doesn't help anyone that he doesn't want to help, regardless of McGrant or anyone else. The fact that he's involved at all with you and the church speaks volumes." He rose from his chair. "Just be careful, Miss Whitaker. McGrant doesn't confront his obstacles directly, he undermines them gradually until they collapse. Rather like those support beams in his mine."

With that sobering comparison, he bid her good day and departed, leaving Abigail with her cooling tea and troubling thoughts.

# Chapter 20

The rhythmic clang of Jonah's hammer against hot metal filled the shop, each strike precise and controlled despite the force behind it. He was fashioning new hinges for the church's side door, the existing ones having rusted beyond repair. It was practical work, necessary work, he told himself. Nothing more.

The sound of approaching footsteps didn't register through the noise, but the familiar figure entering his workshop made him pause mid-strike. Sheriff Luke Holden removed his hat as he stepped into the relative dimness of the shop, waiting for Jonah to acknowledge him.

Jonah thrust the metal back into the forge and straightened, nodding to the lawman. "Sheriff."

"Jonah," Luke replied, moving further into the shop. "Got a minute?"

Jonah gestured to a workbench where they could sit. The two men had known each other since Jonah's arrival in Clear Springs, maintaining a relationship of mutual respect. Luke was one of the few people Jonah considered trustworthy in town.

"Mine accident yesterday," Luke began without preamble. "Axel Frazier's laid up at Doc's place with injuries that'll keep him from working for months, if he ever fully recovers."

Jonah nodded. "Heard about it."

"Did you hear three men got fired for suggesting the support beams might have been tampered with?"

"No."

Luke sighed, rubbing a hand across his face. "That's not the half of it. I got word this morning that McGrant's bringing in replacements from outside. Men with... reputations."

Jonah's eyes narrowed. "What kind of reputations?"

"The kind that involves breaking strikes in Lewisville. Intimidating workers in Silverton." Luke's jaw tightened. "Enforcers, not miners."

"Why tell me?"

"Because things are changing quickly at the mine, and not for the better." Luke leaned forward, resting his elbows on his knees. "McGrant's always ruled with a firm hand, but lately, it's becoming something else. Something harder, more desperate."

Jonah considered this. "Silver yield dropping?"

"That's my guess. From what I've been told, the mines are not producing like it used to. McGrant's pushing harder, taking more risks." Luke shook his head. "And now he's got this bee in his bonnet about the church reopening."

"Miss Whitaker's service on Sunday," Jonah stated.

"Exactly. McGrant was in the café this morning, taking names. Deputy Mansfield overheard him telling McCallum they needed to address the church situation." Luke met Jonah's gaze directly. "I'm worried, Jonah. Not just about the town, but about Miss Whitaker specifically."

Jonah's hands clenched involuntarily. "Why?"

"Because she's becoming a symbol of hope. People who wouldn't normally stand against McGrant are finding courage through her example. And McGrant doesn't tolerate resistance."

"What's he planning?"

"Don't know the details. But I've seen that look in his eye before... right before that last circuit preacher's supposed accident." Luke's expression darkened. "We both know that wasn't really an accident."

Jonah remained silent, processing this information with growing unease. He'd suspected as much about Reverend Wither's fall from his horse, but hearing Holden confirm it made the danger to Abigail seem more immediate.

"Can't arrest a man on suspicion," he finally said.

"No," Luke agreed. "And that's the problem. McGrant's too smart to leave evidence. Works through others, maintains distance from the dirty work." He stood, replacing his hat. "Just wanted you to know what's brewing. Figure you've got as much stake in this as anyone."

"Don't know what you mean."

Holden's mouth quirked in a humorless smile. "Sure you don't." He moved toward the door, then paused. "One more thing. McCallum's daughter was seen lingering near the church yesterday. The girls never shown an interest in anything before, but now she's visiting when she thinks no one's watching. If McGrant finds out..."

The implications hung in the air between them. Hannah McCallum's interest in the church would be seen as a direct betrayal by her father and, by extension, by McGrant himself.

"I'll keep an eye out," Jonah said shortly.

After Holden departed, Jonah returned to the forge, but his mind was no longer on the hinges. The sheriff's warnings had crystallized a sense of foreboding that had been building for days. McGrant was moving, gathering his forces, preparing to extinguish the small flame of independence that Abigail had kindled.

Jonah's hammer struck the metal with renewed force, each blow punctuating his thoughts. He'd warned her about McGrant. Told her the risks. She'd understood, but proceeded anyway.

And now she was in danger. Real danger, not just the abstract threat he'd cautioned her about.

Jonah thrust the metal back into the forge with more force than necessary, watching the flames leap higher.

# Chapter 21

Abigail knelt in the church, carefully arranging the hymnals in the pew racks. After her conversation with Dr. Carpenter earlier, she'd needed the solace of purposeful work inside the church, the comfort of the sanctuary despite its still evident damage.

The side door opening made her look up. She was surprised to see Hannah McCallum slip inside, her slender figure silhouetted against the afternoon light.

"Hannah," Abigail greeted her warmly, rising to her feet. "What a pleasant surprise."

The girl hesitated just inside the doorway, clearly uncertain of her welcome. "I... I shouldn't be here. Father would be furious if he knew."

"Then we won't tell him," Abigail replied simply. "You're welcome here, Hannah. Always."

Hannah took a few tentative steps forward, her gaze traveling over the church interior.

"It's looking nice," Hannah observed. "I remember coming here, before..." she trailed off.

"Before the church closed?" Abigail supplied gently.

"Before Mother died. Before Father forbade it." She moved closer to the altar, reaching out to touch it with delicate fingers. "She loved services. Said it was the one place she felt truly at peace."

Abigail's heart ached for the girl, recognizing the loneliness in her voice. "Your mother sounds like she was a wonderful woman."

"She was," Hannah whispered. "Father was different when she was alive. Stricter than other parents, perhaps, but not..." She stopped, seemingly afraid to criticize her father even here.

"Not as he is now?" Abigail suggested carefully.

Hannah nodded, her eyes downcast. "After she died, he changed. Became harder. Said faith was a weakness that had failed her, failed them both." She looked up, a flash of defiance in her eyes. "But I don't believe that. I think faith was what gave her strength, especially at the end."

Abigail approached slowly, sensing the girl's need to talk but not wanting to press too hard. "Faith often provides comfort in difficult times. A sense that we're not alone in our struggles."

"That's what I miss most," Hannah admitted. "The feeling of... belonging to something larger than myself." She glanced toward the back doors nervously. "Your service on Sunday. The singing. It reminded me of mother so much."

"You're welcome to join us this coming Sunday," Abigail offered. "Or to come here anytime you need a quiet place to think or pray."

Hannah's expression clouded. "Father would never allow it. Says the mine is our true provider, not some distant God who let Mother suffer."

Abigail considered her words carefully. "Faith doesn't promise an absence of suffering, Hannah. It offers meaning within suffering, and hope beyond it." She smiled gently. "But I understand your situation.

The church doors will remain open for you whenever you feel safe to enter."

The girl seemed to struggle with some internal decision. Finally, she reached into her pocket and withdrew a small, worn book. "I've kept this hidden since Mother died. Father would burn it if he found it." She held it out to Abigail.

It was a small devotional, its leather cover softened with use, the gilt edges of its pages worn from frequent turning. Abigail recognized it as the kind of personal prayer book many women carried.

"I read from it sometimes when I'm alone. But I thought... perhaps it belongs here now. Where others might benefit from it."

Abigail understood the magnitude of what Hannah was offering, not just the book itself, but the connection to her mother it represented. "Are you certain you want to part with it? It's a precious keepsake."

Hannah nodded, her eyes bright with unshed tears. "Mother would want it to be used, not hidden away. And I've memorized the passages that meant the most to her." She pressed the book into Abigail's hands. "Please. Keep it here, where it can be part of worship again, and it's safe."

Abigail accepted the book with the reverence it deserved. "I'll treasure it, Hannah. And perhaps, when you visit again, you can show me which passages were special to your mother."

A small smile transformed Hannah's face. "I'd like that."

The church door opened again, startling them both. Hannah's expression immediately shifted to one of alarm, but it was only Ethan, carrying a toolbox.

"Miss Whitaker, Mr. Brooks sent me to fix the loose floorboards by the—" He stopped short upon seeing Hannah. "Oh! Sorry, didn't mean to interrupt."

"It's all right, Ethan," Abigail assured him. "Hannah was just leaving, I believe."

Hannah nodded quickly, already moving toward the side door. "Thank you for... for everything," she said to Abigail, before slipping out into the afternoon sunlight.

Ethan watched her go with curiosity. "Was that Hannah McCallum? Mr. McCallum's daughter?"

"Yes," Abigail confirmed, carefully placing Hannah's mother's devotional on the altar.

"Huh," Ethan replied, setting down his toolbox. "Mr. McCallum keeps her pretty close to home usually."

"Sometimes people find their way to places they need, regardless of restrictions," Abigail said thoughtfully. "Now, which floorboards need attention?"

As Ethan showed her the loose boards near the altar steps, Abigail's mind remained on Hannah and the precious gift she'd entrusted to her. The girl's situation reflected the broader dynamics in Clear Springs. The souls yearning for connection and meaning, constrained by fear and control.

"Mr. Brooks said he'll be by later to install those new hinges on the side door," Ethan mentioned as he knelt to examine the floorboards. "Said it's important to have multiple exits secure."

Abigail smiled. "He's right, of course. Please thank him for his thoughtfulness."

"You could thank him yourself when he comes," Ethan suggested with a grin. "He pretends not to care about the church, but he's been working on those hinges all morning. Making them special, stronger than regular ones."

"I'll be sure to express my appreciation properly."

Ethan hammered the loose floorboards back into place, chatting about other repairs Jonah had mentioned might be needed at the church. Abigail listened with half an ear, her thoughts divided between Hannah's secret visit, Dr. Carpenter's warnings, and now the news that Jonah would be coming later.

# Chapter 22

The afternoon shadows were lengthening when Jonah arrived at the church, the new hinges wrapped carefully in oilcloth. He'd taken particular care with these hinges, forging them stronger than standard, designing them to withstand force if necessary.

He found Abigail alone in the sanctuary, arranging wildflowers in simple glass jars along the windowsills. The late afternoon light caught in her hair, turning the blonde strands to gold. For a moment, he simply stood in the doorway, watching her work.

She sensed his presence and turned, a smile lighting her face. "Mr. Brooks. Ethan mentioned you'd be coming."

"The hinges," he explained unnecessarily, holding up the wrapped package. "For the side door."

"Thank you," she replied, moving toward him. "I appreciate your attention to such details."

Jonah nodded, suddenly uncomfortable with her gratitude for what seemed to him a basic precaution. "Side exit should be secure. Basic safety."

Abigail studied him with those perceptive eyes that always seemed to see more than he intended to reveal. "Of course. Safety is important, especially these days."

Something in her tone made him look at her more closely. "Meaning?"

She hesitated, then gestured to a pew. "Would you sit with me for a moment? There's something I'd like to discuss."

Jonah set down his tools and followed her to the front pew. They sat with a respectful distance between them, Abigail smoothing her skirts as she gathered her thoughts.

"I had an interesting conversation with Dr. Carpenter today," she began. "About the recent accident at the mine."

Jonah's jaw tightened.

"He believes it may not have been an accident at all." Abigail's voice was low, though they were alone in the church. "That the support beams may have been deliberately weakened to target workers who had spoken up about safety concerns."

"Carpenter said this outright?"

"He was careful with his words, but his meaning was clear." She met his gaze directly. "Sheriff Holden spoke with you today as well, didn't he? About McGrant?"

"How did you know?"

"Because you're here with specially made hinges, looking more concerned than usual," she replied with a small smile. "And because the sheriff strikes me as a man who would warn those he trusts about potential dangers."

Her assessment was accurate, both of Holden and himself. Jonah found himself once again impressed by her ability to read situations and people.

"He's worried," Jonah admitted. "McGrant's bringing in men with reputations for handling problems. Word has it, the mine may be producing less silver, and he's getting desperate."

"And furthermore, the church represents a problem to him. A gathering place outside his control."

"You represent a problem," Jonah corrected bluntly. "You're giving people something McGrant can't match... hope, community, and purpose beyond survival."

Abigail absorbed this, her expression thoughtful. "Hannah McCallum visited today," she said, changing the subject slightly. "She came to the church when she thought no one would see her."

Jonah frowned. "That's dangerous for her. McCallum's completely under McGrant's thumb. Treats his daughter like property."

"She's seeking a connection to her mother's faith," Abigail explained. "Something her father has forbidden since her mother's death." She gestured to a small book resting on the altar. "She gave me her mother's prayer book to keep here, where it would be part of worship again, as she put it."

"The girl's risking a lot."

"Yes. But she feels it's worth the risk. That's what faith does, Mr. Brooks. It provides courage when fear would be easier."

"McGrant won't see it that way. To him, it's defiance, plain and simple."

"Perhaps it is," Abigail conceded. "But sometimes defiance is necessary when what's being demanded is wrong." She sighed, looking around the church interior. "I didn't come to Clear Springs seeking conflict, Mr. Brooks. I came to restore this church, to serve a community in need of spiritual guidance. And I understand that those goals conflict with McGrant's control."

"And knowing that? What will you do?"

"Continue," she replied without hesitation. "With greater awareness of the risks, certainly. With prudent precautions, like these excellent hinges you've crafted." She smiled briefly. "But I won't abandon what God has called me to do because a man like Silas McGrant finds it inconvenient for his purposes."

"It's more than inconvenient for him. It's threatening. A man like McGrant doesn't distinguish between spiritual matters and business interests. It's all about control."

"I understand that now," Abigail acknowledged. "Dr. Carpenter made that quite clear." She looked at him directly. "What I don't fully understand is why you're involved, Mr. Brooks. You've made it clear you have little interest in church matters, yet here you are, crafting special hinges and sending Ethan to fix floorboards."

The directness of her question caught him off guard. Jonah looked away, uncomfortable with examining his own motivations too closely.

"Practical concerns," he muttered. "Building should be sound."

"Is that all?"

Jonah stood abruptly, moving toward the side door where he intended to install the hinges. "Should get these in before dark."

Abigail didn't push further, rising gracefully and nodding. "Of course. I'll leave you to your work."

As she moved away, Jonah felt an unexpected urge to explain himself, to offer something more honest than his gruff deflection. "Miss Whitaker," he called, causing her to turn back. "What you're doing here... it matters. To more people than you know."

"Thank you for saying so, Mr. Brooks."

"McGrant won't stop," he continued, the words coming reluctantly but honestly. "He'll keep pushing, testing, looking for weaknesses. A man like that can't abide what he can't control."

"I'm aware of the risks."

"Are you?" Jonah challenged, moving closer. "The last circuit preacher, Reverend Wither's... he had an accident that sent him running... and it wasn't random. The sheriff and I both believe McGrant was behind it, wanted him gone when he started speaking against mine conditions."

Abigail's eyes widened slightly. "You and the sheriff think he would harm a preacher?"

"Through others, keeping his hands clean. But yes." Jonah held her gaze, needing her to understand the reality of what she faced. "You need to be careful. Very careful."

"I will be," she promised. "But I won't live in fear, Mr. Brooks. That's what men like McGrant want, for people to be so afraid they surrender their own judgment, their own faith."

Jonah shook his head, both frustrated and impressed by her determination. "Just... watch your back. And maybe accept all help when it's offered."

A small smile curved her lips. "Like specially crafted hinges and fixed floorboards?"

"Something like that."

"I'm grateful for your help, Mr. Brooks. More than you know." Her voice had softened, and something in her expression made his chest tighten unexpectedly.

To hide his discomfort, Jonah turned back to his tools. "Should get these installed before the light fades."

Abigail nodded, understanding his need to retreat into practical matters. "I'll be in the parsonage if you need anything. I'll have fresh coffee waiting."

As she departed, Jonah began working on the hinges. Physical labor had always been his refuge, the place where his thoughts cleared and his purpose sharpened.

But today, even as his hands worked with practiced precision, his mind remained unsettled. The warnings from Holden, the implications of McGrant's growing desperation, and above all, Abigail's quiet courage in the face of mounting danger, all these thoughts circled relentlessly.

The realization that he cared about what happened to Abigail, and to this town, struck him with unexpected force. He'd spent so long shutting out such feelings that their return was almost painful in its intensity.

He paused his work and looked at the altar. Setting his tool aside, he walked toward it and knelt to pray.

"Lord, I know I've been distant from you for too long. I'm uncertain whether you're calling me back or what stirs within me. But I need you."

# Chapter 23

Jonah tightened the final screw on the new hinges, giving the side door a firm push to test its stability. The door swung smoothly, then closed with a satisfying thud. He ran his hand along the edge of the door, nodding with approval.

He gathered his tools, placing them in his leather case. The evening had grown dim, and light glowed from the parsonage windows. Jonah hesitated, debating whether to simply leave now that his work was done or let Abigail know he was finished.

He made his way toward the parsonage. The small house looked welcoming in the fading light. The porch had been repaired and the shutters that had once hung askew were now fixed. As he approached, he saw Abigail sitting in a rocking chair, a steaming cup in her hands, gazing thoughtfully toward the mountains.

Jonah paused at the bottom of the steps, removing his hat. "Miss Whitaker."

Abigail turned, her expression brightening when she saw him. "Mr. Brooks. Have you finished with the hinges?"

"Yes, ma'am. The door's secure now."

"Would you care to join me?" She gestured to the empty chair beside her. "The coffee's still hot."

Jonah shifted his weight, uncomfortable with the invitation, despite finding himself oddly drawn to accept it. "Don't want to intrude on your evening."

"You wouldn't be intruding at all," she assured him, already rising to fetch another cup. "Please, sit. It's a lovely evening for conversation."

Before he could formulate an excuse, Abigail had disappeared inside. Jonah climbed the steps and lowered himself into the vacant chair, placing his hat on his knee. He felt strangely out of place, sitting on a porch, as if he were a social caller.

Abigail returned with a second cup of coffee and handed it to him. "Cream or sugar?"

"Black is fine, thank you," he replied, taking a sip of the coffee. It was good—rich and strong, not the weak brew many served to stretch their supply.

"I appreciate your thoroughness in all the work you've done for the church." She smiled, her eyes reflecting the last light of day. "You're a man who thinks ahead, Mr. Brooks."

Jonah shrugged. "Just practical."

They sat in silence for a moment, the only sounds the creak of Abigail's rocking chair and the distant call of birds settling for the night. Jonah found himself unexpectedly content in the quiet moment, the coffee warming his hands, the day's labor satisfyingly complete.

"What was Boston like?" he asked.

Abigail looked at him, clearly pleased by his interest. "Very different from Clear Springs. Bustling, crowded, with buildings so tall they block the sky in places. There's a constant noise... carriages, vendors, church bells, and ships in the harbor."

"You miss it?"

She considered this; her gaze returning to the mountains. "I miss certain aspects. The libraries, the concerts, the comfort of familiar routines. But Boston never felt entirely like home to me. My parents were often away on missionary work, and I was frequently left in the care of hired nannies or assistants or at boarding school."

"Your parents traveled often?"

"Yes, they were deeply committed to missionary work. They would return to Boston between assignments, but their hearts were always drawn to places of need." A wistful smile touched her lips. "I admired their dedication, though as a child, I sometimes resented sharing them with strangers. As I got older, they sometimes let me travel with them while on mission trips. Those are some of my favorite memories."

Jonah nodded, understanding the complexity of loving people whose calling took them away. "Must have been hard when they were gone."

"It was, especially when I was younger. But as I grew older, I came to understand their passion. They believed so deeply in bringing hope to desperate places." She looked at him directly. "That's why this church meant so much to them. They saw Clear Springs as a community that needed a spiritual foundation to thrive. This place meant something to them. Clear Springs was deeply embedded in their hearts."

"And now you're carrying on their work."

"I'm trying to. Though I'm discovering it is more challenging than I anticipated." She laughed softly, the sound warm in the gathering dusk. "My parents spoke of the physical hardships, the primitive conditions, the isolation, but they never mentioned the... political complications."

"McGrant, you mean."

"Yes. And the complex dynamics of a town so dependent on a single industry controlled by one man." She shook her head. "In Boston, power is diffuse, spread among many influential families and institutions. Here, it's concentrated so intensely."

"Frontier towns are often that way," Jonah said. "One man with money or vision establishes a foothold, others follow, seeking opportunity. Before long, the founder or a person with money controls everything... water rights, land, commerce."

"You sound like you've seen it before."

"Traveled some after the war. Saw similar patterns in different places." He took another sip of coffee, realizing he'd said more than he intended.

"The war... you fought for the Confederacy?"

"Yes."

"That must have been difficult. The war divided so many families, communities."

"It did." He looked down at his cup, unwilling to elaborate further.

Abigail seemed to sense his reluctance. She changed the subject gracefully. "And after the war? Did you come directly to Clear Springs?"

"No. Drifted for a while. Worked where I could... ranches, railroads, and smithies when the opportunity arose. Spent time in Kansas, Nebraska, and Wyoming before reaching Colorado."

"What brought you here specifically?"

Jonah considered the question, realizing he'd never fully examined his own motivations for settling in Clear Springs. "Nothing in particular. The town needed a blacksmith. I had the skills. Seemed as good a place as any to stop moving."

"And you've been here four years now?"

"Going on five."

Abigail nodded, studying him with those perceptive eyes that made him feel oddly exposed. "Do you have family elsewhere, Mr. Brooks?"

The question, innocent as it was, struck like a blow. Jonah set his coffee cup down carefully on the small table between them, his fingers tightening around the handle before he let go. "No. Not anymore."

Abigail's expression softened. "I'm sorry. I didn't mean to stir up painful memories."

Silence settled between them, but the quiet comfort of earlier had vanished. Grief stirred inside him, memories pressing in—ones that still had the power to drag him under if he let them.

Abigail didn't press, didn't judge—just sat there, steady and understanding. And for the first time in a long while, the urge to speak, to lay down the weight he had carried alone for so long, nearly overpowered his instinct to hold it in.

"Had a family once," he said abruptly. "Back in North Carolina."

"North Carolina is beautiful, I've heard."

"It was. Small farming community miles outside of Raleigh. Nothing grand, but good land. Fertile." Jonah stared into the distance, seeing not the Colorado mountains but the rolling hills of his homeland. "My father built the house himself when he married my mother. Added rooms as children came—myself, then my brother Josiah, and sister Bessie after that."

"You were the eldest, then?"

"Yes. Expected to take over the farm, eventually. Continue what my father started." A bitter smile crossed his face. "Had different ideas at first. Felt called to preach."

Abigail's surprise was evident in her voice. "You were a preacher?"

"Training to be. Worked alongside my father at our small church. He was the minister there, though he farmed to support the family.

The church couldn't pay much." Jonah shook his head at the memories. "I was young, full of conviction. Thought I knew God's plan clearly."

"What changed?"

Jonah fell silent, the familiar pain rising like a tide. Part of him wanted to stop here, to retreat from memories he'd spent years trying to avoid. But another part, one he barely recognized anymore, urged him to continue, to share the burden he'd carried alone for so long.

Abigail seemed to sense his internal struggle. Gently, she placed her hand on his forearm, the touch light but steady. "Whatever it is, Mr. Brooks, you don't have to carry it alone."

Her gesture, simple and compassionate, broke something loose within him. Jonah looked at her hand resting on his arm, then into her eyes, finding nothing but genuine concern there.

"I enlisted in '63," he began, his voice low. "The War was going badly for the Confederacy by then, but I still believed in defending my home, my state. Emily, my wife, was expecting our first child when I left." He paused, the words becoming more difficult. "Promised I'd be back soon. Made all sorts of promises I couldn't keep."

Abigail's hand remained on his arm, a steady anchor as he navigated the painful waters.

"War wasn't what I expected. Nothing noble or glorious about it. Just death and suffering on both sides." Jonah's jaw tightened at the memories. "Still, I tried to maintain faith. Led prayers for my unit. Offered comfort to dying men and boys far from home."

He took a deep breath before continuing. "When the war ended in '65, I headed home immediately. Eager to meet my child, see Emily again. Dreaming of returning to normal life, to preaching, to family." His voice grew hollow. "But there was nothing to return to."

Abigail's fingers tightened slightly on his arm. "What happened?"

"Fire. While I was away. Swept through our farm, the house…" Jonah swallowed hard. "Everyone had been inside. Emily, our child. My parents. Josiah and Bessie. All gone."

"Oh, Jonah," Abigail whispered, using his first name without seeming to notice. "I'm so sorry."

"Wasn't just my family," he continued, the words coming faster now, as if a dam had broken. "Much of the town burned, too. Raiders, they said. Union or Confederate, no one knew for certain. Just men taking advantage of chaos to destroy and steal."

He looked directly at her, his eyes burning with long-suppressed grief. "I went to the church, looking for… something. Comfort. Answers. Meaning. It was gone too. Burned to the foundation."

Abigail's eyes glistened with tears. She didn't try to hide them.

Jonah looked away, unable to bear her compassion. "I couldn't reconcile it, how God could let it happen. All those innocent lives. The church itself. Everything I believed in, destroyed while I was away fighting for what, I thought, was right."

"Faith often faces its greatest test in suffering," Abigail said gently. "It's not wrong to question, to struggle."

"Did more than question. Rejected it entirely. Decided if that was God's plan, I wanted no part of it." Jonah's voice hardened. "Spent the next year drinking, fighting, and trying to forget. When that didn't work, I started moving west. To new places where no one knew me. Where I didn't have to explain or remember."

He fell silent, emotionally exhausted by the telling. The night had fully descended now; the porch illuminated only by the soft light spilling from the parsonage windows.

Abigail hadn't removed her hand from his arm, her touch a constant, comforting presence. "Thank you for telling me," she said quietly. "I know it wasn't easy."

"Don't know why I did," Jonah admitted. "Haven't spoken of it to anyone. Ever."

"Sometimes the heart knows when it's safe to share its burdens," she replied. "And sometimes God provides the right person at the right moment to hear what needs to be said."

Jonah looked at her, studying her face in the gentle light. There was no pity there, only understanding and a quiet strength that continued to surprise him.

"Is this why you're helping with the church? Did you feel called to help me?" she asked. "Despite your feelings about faith?"

"Maybe. When I first saw you determined to restore it, I thought you were naïve. I thought you wouldn't last. But something about your persistence..." He trailed off, unable to articulate the complex emotions her efforts had stirred in him.

"Reminded you of what you once believed in?" she suggested.

Jonah shook his head and looked down at the porch floor.

"Faith isn't about going back, Jonah. It's about moving forward, carrying our experiences, even the painful ones, with us into a new understanding." Abigail's voice was gentle but firm. "God doesn't ask us to pretend our suffering didn't happen, or that it didn't change us."

"Then what does He ask?"

"That we remain open to healing. Open to purpose beyond our pain. Open to the possibility that what seems destroyed might yet be rebuilt."

The parallel to the church renovation wasn't lost on Jonah. He looked toward the shadowy outline of the church building, its steeple a dark silhouette against the night sky.

"That's a lot to ask."

"It is," Abigail agreed. "But perhaps not all at once. Perhaps just one small step at a time."

Jonah felt strangely lightened, as if sharing his burden had physically relieved some of the weight he'd carried for years.

"It's getting late," he said, reaching for his hat. "Should let you get your rest."

Abigail nodded, though she seemed reluctant for the evening to end. "Thank you for the hinges, Mr. Brooks. And for your company."

"Jonah," he corrected her, surprising himself. "I think, after what I've shared, you might as well use my given name."

A smile brightened her face. "Then you must call me Abigail."

"Abigail," he repeated. He stood, placing his hat on his head. "Thank you for listening. And for the coffee."

"You're welcome anytime, Jonah. For coffee or conversation."

He nodded, suddenly awkward now that the moment of intimate sharing had passed. "Goodnight, then."

"Goodnight."

As Jonah descended the porch steps, he felt her watching him. He turned back. "Abigail?"

"Yes?"

"What I told you tonight... about my past, what happened..." He hesitated, unaccustomed to making requests. "Would appreciate it if it stayed between us."

"Of course," she replied immediately.

He nodded once more before turning toward town. His mind was too full of the evening's conversation, of memories long suppressed now brought into the open, of the strange relief that came with sharing them.

As he walked through the quiet town, Jonah realized with sudden clarity that for the first time in years, he didn't feel entirely alone.

# Chapter 24

From the wide doorway of his shop, Jonah watched the steady stream of townspeople heading toward the church. Timothy Wells' wagon loaded with lumber, followed by three miners he recognized as men who rarely ventured anywhere but between the mine and the saloon. They headed in that direction.

"Quite a turnout," Ethan remarked behind him, pumping the bellows to maintain the forge's heat. "Seems like half the town's heading to help Miss Whitaker."

Jonah resumed hammering the horseshoe he was shaping, his blows perhaps harder than necessary. "Town's full of people with nothing better to do on a Saturday, apparently."

Ethan grinned. "You know, those front steps they're replacing would benefit from proper iron brackets. The old ones were completely rusted through."

"Not my concern," Jonah replied curtly, though his eyes drifted toward the church again.

"Miss Whitaker mentioned yesterday that they're short on tools," Ethan continued casually. "Especially sandpaper for the pews and hammers for repair work."

Jonah plunged the horseshoe into the water barrel, where it hissed and steamed. "Shop's open today. We got three horses waiting for shoes and that wagon axle to be repaired. I don't have time."

"I could take some tools over," Ethan suggested. "Maybe stay for an hour to help. You could manage without me for a bit, couldn't you?"

Jonah straightened, wiping sweat from his brow with his forearm. He studied his apprentice's eager expression. The boy's enthusiasm reminded him too much of his own youthful idealism, before life had taught him harsh lessons.

The days since his unexpected conversation with Abigail on her porch, since he'd shared burdens he'd carried alone for years, Jonah had found himself increasingly unsettled.

"Go if you want," he said, returning to the forge. "Take whatever tools they need. But be back by noon."

Ethan's face lit up.

As the young man hurried to collect tools, Jonah called after him, "And tell Wells those steps need proper bracing if they're going to last."

Ethan paused, a knowing smile playing at his lips. "I'll tell him you said so."

After Ethan departed with an armful of tools, Jonah found himself working with half his attention, his gaze repeatedly drawn to the church. The sound of hammering and occasional bursts of laughter carried down the street. A wagon arrived with several women bearing covered dishes, presumably for a midday meal.

Jonah wondered how the work was progressing. Whether the roof repairs he'd made earlier had held against the recent torrential rains. Whether Abigail was trying to do too much herself, as was her habit.

His thoughts were interrupted by the sight of Hannah McCallum slipping furtively toward the church, glancing over her shoulder as if concerned about being followed. The girl was taking an enormous risk.

Jonah set down his tools with a sigh of resignation. The horseshoes could wait.

***

Hannah hovered at the edge of the churchyard, her slender form partially hidden behind a large oak tree. She watched the bustling activity with longing evident in her posture, shoulders tense with indecision, hands clasped tightly at her waist.

Abigail noticed her and approached, wiping her hands on her apron. "Hannah, I'm so glad you came. Would you like to help us?"

"I shouldn't stay long. Father thinks I'm visiting Missy Jenkins to borrow a book."

"Then we'll make your time count," Abigail said. "Come, we're planting flowers around the church sign."

Hannah hesitated, then followed Abigail to where Bonnie Carpenter knelt on the soft earth, creating holes for seedlings. The doctor's wife smiled kindly at the nervous girl.

"Perfect timing! These marigolds need gentle hands. Have you gardened before, Hannah?"

"A little. My mother loved flowers." Hannah knelt beside the woman, accepting a trowel with tentative enthusiasm.

Abigail was about to join them when Ruth called from the front steps, where Timothy and his helpers were struggling with a particularly stubborn section of rotting wood.

"Miss Whitaker!"

As Abigail hurried their way, she nearly collided with Ethan, who arrived carrying an assortment of tools.

"Mr. Sheldon! What a pleasant surprise."

Ethan grinned, setting down his burden. "Jonah sent me with these."

Timothy Wells looked up from his crouched position by the steps. "Jonah Brooks parting with his precious tools? Now there's a miracle to rival any in scripture."

"He also said to tell you that these steps need proper iron brackets, Mr. Wells, and better bracing if they're going to last," Ethan added.

"Did he now? Well, if the man's so concerned, he should come supervise personally!"

"He's busy with horseshoes and a broken wagon axle," Ethan explained.

Abigail surveyed the tools Ethan had brought, finely crafted hammers, chisels, planes, and even several specialized implements whose purposes she couldn't immediately identify.

"Please thank Mr. Brooks for his generosity," she said.

"You can thank him yourself," Ruth interjected, pointing toward town. "Looks like he's decided to join us."

Abigail turned to see Jonah approaching, his stride purposeful. He'd removed his blacksmith's apron but still wore his work clothes, the sleeves of his shirt rolled up to reveal muscular forearms. He carried what appeared to be metal brackets and additional tools.

Her heartbeat quickened at the sight of him. Since their conversation on her porch three nights ago, she had held a newfound understanding of the gruff man walking toward them that felt both fragile and significant.

"Wells," Jonah called as he approached the steps. "Those supports won't hold through the first snow if you set them that way."

Timothy straightened, wiping sweat from his brow. "Well now, the master craftsman arrives to enlighten us mere mortals." Despite his teasing words, he stepped aside willingly. "Show us how it's done then, Brooks."

Jonah knelt to examine the partially dismantled steps, running his hand along the wood. "Foundation's still solid. That's something." He glanced up at Abigail. "Thought you might need these." He indicated the metal brackets he'd brought.

"Thank you," Abigail said. "I didn't expect to see you today."

Jonah's expression remained impassive, but something in his eyes softened slightly. "Saw Hannah heading this way. Girl's taking a risk being here. Thought I'd keep an eye out for trouble."

The practicality of his explanation didn't entirely mask the voluntary nature of his presence, and Abigail smiled. "Well, whatever your reasons, we're grateful for your expertise."

For the next hour, Jonah worked alongside Timothy and two miners, rebuilding the church steps with meticulous care. His instructions were concise but clear, his movements efficient. Occasionally, he glanced toward the road leading from town, his concern for Hannah's safety evident.

Inside the church, Reverend Blake was directing the sanding of pews while Doc Carpenter sanded the pulpit.

Margaret and several other women prepared a lunch table under a large oak tree, spreading tablecloths over hastily assembled plank tables.

Abigail moved between groups, coordinating efforts and expressing gratitude to each volunteer. When she returned to check on the steps' progress, she found Jonah demonstrating to a young miner how to properly set the iron brackets he'd crafted.

"These will prevent the wood from splitting when it expands in wet weather," he explained patiently. "See how the curve matches the natural grain?"

The miner nodded, clearly impressed both by the craftsmanship and by receiving direct instruction from the usually taciturn blacksmith.

"You're quite the teacher, Mr. Brooks," Abigail said.

Jonah straightened, brushing wood shavings from his hands. "Just showing him the right way to do it."

"Nevertheless, you have a gift for explanation. Clear, precise, respectful of your student." She smiled. "Ethan is fortunate to have such a teacher."

"The boy's a natural with metal. Makes teaching easy."

"I doubt that's entirely true. The best students still need capable guidance." Abigail gestured toward the nearly completed steps. "These look wonderful, sturdy enough to welcome congregants for many years to come."

"Should hold," he agreed, his tone matter-of-fact, though his eyes revealed satisfaction with the work. "They need a coat of linseed oil before winter sets in."

"I'll add it to my ever-growing list," Abigail said with a small laugh. "Sometimes I wonder if I'll ever truly finish."

"Buildings are never really finished. They need constant care, maintenance. Neglect them, and they fall apart quickly."

"Like faith. It requires regular attention and care to remain strong."

"Maybe so."

Margaret called from beneath the oak tree: "Lunchtime, everyone! Come while it's hot!"

The workers gratefully set aside their tools and gathered around the makeshift tables laden with food. Anne's meat pies, Ruth's bread,

Libby's apple tarts, and contributions from a dozen other households created a feast unlike anything Clear Springs had seen in years.

Abigail noticed Hannah hanging back, clearly uncertain whether to join the communal meal. She approached the girl gently. "Please eat with us, Hannah. Everyone would enjoy your company."

"I should go," Hannah replied reluctantly. "If father discovers I'm here..."

"At least take some food with you," Abigail insisted, wrapping a meat pie and two apple tarts in a cloth napkin. "A small thank you for your help with the garden."

Hannah accepted the package with a grateful smile. "The church looks beautiful, Miss Whitaker. Like it did when my mother used to bring me."

"You're welcome here, Hannah. Remember that."

The girl nodded, then slipped away, taking a circuitous route back toward town to avoid being seen.

Abigail watched her go, heart heavy with concern for the girl's situation.

When she turned back toward the lunch gathering, she was surprised to see Jonah still present, standing somewhat apart from the group.

"Will you join us for lunch, Mr. Brooks?" she asked, approaching him. "There's certainly plenty to go around."

Jonah hesitated, glancing toward his shop down the street. "Jonah... not Mr. Brooks. I should get back to work."

"Surely, even the most dedicated blacksmith deserves a meal after his labor," Abigail pressed gently. "The horses won't mind waiting a little longer for new shoes, Jonah."

Something in her expression must have swayed him, for he nodded reluctantly. "Suppose I could eat quickly."

They joined the others beneath the oak tree. Abigail sat beside Jonah, with Reverend Blake across from them and Margaret at the reverend's side.

"Jonah! Good to see you joining in community affairs," Reverend Blake said warmly, passing him a plate. "Your craftsmanship on those steps is remarkable."

Jonah accepted the plate with a nod of acknowledgment. "Just practical work."

"Practical work done exceptionally well," the reverend insisted.

"The Lord appreciates quality workmanship," Margaret said, serving Jonah a generous portion of stew. "And so do these old bones that will be climbing those sturdy new steps tomorrow morning."

Jonah seemed uncomfortable with their appreciation, but managed a polite nod.

The conversation flowed around them as they ate. The townspeople discussing the morning's progress, planning afternoon tasks, and sharing news and observations. Abigail noticed that while Jonah remained largely silent, he listened attentively, occasionally nodding at practical suggestions or technical discussions about the remaining repairs.

"The floor in the back corner still needs attention," Doc Carpenter was saying to Timothy. "Some of those boards are rotting from underneath. We'll need to pull them up."

"That's a two-man job, at least," Timothy replied. "And we're short on experienced hands for that kind of precision work."

"I can help with that," Jonah said, drawing surprised glances from those nearby.

"We'd be most grateful," Abigail said.

Jonah replied with a shrug. "Dangerous to have unstable flooring in a public building."

"It's kind of you to offer your time," Reverend Blake said. "Especially when I know how busy your shop keeps you."

Jonah shifted uncomfortably. "Horseshoes can wait a few hours."

After lunch, the work resumed with renewed energy. Jonah and Timothy began the painstaking process of removing the damaged floorboards, while others continued sanding pews, sealing walls with linseed oil, and tending to countless other restoration tasks.

Abigail moved between groups, offering assistance where needed, but found herself repeatedly drawn to observe Jonah's careful work on the floor. His strong hands moved with surprising gentleness as he examined each board, his focus complete.

When the afternoon grew warm, workers shed jackets and rolled up sleeves. Abigail organized a water station, ensuring everyone stayed hydrated. As she approached Jonah with a dipper of cool water, she found him kneeling alone, Timothy having gone to fetch additional lumber.

"Water?" she offered, extending the dipper.

Jonah looked up, wiping sweat from his brow with his forearm. "Thank you." He accepted the dipper and drank deeply.

"How bad is the damage?" Abigail asked.

"Could be worse. The main supports are sound, just the cross-beams are rotted." He pointed to the darkened wood. "Water damage from that leaky roof before we fixed it. Fixable, though."

"That's a relief. I feared we might need to replace the entire floor."

"No need to go that far. Just targeted repairs." Jonah handed back the empty dipper. "Should have it secure by day's end."

"You don't need to stay that long. You've already done more than I could have hoped for."

"Started the job. Might as well finish it properly." He hesitated, then added, "Besides, more hands make the repairs go faster."

Abigail smiled. "Indeed it does."

Jonah returned to his work and Abigail remained kneeling beside him, watching his methodical assessment of each board and support.

"My father was a carpenter as well as a farmer and a minister," Jonah said suddenly, surprising her with the voluntary personal information. "He taught me to respect wood, understand its grain and natural strength." He ran his hand along an exposed beam. "Said you couldn't rush woodwork any more than you could rush faith. Both needed time and attention to detail."

Abigail remained quiet, recognizing the rare gift of his sharing.

"He built our church back home," Jonah continued, his focus on the floor before him. "Small place, nothing grand. But solid. Sturdy." His voice softened almost imperceptibly. "It was a beautiful church."

"Like this church will be again soon," Abigail said.

As she walked away, Abigail felt a warmth that had little to do with the afternoon sun. The armor Jonah maintained around himself had lowered more today, first with his unexpected appearance, then with his voluntary assistance, and finally with that small but significant sharing of his past.

# Chapter 25

The afternoon progressed steadily, with remarkable transformations occurring throughout the church. The pews were sanded smooth and gained a warm glow from fresh beeswax polish. The inside walls brightened with fresh paint. The windows sparkled, and the small garden around the church sign would soon burst with newly planted flowers.

By late afternoon, most volunteers had completed their tasks and departed with tired smiles and promises to return for Sunday's service. Reverend Blake blessed the day's work before allowing Deputy Mansfield to escort him home. Margaret and Ruth organized the remaining food for workers to take home, while Libby helped clean and return borrowed tools and supplies.

Jonah and Timothy had worked diligently on the floor repairs inside the church, and the new cross-beam was securely in place. When the final board was secured, Timothy straightened with a groan, pressing his hands against his lower back. "That should hold until judgment day," he declared with satisfaction. "Fine work, Brooks. Didn't know you had such good carpentry skills alongside your blacksmithing."

Jonah shrugged as he gathered his tools. "Basic knowledge. Nothing special."

"Disagree entirely," Timothy replied good-naturedly. "But I won't argue with a man who saved me hours of difficult work if I had to do it alone." He glanced toward the darkening windows. "Best get home before Wilma sends out a search party. Shall I let Miss Whitaker know we're finished?"

"I'll let her know," Jonah replied.

Timothy nodded, gathering his own tools. "Good man. See you tomorrow at service, perhaps?"

Jonah's expression remained neutral. "Got work to catch up on."

"Of course," Timothy replied. "Good evening to you, then."

After Timothy departed, Jonah sat alone in the church's main sanctuary. The space felt different now, warmer, more welcoming than when he'd first entered it weeks ago. The pews gleamed, and the altar stood strong and dignified. Even the air seemed changed, the mustiness replaced by the clean scents of beeswax, fresh paint, and wood polish.

He moved slowly toward the front, his footsteps echoing slightly. The pulpit where Abigail would stand tomorrow had been polished to a soft glow. Beside it, someone had placed a simple arrangement of wildflowers in a large blue jar.

Without conscious intention, he turned to sit on the front pew, his tools resting beside him.

"I wondered if I might find you here."

Abigail's soft voice from the doorway drew him from his thoughts. She approached slowly, as if concerned about intruding on a private moment.

"The floor's finished," Jonah explained, rising quickly. "It was straightforward work."

"Perhaps to someone with your abilities." Abigail smiled, stopping beside him to survey the sanctuary. "Isn't it remarkable what's been accomplished today? I scarcely recognize it as the same place."

"Everyone did good work."

"They did indeed." She turned to face him directly. "Thank you, Jonah. Not just for the floor or the steps, but for being here today. Your presence meant a great deal to the project and to me personally."

Her gratitude, expressed so directly and with such warmth, created a lightness in his chest.

"Wasn't planning to stay all day. Just meant to check on Hannah, maybe help with the steps for an hour."

"Yet you stayed. And contributed far more than you intended."

"The church needed proper work. And it was... not unpleasant... working alongside folks."

Abigail's smile deepened at his hesitant admission. "Community has a way of surprising us, doesn't it? There's something powerful about working together that transcends individual effort."

"Suppose so." Jonah glanced toward the windows, where twilight was gathering. "I should check those front steps one last time."

"Of course. I'll walk with you if you don't mind."

They moved together toward the entrance, their footsteps creating a synchronized rhythm on the floor. Outside, the evening air carried the scent of fresh earth from the newly planted garden and the lingering aroma of pine from the cut lumber.

Jonah knelt to examine the steps, running his hand along the joints and brackets with practiced assessment. "Solid work. Should serve well."

"They're beautiful," Abigail said, standing beside him. "Sturdy yet welcoming. Exactly what church steps should be."

Rising, Jonah brushed dust from his hands. "Might want to add a handrail, eventually. For the elderly or those unsteady on their feet."

"Another excellent suggestion. Perhaps during our next community workday?"

The casual use of "our" wasn't lost on Jonah, but he didn't reject the inclusion.

"Might be able to forge some brackets for that. When time allows."

"That would be wonderful." She hesitated, then added, "Would you like to come join me for a cup of coffee? It's been a long day, and I've just brewed a fresh pot."

Part of Jonah urged caution, warned against further entanglement in Abigail's world with its demands on his carefully maintained emotional distance. Yet another part, growing stronger by the day, recognized that something fundamental had shifted within him since their conversation on her porch, since he'd spoken aloud of losses he'd buried for years.

"Coffee would be welcome. If it's no trouble."

"No trouble at all." The pleasure in her voice was evident as she led the way toward the parsonage. "I've been on my feet since dawn, and I suspect you have to. We've earned a moment of rest."

The parsonage glowed with warmth as they entered, a lamp already lit on the small table in the kitchen. The main room was simple but cozy, with Abigail's feminine touches evident in the lace curtains, carefully arranged bookshelves, and small vases of wildflowers on various surfaces.

"Please, sit," Abigail gestured to a chair at the table while she moved to the stove, where a coffee pot simmered. "Black?"

"Black is fine," Jonah replied, setting his hat on his knee and looking around the room. He was struck by how Abigail had transformed this once-neglected space into a home.

She set a cup of coffee before him before taking the chair opposite. "I must admit, I'm more exhausted than I realized," she said with a small laugh. "But it's a satisfying kind of tiredness."

"Productive work does that," Jonah agreed, warming his hands around the cup. "Different from just being worn out."

"I agree." Abigail took a sip of her coffee, studying him over the rim of her cup. "Did you notice how happy everyone seemed today, despite the hard work? There was such joy in the shared purpose."

Jonah nodded. "Been a while since this town had much to unify around besides surviving McGrant's control."

"That's precisely it," Abigail said eagerly. "Today wasn't just about restoring a building. It was about continuing to restore a sense of community, of shared ownership in something larger than individual concerns."

"McGrant won't like that."

"I know." Abigail's expression sobered. "I worry he'll find ways to punish those who helped."

"Probably will." Jonah took a long drink of his coffee before continuing. "But maybe that's changing, too. More folks standing together makes it harder for him to single out individuals."

"I hope you're right." Abigail absently traced the rim of her cup with her finger. "I never intended to create conflict when I came here. I simply wanted to honor my parents by continuing their work."

"Some work naturally creates conflict," Jonah replied. "Especially when it challenges how things have been."

Abigail looked up, surprised by his insight. "That's very true. Change, even good change, often meets resistance."

A comfortable silence fell between them as they sipped their coffee, the day's exertions settling into tired muscles and the satisfaction of work well done.

"Hannah seemed happy today," Abigail said eventually. "For those brief hours working in the garden, she looked like any other young girl, carefree and enjoying life."

"She's taking risks."

"I know. I worry about her." Abigail sighed. "But I can't turn her away when she so clearly needs connection to her mother's faith, to something beyond her father's control."

"Not suggesting you should," Jonah clarified. "Just saying we should be watchful. McCallum has a temper, especially when he's been drinking."

The casual use of "we" wasn't lost on Abigail, but she didn't draw attention to it.

"I've been praying for wisdom in how best to help her," she said instead. "And for her protection."

Jonah nodded, his expression thoughtful. After a moment, he asked, "Will tomorrow's service go forward as planned? Even with some work still unfinished here?"

"Yes," Abigail confirmed. "Reverend Blake feels strong enough to deliver a short sermon, and really, the essential repairs are complete. The remaining work can continue in the weeks ahead."

"Expect you'll have a full house," Jonah said.

"I hope so." Abigail smiled. "It would be wonderful to see those pews filled, to hear hymns sung by many voices instead of just a few."

Jonah studied her, struck by the genuine joy that illuminated her features at the prospect. Her anticipation wasn't about seeking praise or attention. Just a sincere hope for the community's spiritual renewal.

"You truly believe in this, don't you? In what this church can mean for Clear Springs."

"With all my heart," she replied without hesitation. "Not just the building, but what it represents—hope, community, and a reminder that we're not alone in our struggles." Her gaze met his directly. "That's what faith offers, Jonah. Not protection from life's hardships, but companionship through them, purpose within them, and hope beyond them."

He felt an unexpected resonance with her description. It reminded him of the faith he'd once known, before grief and anger had buried it beneath protective layers of cynicism and doubt.

"Your parents would be proud," he said. "Of what you've accomplished here."

"I think they would be."

Jonah nodded, finishing his coffee and setting the cup down gently. "I should let you rest. Been a long day."

"It has," Abigail agreed, rising as he did. "But a good one."

They moved toward the door, both suddenly awkward in the transition from their comfortable conversation to departure.

At the threshold, Jonah turned, hat in hand. "About tomorrow's service..."

"Yes?" Abigail prompted when he hesitated.

"Those new steps should be tested properly. Make sure they hold up under regular use." He cleared his throat. "Might stop by. Briefly. To check my work."

A smile bloomed on Abigail's face.

# Chapter 26

As Abigail climbed the church steps the next morning, a glint of something unusual caught her eye. Glass fragments scattered across the landing, along with mud and what appeared to be smears of paint. Her pace slowed, a sense of unease rising within her. The doors stood partially ajar, though she distinctly remembered locking them the previous evening.

Abigail pushed the door open and froze.

Devastation greeted her. Shattered glass from broken windows littered the floor, catching morning light in cruel sparkles. The newly polished pews bore splashes of dark paint that had dripped onto the floor like blood. Hymn books lay strewn about, pages ripped out and trampled. The altar had been overturned, and the cross that hung above it torn down and broken in two.

"No," Abigail whispered, her voice faltering as she stepped inside. "Dear Lord, no."

Her feet crunched on broken glass as she moved deeper into the sanctuary, each step revealing more destruction. The flowers so carefully arranged yesterday had been tossed about. The pulpit lay on its side, cracked down the middle.

In the center of it all, nailed to a splintered pew, was a piece of paper with crude lettering: "CLOSE THE CHURCH OR SUFFER WORSE. GO HOME, MISSIONARY WOMAN."

Abigail's hand flew to her mouth, stifling a sob. All the work, all the community's efforts, all her hopes, desecrated in a single night of malice.

For a moment, she stood immobilized by shock and grief. Then, as if her legs could no longer support her, she sank to her knees among the broken glass and torn pages, heedless of the damage to her Sunday dress.

"Why?" she whispered, tears flowing freely now. "Father, why would someone do this?"

Her prayer was interrupted by a gasp from the doorway. Margaret stood there, a basket of freshly baked bread for communion dangling forgotten from her arm.

"Merciful heavens," Margaret breathed. "Abigail, child—are you hurt?"

"No," Abigail managed, wiping tears with trembling hands. "No, I'm not hurt. Just... the church..."

Margaret set her basket down and hurried to Abigail's side, helping her to her feet. "Come away from this glass, dear. You'll cut yourself."

"I don't understand," Abigail said, allowing herself to be guided to a relatively undamaged section of a pew. "Who would—" She stopped, the answer obvious. "McGrant."

Margaret's face hardened. "Or his men, more likely. Keeping his hands clean while his dirty work gets done." She surveyed the destruction, her expression shifting from shock to anger.

"What do we do now?" Abigail asked, her voice small.

Before Margaret could answer, more voices sounded from outside. Ruth appeared at the door with her children, her shocked exclamation drawing attention from others who were arriving for the service.

Within minutes, a crowd had gathered: Doc Carpenter and his wife, Timothy Wells and his family, Deputy Mansfield, Libby, and dozens of other townspeople. Each new arrival registered shock, then outrage at the devastation.

"Who would do such a thing?" Libby demanded, her arm around Abigail's shoulders.

"We all know who," Timothy replied grimly, examining the broken windows.

"It's McGrant's doing, sure as sunrise," Ruth agreed, keeping her children close. "This has his mark all over it."

Deputy Mansfield moved methodically through the space, examining the damage with a lawman's eye. "Nobody heard anything during the night?"

Heads shook. The church stood just far enough from town that nighttime disturbances might go unnoticed, especially if the perpetrators were careful.

"What about the service?" someone asked. "Should we cancel?"

"Absolutely not," Abigail said. Despite her tear-stained face, determination replaced her initial shock. "I will not let whoever did this drive us from worship."

"But Miss Whitaker," Timothy gestured to the destruction, "the place is in shambles."

"Then we'll worship in shambles," she replied firmly. "The church isn't the building—it's the people. And I won't let this act of hatred prevent us from gathering as a community of faith."

A murmur of approval went through the gathering. Reverend Blake arrived then, leaning heavily on his cane. His face paled at the sight of the vandalism, his aged features crumpling in distress.

"Who would desecrate God's house this way?" he asked, his voice breaking. "What manner of hatred drives such an act?"

"The same that drove the moneychangers into the temple," Abigail replied gently. "Greed and fear of losing control."

The reverend nodded slowly, visibly struggling to compose himself. "You're right, of course. And like our Lord, we must not be deterred." He straightened as much as his ailing body allowed. "We will hold service today, as planned."

"But where?" Margaret asked practically. "The glass alone makes it dangerous."

"Outside," Abigail suggested. "The new steps are wide enough for Reverend Blake to stand on the landing, and the congregation can gather in the yard. It's a beautiful morning."

Agreement spread through the crowd, and with remarkable efficiency, they began adapting to the new circumstances. Timothy and two miners carefully brought the damaged pulpit outside, positioning it on the landing. Margaret and Ruth rescued what communion elements they could, while others salvaged unharmed hymn books.

As they worked, more townspeople arrived, each reacting with shock and then determination to the vandalism. Word spread quickly through town, drawing even those who hadn't planned to attend. Nearly half the town had gathered in the churchyard, their faces solemn but resolute.

Abigail stood to the side, organizing the impromptu outdoor service, when she felt a presence beside her. She turned to find Jonah, his expression thunderous as he surveyed the scene.

"When did you find it this way?" he asked, his voice tight with controlled anger.

"I came a few minutes early to prepare…"

Jonah's jaw clenched as he looked at the broken windows, the paint-splattered walls visible through the doorway. "McGrant's work."

"I believe so, though there's no proof."

"Don't need proof. Nobody else would dare." His gaze shifted to the torn note in her hand. "What's that?"

Abigail hesitated, then handed him the warning. Jonah read it quickly, his face darkening further.

"This isn't just vandalism," he said. "It's a direct threat against you."

"Against the church," Abigail corrected, though she knew he was right.

"Against you," Jonah insisted.

Reverend Blake called for the service to begin. The congregation gathered on the lawn, some sitting on the grass, others standing solemnly. Despite the circumstances, the atmosphere was one of quiet determination.

Abigail moved to join them, but Jonah caught her arm gently. "This isn't over," he warned. "McGrant's escalating. First warnings, then vandalism. What's next?"

"I can't think about that now. We have a service to conduct."

Jonah nodded reluctantly, releasing her arm. To her surprise, instead of departing, he found a place at the back of the gathering, in the yard, separate from the townspeople, leaning against a tree with arms crossed, his watchful gaze scanning the perimeter as Reverend Blake began to speak.

The service was necessarily abbreviated. Reverend Blake, visibly affected by the destruction, struggled to find his usual eloquence. His sermon became a meditation on perseverance through trials.

"We are reminded today," he said, his voice gaining strength as he spoke, "that opposition often follows faithful work. When the Israelites rebuilt Jerusalem's walls under Nehemiah's leadership, they faced mockery, threats, and planned attacks. Yet, they persisted, working with tools in one hand and weapons in the other."

He looked out over the congregation, many of whom had labored at the church just yesterday. "Like them, we will not be deterred. We will rebuild what has been damaged, restore what has been defiled. And we will do so not with bitterness, but with the conviction that God's work will prevail despite human opposition."

Abigail watched the faces of those gathered, miners, shopkeepers, farmers, and women with children clutching their skirts. Despite the outrage that had greeted the vandalism, she saw no defeat in their expressions, only a strengthened resolve.

When Reverend Blake faltered, overcome by emotion, Abigail stepped forward at his gesture.

"Friends," she began, her voice clear despite the emotion tightening her throat, "what we witnessed this morning was an act of destruction meant to intimidate and divide us. But look around—" she gestured to the gathered crowd, larger than any previous service, "—it has only brought us closer together."

Murmurs of agreement rippled through the assembly.

"We have worked side by side restoring this building. Today, we face the heartbreaking reality that what can be built can also be damaged. But while hands can tear down a building, they cannot destroy the faith and community that gives it meaning."

Abigail felt tears threatening again, but continued steadily. "I suggest we adjourn briefly now. Return to your homes, change into work clothes if you wish, and let us gather again to begin repairs. Not because the building itself matters most, but because in rebuilding together, we demonstrate that acts of destruction cannot overcome our commitment to one another and to God's purposes in Clear Springs."

A chorus of "amens" sounded, along with nods of determination.

"Let us pray," she concluded, "not just for the restoration of wood and glass, but for the hearts of those responsible. And for our own hearts, that we might respond with justice tempered by mercy, with righteous indignation that doesn't descend into hatred."

As she prayed, Abigail felt the congregation's unity tangibly, a shared purpose transcending the day's shock and disappointment. When she finally said "Amen," the response was strong and unified.

People dispersed with purpose, many heading home to change clothes and gather tools. Some remained, already beginning to clean up broken glass and debris. Reverend Blake, exhausted by the emotional service, accepted Doc Carpenter's offer to escort him home to rest.

Abigail stood watching the activity, simultaneously heartbroken at the destruction and heartened by the response. She became aware of Jonah still present, now examining the broken window frames.

"They'll need complete replacement," he said when she approached. "Not just the glass, but the casings, too. They've been deliberately damaged to weaken them."

"Thorough in their destruction," Abigail observed sadly.

Jonah turned to her, his expression grave. "This wasn't random vandalism, Abigail. This was calculated. They knew exactly how to cause maximum damage with minimum effort."

"You think it was planned carefully?"

"Yes." He gestured to various points of damage. "See how they've hit the parts we just repaired? The new steps are scored deeply—not just defaced, but structurally weakened. The floor we fixed yesterday has been pried up in places."

The implications settled heavily on Abigail. "Someone who knew exactly what we'd repaired. Someone who was watching yesterday."

Jonah nodded in agreement.

Abigail sank onto the grass, overwhelmed by the deliberate malice behind the attack. "All that work, all the community effort—"

"—will happen again," Jonah finished firmly.

He sat beside her on the church lawn, closer than propriety might dictate, but Abigail found his presence steadying rather than concerning.

"You gave them hope," he continued, his voice softening. "Before you came, this town was fractured. Everyone looked out for themselves, tried to stay in McGrant's good graces, or at least avoid his notice. Today will only strengthen the people's hope and solidarity."

Abigail looked at him. "You truly believe that?"

"I do." Jonah's gaze held hers steadily. "McGrant made a serious miscalculation. He thought destroying the church would break the community's spirit. Instead, he's given them something to rally around."

"That's remarkably optimistic coming from you, Mr. Brooks."

A hint of answering warmth touched his stern features. "Don't get used to it, Miss Whitaker."

They watched as Timothy and two miners carefully removed broken glass from window frames.

"I still don't understand such deliberate cruelty," Abigail said. "What kind of hatred destroys a place of worship?"

"The kind that fears what it represents," Jonah replied. "McGrant doesn't hate the church because it's a church. He hates what it means for his control over this town."

"That makes sense, but it doesn't make it easier to bear."

"No, it doesn't." Jonah's hand moved as if to cover hers where it rested on the ground between them, then withdrew. "You need to be careful, Abigail. This warning—" he nodded toward the note she still held, "—it's not just words."

"What would you have me do? Abandon the church? Leave Clear Springs?"

"No." His answer came swiftly, with a conviction that surprised her. "But you need protection. Someone watching the church, the parsonage. Especially at night."

"Deputy Mansfield can't spare the time to guard everything, and neither can Sheriff Holden."

"I wasn't thinking of Mansfield or Holden." Jonah met her questioning gaze directly. "I have a cot in my home behind my shop. I will move it to the front of my shop each evening and sleep outside so that I can be close enough to hear or see trouble."

Abigail was momentarily speechless at his offer. "Jonah, I couldn't ask that of you."

"You didn't ask. I'm offering." His tone brooked no argument. "I know how to handle trouble if it comes."

Jonah Brooks was offering not just observation but protection, potentially violent protection if necessary. The thought should have disturbed her more than it did.

"I don't want anyone hurt because of me," she said finally.

"Then accept my help to prevent that." His gaze was unwavering. "McGrant's men won't stop with property damage if they think they can get away with more. But they're cowards at heart. The knowledge someone's watching will likely be enough."

Abigail considered his words carefully.

"Very well," she agreed. "But only until we can arrange something more permanent. I won't have you sleeping outside your shop indefinitely."

Relief flickered across his features. "Good. I'll begin my watch tonight."

Deputy Mansfield approached, his expression grave.

"Miss Whitaker, Mr. Brooks," he nodded to them both. "I've examined everything thoroughly. This wasn't ordinary vandalism."

"We've reached the same conclusion," Abigail replied, rising from the lawn.

"I'll file a report, of course, but—" he hesitated, glancing at Jonah, "—without witnesses, there's little I can officially do. Sheriff Holden's out of town for the next week or so."

"And you can't act without him," Jonah stated flatly.

Mansfield's frustration was evident. "My hands are tied legally. McGrant has too many connections in the county seat. One wrong move, and he could have the sheriff's office investigating me instead."

"So they get away with it," Jonah's voice held controlled anger.

"For now," Mansfield agreed grimly. "But I'll keep my eyes open. And Miss Whitaker—" he turned to her directly, "—I'd advise extreme caution. This level of calculated damage suggests dangerous intent."

"Jonah has offered to keep watch," Abigail informed him.

Relief crossed the deputy's face. "Good."

"That's settled, then," Abigail said with more confidence than she felt. "Now, if you'll excuse me, I should help organize the cleaning efforts before everyone returns."

As she moved away, she heard Mansfield speaking quietly to Jonah. "Watch her closely, Brooks. This isn't just about the church. Mc-Grant's made it personal."

"I know," Jonah replied, his voice hard. "Trust me, nothing will happen to her while I'm watching."

The certainty in his tone sent an unexpected shiver down Abigail's spine—not of fear, but of something more complex than she was ready to examine too closely.

## Chapter 27

By mid-afternoon, the church grounds hummed with activity. True to their word, townspeople had returned in work clothes, bringing tools, supplies, and determined spirits. The broken glass had been cleared, damaged pews moved outside for repair, and the interior swept clean of debris.

Timothy led a team measuring the window frames for replacement, while another group, led by his son, restored the altar to its proper position. Women worked in teams, removing paint from surfaces.

Abigail moved among them, organizing efforts, expressing gratitude, and occasionally pausing to offer encouragement where spirits flagged. Despite her outward composure, the emotional toll of the morning weighed heavily. Each piece of deliberate damage revealed more upon closer inspection—hymn books soaked in water before being torn, crosses splintered rather than simply knocked down. Even the wildflowers that were in glass jars had been trampled with evident malice.

She retreated to the parsonage porch for a moment alone, a temporary escape from the emotional demands. The community needed to see her present and undeterred.

She sank into the rocking chair, closing her eyes, allowing herself just five minutes of quiet reflection.

"You should rest properly."

Abigail started at Jonah's voice. He stood at the bottom of the porch steps, a cup in his hand.

"I'm fine," she assured him. "Just catching my breath."

Jonah climbed the steps and extended the cup. "Margaret insisted you drink this."

The cup contained cool water sweetened slightly with honey. Abigail accepted it gratefully, only now realizing how thirsty she was.

"Thank you." She sipped slowly, appreciating the thoughtfulness. "And thank Margaret for me."

Instead of leaving, Jonah leaned against the porch railing, his gaze focused on the church. "Windows could probably be ready by Wednesday. Timothy knows a glazier in the next town over who owes him a favor."

"That's remarkably fast."

Jonah's eyes tracked the bustling activity. "Never seen this town move so quickly on anything."

Abigail followed his gaze. "It's as if everyone instinctively knows their role."

"Common purpose does that," Jonah observed.

They watched as Doc Carpenter arrived with Reverend Blake. The elderly minister moved among the workers, offering encouragement and occasional prayers that were received with respectful attention even by those not normally church-attenders.

"He's a good man," Jonah said. "The reverend. Reminds me of my father in some ways."

Abigail glanced at him.

"In what ways?"

"The dignity, I suppose. The way he speaks to people, not down to them, not with false piety, just... genuine concern."

"Your father was like that? As a minister?"

"Yes." A ghost of a smile touched Jonah's lips. "He used to say the pulpit was no place for a man who thought himself better than his congregation. Said a preacher should be among equals, not set apart."

"Wise words," Abigail agreed. "And true. Pride has no place in service."

Jonah nodded, his gaze still on the reverend. "My father would have liked you," he said. "He would have appreciated your... authenticity."

The simple statement warmed Abigail deeply.

"I wish I could have met him," she replied. "And your mother. They must have been remarkable people to raise a son with such integrity."

He cleared his throat, clearly uncomfortable with the praise.

"You should finish that," he said, nodding to the cup she still held. "Margaret will have my hide if you don't."

Abigail complied, drinking the last of the sweetened water. As she lowered the cup, movement near the church caught her attention. Hannah slipping cautiously around the side of the building, her expression a mixture of horror and determination as she surveyed the damage.

"Hannah's here," Abigail said quietly. "It is dangerous for her to be here."

Jonah followed her gaze, his posture tensing. "Very."

"I should speak with her."

"I'll keep watch," Jonah offered. "I'll signal if anyone from town approaches who might report back to her father."

Grateful for his understanding, Abigail handed him the empty cup and made her way across the churchyard to where Hannah stood, partially concealed by the building's shadow.

"Hannah," she called softly.

The girl startled, then relaxed slightly at the sight of Abigail. Her eyes were filled with tears. "Who would do such a terrible thing?"

"We don't know for certain," Abigail replied. "But we're already repairing the damage. See how many have come to help?"

Hannah nodded, watching the activity with wonder. "I wish I could help too."

"You must be careful, Hannah. Your father—"

"Believes I'm helping Mrs. Jenkins with mending," Hannah finished.

The girl's hand went to the pocket of her dress. "I brought something. For the church." She withdrew a small cloth pouch. "It's not much, just some coins I've saved from errands. But I wanted to make a donation."

Abigail was deeply touched by the gesture. "Hannah, that's incredibly generous, but your savings—"

"Please," Hannah interrupted, pressing the pouch into Abigail's hand. "The church was special to my mother."

Understanding the profound meaning behind the gift, Abigail nodded. "Thank you. We'll use it for something special, perhaps new hymnals, to replace those damaged."

Hannah's face brightened. "I'd like that. My mother loved hymns."

A sharp whistle drew their attention. Jonah stood on the parsonage porch, giving a subtle hand signal.

"You should go," Abigail said quickly. "Mr. Brooks is warning us someone's coming."

Hannah nodded, clutching Abigail's hand briefly. "I'll try to come to service next Sunday. If I can find a way."

"Be careful, Hannah. Your safety matters more than attendance."

The girl slipped away. Abigail watched until she was out of sight, then returned to the parsonage.

"Tom Higgins was heading this way," Jonah explained when she reached the porch. "He's not reliable where McCallum's concerned."

"Thank you for the warning."

Jonah nodded, his expression troubled. "She's taking significant risks..."

He didn't need to finish the thought.

"She gave me this." Abigail showed him the small pouch of coins. "Her savings, as a donation."

Jonah's expression softened. "Brave girl."

"Indeed." Abigail carefully tucked the pouch into her pocket. "I worry for her, Jonah. Her home situation seems... difficult."

"It is." His jaw tightened. "McCallum's not known for gentleness at the best of times. When drinking, he's worse."

"Has he ever...?" Abigail couldn't bring herself to complete the question.

"Hurt her? Not that I've seen evidence of." Jonah's tone suggested he'd been watchful. "But emotional cruelty leaves fewer visible marks."

Abigail nodded sadly. "We must pray for her protection, and for wisdom in how best to help without worsening her situation."

"Prayer's a start," Jonah agreed, though something in his tone suggested he was thinking of more direct interventions if necessary.

Before their conversation could continue, Margaret called from the churchyard, requesting Abigail's input on arrangements for the workers' late afternoon meal. With a nod to Jonah, Abigail returned to her duties, her heart heavy with concerns for Hannah but warmed by the girl's courage and generosity.

# Chapter 28

Evening approached with remarkable progress made. While much remained to be done, the most visible signs of destruction had been addressed. The broken pulpit had been temporarily mended, awaiting proper repair. Most of the paint had been cleaned from the pews and walls. The damaged floor had been secured.

Workers began departing as the light faded, promising to return when possible to continue restoration efforts. Margaret organized the last of the food distribution, ensuring everyone departed with a share of the communal meal that had sustained them throughout the day.

As the churchyard emptied, Abigail stood in front of the church, exhaustion finally catching up with her. The emotional swings of the day, from anticipation to shock, from grief to determination, from gratitude for community support to lingering sorrow at the deliberate destruction, left her drained beyond measure.

"You should rest," Jonah's voice came from behind her. "It's been a long day."

Abigail turned to find him carrying a lantern, its warm light illuminating his concerned expression.

"It has," she agreed wearily. "But also a hopeful one. The people here care more deeply about this church than I realized." Abigail gazed up at the church's outline against the darkening sky. "Or perhaps they care about what it represents, something McGrant can't control or corrupt."

"Both, likely." Jonah moved to stand beside her. "You've given them something worth defending."

His simple statement touched her deeply. "Thank you for saying that."

They stood for a moment, the day's events settling around them like dust after a storm.

"I've moved my cot," Jonah said. "Set up where I can see both the church and parsonage clearly."

Abigail nodded, grateful yet still uncomfortable with his sacrifice. "I still wish there was another solution."

"There isn't." His tone left no room for argument. "I'll keep watch tonight. You should get some sleep."

"I doubt sleep will come easily," Abigail admitted. "I know when I close my eyes, I will see the destruction. The deliberate hatred of it."

Jonah studied her face in the lantern light. "You need rest regardless. Tomorrow will bring new challenges."

"I know." She sighed deeply. "I just need a few more minutes here. To pray, to process."

Understanding her need for solitude, Jonah nodded. "I'll be at the shop."

Jonah lingered a moment longer, seeming reluctant to leave her alone, then turned toward his shop.

"Wait," Abigail called.

Jonah turned to face her.

"Please sit with me on the church steps while I pray."

Jonah walked back and settled on the bottom step beside her.

"Father," she prayed softly, "I don't understand such malice. Help me respond with wisdom rather than fear, with determination rather than discouragement. And please protect those who've stood with us today. Shield them from retribution."

The quiet prayer steadied her only for a moment. And then she wept. Deep, guttural sobs and tears wracked her body. Jonah wrapped his arm around her and pulled her close as the day's emotional burden finally broke free.

# Chapter 29

J onah settled on the narrow cot just inside the wide doorway of his shop, positioned to give him clear views of both the church and parsonage. He'd moved his workbench to create this vantage point, rearranging the shop's interior to serve his new purpose as watchman.

The day's events replayed in his mind. Abigail's face when he'd first seen her among the destruction, the quiet dignity with which she'd addressed the congregation despite her evident heartbreak, her unwavering determination throughout the long hours of cleanup and initial repairs, and her eventual emotional breakdown.

Her resilience both impressed and concerned him. She pushed herself too hard, took too much responsibility on her slender shoulders. Yet, she never complained, never sought pity or special consideration.

Movement at the parsonage window caught his attention. Abigail's silhouette was visible against the lamplight. She closed the curtain, fulfilling her promise to signal her safe retirement for the night.

As her light dimmed, Jonah settled more comfortably on the cot, his rifle within easy reach, a cup of coffee at his side to help maintain his vigilance through the night. He hadn't planned this role when he'd first encountered Abigail Whitaker, had actively resisted involvement in her mission. Yet here he sat, voluntarily standing guard over her safety.

The irony wasn't lost on him. After years of careful isolation, of protecting himself from emotional entanglements, he now found himself the protector of not just Abigail, but the church itself. The very institution he'd turned his back on after losing his faith, along with his family.

Jonah took a sip of coffee, his gaze steady on the darkened buildings surrounding him. Whatever McGrant's next move might be, he would be ready. Abigail would not face it alone, not while he drew breath.

With that resolution firmly in mind, he settled in for the long night's watch, his determination as solid and unwavering as the iron he forged in his daily work.

Jonah rubbed his tired eyes, gaze still fixed on the darkened parsonage. A coyote howled somewhere in the distance, the sound echoing his own inner solitude.

Four years he'd lived in Clear Springs. Four years of minimal connections, of existence rather than living. He'd made his peace with that emptiness, or so he'd told himself. The shop provided purpose enough; the rhythmic beating of metal, the controlled fury of the forge, the satisfaction of creating useful things all served as adequate substitutes for genuine human connection.

Until Abigail Whitaker stepped off that stagecoach.

He exhaled slowly, acknowledging what he'd been fighting since her arrival. The woman had disrupted everything. His routine, his carefully maintained distance, his emotional numbness that had become as much a shield as his physical strength.

Her tears tonight had undone him completely. Holding her while she wept had awakened something he'd thought long dead. The protective instinct had been immediate and overwhelming, but underneath it lay something unsettling and yet welcoming all at the same time. A longing he hadn't allowed himself to feel in years.

"Fool," he muttered to himself, shifting on the uncomfortable cot. "She's a missionary, not some frontier woman looking for a husband."

Yet, he couldn't deny the growing attachment. It wasn't just physical attraction, though he'd be lying if he denied her beauty hadn't affected him. No, it was her spirit that drew him. Her unwavering commitment to her calling, her genuine concern for others, her refusal to abandon her mission despite very real danger.

Jonah took another sip of cooling coffee, grimacing at the bitter taste. Abigail had gotten under his skin, made him care again when caring meant vulnerability. Made him hope again when hope had been buried alongside Emily and their unborn child.

The thought of Emily no longer brought the searing pain it once had. Instead, a gentle sadness, a memory of love rather than its brutal loss. When had that shifted? He couldn't pinpoint the moment, but somehow Abigail's presence had begun healing wounds he'd assumed would remain raw forever.

He stood, stretching his tall frame, and paced the length of the shop's entrance. The night was quiet, peaceful in a way that belied the day's violence and destruction. Stars scattered across the clear sky, indifferent to human struggles below.

God's handiwork, his father would have called it. The thought came unbidden, surprising him. He'd spent years avoiding such reflections, such terminology. Yet here it was, rising naturally to mind, as if the long estrangement from faith had begun to thaw alongside his frozen heart.

That was Abigail's influence, too. Not through preaching or judgment. She never pushed her beliefs on him directly, but through living them so authentically that they became impossible to dismiss. She embodied the faith he'd once held dear, the convictions his parents had instilled in him, the calling he'd once believed was his own.

Jonah returned to the cot, rifle across his knees, and faced the uncomfortable truth. He was falling in love with Abigail Whitaker. Not just physical attraction or admiration, but the deep, transformative love that changes a person's very being. The kind of love he'd sworn never to risk again after losing everyone who mattered to him.

The realization should have terrified him. Instead, it settled into his chest with the solid weight of truth. He couldn't fight it anymore than he could stop breathing. Whatever came next, whether McGrant's threats escalated, whether Abigail could ever return such feelings, whether this fragile community survived the power struggle unfolding, Jonah knew he'd crossed a line from which there was no retreat.

His solitary existence had ended the moment he'd allowed himself to care about the church, the town, and most significantly, the remarkable woman who'd awakened his dormant heart. For better or worse, Jonah Brooks had rejoined the world of the living.

With that knowledge came both vulnerability and strength. If McGrant or his men appeared tonight with ill intent, they would face not just a skilled fighter protecting property, but a man defending something far more precious, hope, purpose, and the possibility of love reborn from ashes long cold.

Jonah settled back, eyes alert, senses attuned to the slightest disturbance. "Sleep well, Abigail," he whispered to the quiet night. "I'm right here."

# Chapter 30

The next morning dawned clear and bright, a stark contrast to the somber mood that had pervaded the previous day. Abigail rose early, her body aching, but her spirit somewhat restored by restful sleep, a blessing she hadn't expected after such turmoil.

She dressed quickly and moved to the window, drawing aside the curtain. The sight that greeted her brought an unexpected smile to her lips. Jonah sat on a chair he'd positioned outside his shop, whittling something with a small knife. Even from this distance, she could see his vigilant posture, his eyes regularly scanning the area.

He'd kept his watch through the night. The knowledge touched her deeply.

Abigail prepared a quick breakfast, then gathered coffee and some of Margaret's bread onto a tray. The least she could do was ensure her self-appointed guardian didn't go hungry.

As she walked down the street toward the shop, Jonah rose to his feet, tucking away his knife and the small carving.

"Good morning," she called. "I thought you might appreciate breakfast."

"Thank you," he replied, taking the tray from her hands. "Though you needn't have troubled yourself."

"It's no trouble." Abigail studied his face, noting the slight shadows beneath his eyes. "Did you sleep at all?"

"Enough." He set the tray on a small table near his chair. "No disturbances during the night."

"Thank God for that small mercy." She glanced toward the church, its damaged windows stark in the morning light. "And thank you, Jonah. You brought me comfort, knowing you were keeping everything safe."

He nodded acknowledgment, pouring coffee from the pot she'd brought. "What are your plans for today?"

"Continue repairs, of course. Timothy and the others will return after their workday this evening to help. Reverend Blake has requested we hold a midweek service, possibly on Tuesday, even if the church isn't fully restored by then."

"A statement," Jonah observed. "Showing McGrant his tactics won't succeed."

"Precisely." Abigail accepted the cup of coffee he offered her. "Will you join us for the service?"

"I'll be there. Though perhaps not seated with the congregation."

"Progress, nonetheless," she replied with a gentle smile. "You're more a part of this community than you realize, Jonah."

He looked away, uncomfortable with her assessment, yet not denying it. "McGrant won't remain quiet for long," he said, changing the subject. "Yesterday's show of community support will only anger him further."

"I know." Abigail sipped her coffee, the bitter warmth fortifying her. "But what more can he do without revealing himself openly as an enemy of the town's welfare?"

"Plenty." Jonah's expression darkened. "He controls livelihoods, housing, credit at the stores. He can make life difficult for those who supported the church without ever connecting his actions to the vandalism."

"Then we must be prepared to support one another even more." Abigail set down her empty cup. "If he targets someone's employment, we find them alternative work. If he restricts credit, we establish a community fund."

Jonah studied her with something like wonder. "You never cease to amaze me, Abigail. Where others see obstacles, you see opportunities."

The compliment warmed her more than the coffee had. "I merely trust that God provides solutions alongside challenges."

"Either way, your determination is... remarkable."

Their conversation paused as Deputy Mansfield approached from the direction of the sheriff's office.

"Morning, Miss Whitaker, Jonah." He nodded to them both, his expression serious. "Any trouble overnight?"

"None," Jonah answered. "Quiet as a cemetery."

"Good." Mansfield shifted uncomfortably. "I've written up the report on the vandalism, but without witnesses, there's little to be done officially."

"We understand," Abigail assured him. "Your support means a great deal, regardless."

"There's something else," Mansfield continued. "McGrant's called a town meeting for tomorrow at noon. Claims it's about 'community safety and welfare' in light of recent 'concerning events.'"

Jonah's posture stiffened.

"Mayor Jenkins has approved the meeting, despite my objections," Deputy Mansfield said.

"Will you attend, Deputy?" Abigail asked.

"Of course. Someone needs to represent law and order." Mansfield's frustration was evident. "But with Sheriff Holden still away, my authority is limited."

"We'll attend as well," Abigail decided. "The church deserves representation."

Jonah looked at her sharply. "That's playing into his hands, Abigail. He wants a public confrontation."

"Then we'll disappoint him by remaining entirely civil and reasonable," she replied firmly. "Running from this meeting would only reinforce whatever narrative he's constructing."

Mansfield nodded. "Miss Whitaker has a point, Jonah. Better to face this directly. I'll be there to ensure things don't get out of hand."

After the deputy departed, Jonah turned to Abigail. "You realize this meeting is a trap of sorts?"

"Of course." She gathered the empty cups onto the tray. "But sometimes walking into a trap with eyes open is better than avoiding it and wondering what's been sprung in your absence."

Jonah shook his head, a reluctant smile tugging at his lips. "Boston society's loss is certainly Clear Springs' gain, Miss Whitaker."

"I'll take that as a compliment, Mr. Brooks." She returned his smile, relieved to see the tension in his features ease slightly. "Now, I believe we both have work awaiting us. The church won't repair itself, and I imagine your customers are wondering why your forge remains cold this morning."

"Let them wonder," he replied with unexpected conviction. "Some things take priority over horseshoes and wagon parts."

The simple statement, delivered with such certainty, affected Abigail deeply. Jonah Brooks, the man who had maintained such careful distance from community entanglements, now prioritized the church's welfare—and hers—above his livelihood.

"Thank you," she said softly, the words inadequate for the emotion behind them. "For everything."

Their eyes met, a moment of connection that transcended the need for further words. Then, with a nod of acknowledgment, Jonah collected the tray from her hands.

"I'll return this to the parsonage," he said. "And I'll check the church's doors and windows again before the workers arrive."

"Always the protector," Abigail observed gently.

"Someone needs to be," he replied, his gaze holding hers with an intensity that sent a flutter through her chest. "Especially for those who are too busy caring for everyone else to look after themselves."

With that, he turned toward the parsonage, leaving Abigail to ponder the shifting landscape between them and the unexpected warmth his concern kindled within her heart.

# Chapter 31

The explosion ripped through the morning air, shattering the peaceful quiet of Clear Springs with a concussive force that seemed to shake the very ground. Jonah was halfway down the street, the parsonage tray still in his hands, when the sound hit him like a physical blow. He spun toward the mine on the hillside, dread pooling in his stomach as a plume of dark smoke billowed skyward.

"No," he whispered, the single word choked with horror.

The tray clattered to the dirt. He stood in shock as people started rushing around him toward the mine. Then he broke into a run, his long legs carrying him swiftly toward the source of the disturbance. Behind him, he heard Abigail's voice calling his name, but he couldn't stop. Years of instinct and training from the war surged to the surface, where there was an explosion. There would be wounded men needing help.

Townsfolk poured from buildings along Main Street, faces stricken with fear as they stared at the ominous cloud rising from the mine entrance. Shouts and screams drifted down from the hillside as miners who'd been outside during the blast scrambled toward the entrance.

Jonah reached the base of the hill, passing women already rushing from their company homes, faces pale with terror. He recognized Ruth among them, her youngest child clutched to her chest as she ran toward the mine where her husband worked.

"Billy!" she screamed, her voice raw with fear. "Billy!"

The path up to the mine was steep, but Jonah's powerful strides ate up the distance. As he approached the entrance, chaos greeted him. Men staggered from the yawning mouth of the tunnel, faces blackened with soot, coughing violently. Others lay on the ground, some moving, some terrifyingly still.

"Get back!" McCallum was shouting at those trying to enter the mine. "Could be another collapse! Nobody goes in!"

"There are men trapped in there!" protested a miner whose face was streaked with blood from a gash on his forehead.

"I said nobody goes in!" McCallum bellowed, his face contorted with something that looked more like fear than concern.

Jonah shouldered his way through the crowd, taking quick stock of the situation. The explosion had come from deep within the mine, but the entrance appeared stable. He'd done enough work reinforcing tunnel supports in his blacksmithing role to know the difference between safe and compromised structures.

"What happened?" he demanded of a dazed miner sitting on a rock, holding a bloodied arm.

"Don't rightly know," the man coughed. "We was working the new vein, and there was this rumbling. Then, all of a sudden, everything broke loose. Fire and noise and... and..." He broke off, coughing violently.

Jonah looked toward the mine entrance again. McCallum was still blocking access, but his eyes darted nervously between the mine and the growing crowd. Something about his demeanor struck Jonah as wrong, not the panic of a man concerned for his workers, but the calculation of someone with something to hide.

"Brooks!" Doc Carpenter's voice cut through the din as the physician pushed his way through the crowd, medical bag in hand. "Help me with the wounded."

Jonah nodded, moving to assist as Doc began triaging the injured men who'd made it out. They worked quickly, Jonah following Doc's terse instructions, applying pressure to wounds, moving men to more comfortable positions, checking for broken bones.

"Where's Sheriff Holden?" Doc asked as they worked.

"He's out of town," Jonah replied grimly. "Mansfield was headed to the sheriff's office when I saw him earlier."

As if summoned by his name, Deputy Mansfield appeared, his face grim as he took in the scene. "What happened?"

Before anyone could answer, a woman's scream pierced the air. Ruth had reached the mine entrance, her eyes wild as she searched frantically for her husband among the wounded.

"Billy!" she cried. "Has anyone seen Billy Patterson?"

The injured miners exchanged glances, but no one spoke. Ruth's face crumpled as she realized what their silence meant. Her husband was still inside.

"He was working the back tunnel with Griffin and Mercer," one man finally said, his voice barely audible.

Ruth whirled toward McCallum. "You have to get them out!" she demanded, grabbing his arm.

McCallum shook her off roughly. "Keep your hands off me! I can't risk sending men in there."

"Those are your workers in there!" Ruth's voice rose with hysteria. "You can't just leave them to die!"

Jonah looked from Ruth's desperate face to McCallum's closed expression, then to the mine entrance. A decision crystallized in his mind.

"Doc," he said quietly, "I'm going in."

"Are you mad, Brooks?" Doc Carpenter grabbed his arm. "That mine could collapse at any moment."

"Men could still be alive in there," Jonah replied firmly. "And I know enough about support structures to avoid the worst dangers."

"I can't let you—" Doc began, but Jonah cut him off.

"You can't stop me." His voice was steady, resolute. "There are men in there with families waiting for them." His eyes flicked briefly to Ruth, who was now on her knees, sobbing. "I won't stand by and do nothing."

Doc Carpenter studied him for a long moment, then nodded once. "Take this." He handed Jonah a clean kerchief from his bag. "Wet it and cover your mouth and nose. The air in there will be foul."

"Jonah!"

He turned to see Abigail pushing through the crowd, her face pale but composed. She carried a bucket of water and clean clothes, ever practical, even in crisis.

"What are you doing here?" he demanded, though he already knew the answer. Abigail would never stay safely away while others suffered.

"Helping," she replied, setting down her supplies near Doc Carpenter. Her eyes widened as she took in Jonah's determined stance. "You're going in, aren't you?"

"I have to." He met her gaze directly, willing her to understand.

Instead of argument, she nodded once. "Be careful." She reached into her pocket and pressed something into his hand—a small wooden cross, simply carved. "For protection."

Jonah's fingers closed around it, the wood warm from her pocket. He nodded once, tucking it securely into his shirt pocket.

"You can't go in there!" McCallum shouted, moving to block Jonah's path. "McGrant's orders. No one enters until he arrives!"

"Move aside," Jonah said, his voice dangerously quiet.

"I said—"

Jonah's hand shot out, gripping McCallum's shoulder with iron strength. "There are men in there, possibly dying. Your men. Move aside, or I'll move you myself."

Something in Jonah's expression must have convinced McCallum of his determination. The foreman stepped back, his face twisted with anger and something else—fear? guilt?

"Your funeral," McCallum muttered.

"Lantern," Jonah called, and someone pressed one into his hand. He lit it quickly, then turned to the assembled miners. "Anyone well enough to come with me?"

Three men stepped forward immediately, faces grim but determined.

"I know where they were working," one said.

"Good." Jonah nodded. "Stay close, follow my lead, and if I say run, you run. Understood?"

The men nodded, and Jonah turned toward the mine entrance. As he did, his eyes met Abigail's once more. Her lips moved in what he recognized as a silent prayer, and he felt a strange calm settle over him. Without another word, he stepped into the darkness of the mine, the other men close behind.

# Chapter 32

The air inside the mine was thick with dust and smoke, making breathing difficult even through the dampened cloth. Jonah held the lantern high, its weak light barely penetrating the gloom. The main shaft seemed intact, but as they moved deeper, evidence of the explosion became more apparent. Support beams had splintered in places, and debris littered the ground.

"They were working a new vein," Abram Daniels explained in a hushed voice, as if afraid the sound might trigger another collapse. "McGrant had been pushing us to work faster, said the silver was richer there."

"How far?" Jonah asked, his eyes constantly scanning for signs of structural weakness.

"Bout a quarter of a mile in, then down the shaft to the left."

They moved cautiously, stepping over fallen timbers and around piles of rock. The air grew worse the deeper they went, and Jonah could hear his companions' labored breathing behind him.

"Careful here," he warned as they reached a section where the ceiling sagged ominously. "One at a time, stay close to the wall."

They navigated the dangerous area successfully, but Jonah's unease grew. The damage was extensive, and he wondered what had caused such destruction.

They reached the turnoff for the left shaft and paused. Smoke curled from the entrance, and the support beams showed significant stress fractures.

"They're down there?" Jonah asked.

Abram nodded grimly. "Four men maybe, five."

Jonah assessed the shaft critically. "This whole section could come down any minute. You men wait here. I'll go first, see if it's passable."

"We're coming with you," one of the others insisted.

Jonah shook his head firmly. "No sense risking all of us. If I don't come back in ten minutes, get yourselves out and tell Deputy Mansfield exactly where I went. Clear?"

The men exchanged glances, then nodded reluctantly.

"Ten minutes," Jonah repeated, then ducked into the damaged shaft.

The destruction was even worse inside. The explosion had originated somewhere nearby. He could smell the residue of blasting powder, far stronger than would be normal for controlled mining operations. The floor sloped downward at a steep angle, making his footing treacherous.

"Hello!" he called, his voice swallowed by the oppressive darkness. "Anyone alive down here?"

For a moment, there was only silence. Then, faintly, he heard a response.

"Here! We're here!"

Jonah moved faster, sliding more than walking down the steep incline. The voice had come from beyond a pile of rubble that partially blocked the passage. He held the lantern higher, searching for a way through.

"How many of you?" he shouted.

"Five!" came the reply. "Griffin is hurt bad, and Mercer's leg is trapped!"

"Patterson?" Jonah called, thinking of Ruth's desperate face.

A pause. "He's here. Breathing, but unconscious."

Relief flooded through Jonah, immediately tempered by concern. He needed to get these men out quickly. The air was growing fouler by the minute, and the groaning of stressed timber warned of imminent collapse.

"I'm coming through," he called, finding a narrow gap in the debris pile. "Stay where you are."

He squeezed through the opening, scraping his shoulders painfully against jagged rock. On the other side, the miners huddled in a small pocket of relative safety beneath a section of roof that had held firm. Patterson lay motionless, while another sat with his leg pinned beneath a fallen beam. A third knelt beside Griffin, whose chest rose and fell in shallow, labored breaths.

"Brooks?" The miner tending Griffin squinted in the lantern light. "Never thought I'd be so happy to see a blacksmith."

"Came to bring you home," Jonah replied, quickly assessing the situation. "What happened?"

"We were setting charges, but something wasn't right. Too much powder, McGrant's orders. Mercer tried to warn McCallum, but he said to follow orders or find new jobs."

Jonah's jaw tightened. "We need to move fast. That support beam won't hold much longer." He gestured to the one intact timber that was keeping the roof from complete collapse.

"Can't leave Mercer," the miner insisted. "His leg's trapped good."

Jonah moved to examine the fallen beam pinning Mercer's leg. It was heavy, but not impossible to lift with enough leverage.

"We'll need something to pry this up," he muttered, scanning the surrounding debris.

"Try this." A miner handed him a length of metal—part of a mining cart rail that had been torn loose in the explosion.

Jonah nodded approval, positioning the makeshift lever carefully. "When I lift, you pull him clear," he instructed the other miner. "We'll only get one chance at this."

The miner nodded, gripping Mercer under the arms.

"Ready?" Jonah positioned himself, bracing his powerful frame for the effort. "One... two... three!"

He heaved against the lever with all his strength, muscles straining as the heavy beam shifted reluctantly. Mercer screamed in pain as his crushed leg was freed, but his companion dragged him clear before Jonah had to release the beam. It crashed back down with a sound like thunder, sending vibrations through the unstable ground.

"We need to move," Jonah urged, already turning to Patterson. "Now."

He lifted Billy Patterson over his shoulders in a fireman's carry, grunting at the weight. "Can you help Griffin?"

The two miners nodded, supporting their injured companion between them. Slowly, they made their way toward the gap in the debris pile. Jonah went first, carefully maneuvering Patterson's limp form through the narrow opening. The others followed, struggling with Griffin, who moaned in pain at every movement.

Mercer came last, dragging his injured leg, his face gray with pain but determined.

The men Jonah had left at the entrance to the left shaft were waiting anxiously, relief washing over their faces as the rescue party emerged.

"Thought you weren't coming back," Abram admitted.

"Almost didn't," Jonah replied grimly. "Let's get out of here before—"

A low rumble interrupted him, the ground trembling beneath their feet. Dust and small rocks showered down from the ceiling.

"Run!" Jonah ordered, already moving, Patterson's weight heavy across his shoulders. "Now!"

They fled through the tunnel, the rumbling growing louder behind them. Jonah's lungs burned, his muscles screaming in protest as he pushed himself forward, determined not to fail when they were so close to safety. The injured men slowed their progress, but none would consider leaving them behind.

The main shaft seemed miles long, each step a battle against exhaustion and the increasingly unstable surroundings. Just as Jonah feared his strength would give out, he saw a glimmer of daylight ahead. With a final surge of desperate energy, he led the group toward the mine entrance.

They burst into the sunlight as a thunderous crash sounded behind them. Jonah staggered forward, carefully lowering Billy Patterson to the ground, where Doc Carpenter immediately rushed to attend him.

Abigail was at Jonah's side in an instant, supporting him as his legs threatened to buckle from exhaustion.

"You did it," she whispered, her voice thick with emotion. "You brought them back."

Jonah could only nod, too winded to speak. His eyes found Ruth, who had fallen to her knees beside her husband, sobbing with relief as Doc confirmed he was alive.

The rescue had been successful, but as Jonah's breathing steadied and his mind cleared, questions began to form.

His eyes found McCallum, who stood apart from the celebration, his face a mask of carefully controlled neutrality. When he noticed Jonah's gaze, the foreman turned away quickly, too quickly.

"Something's very wrong here," Jonah murmured, mostly to himself.

But Abigail heard him. "What do you mean?"

Before he could answer, Doc Carpenter approached, wiping blood from his hands with a cloth.

"Griffin won't make it," he said quietly, his face grim. "Too much internal damage. Patterson has a severe concussion but should recover. Mercer's leg..." He shook his head. "Might have to take it."

"The others?" Jonah asked.

"Cuts, burns, broken bones. Nothing fatal, thank God." Doc's eyes narrowed as he studied Jonah. "You need attention yourself. That cut on your forehead is deep."

Jonah touched his temple, surprised to find his fingers came away bloody. In the intensity of the rescue, he hadn't even noticed the injury.

"It can wait," he replied. "Doc, this wasn't a normal mining accident."

Doc Carpenter glanced around, then lowered his voice. "Not here. Meet me at my office later today. Both of you." His gaze included Abigail. "There are things I've suspected for some time, but after today..." He trailed off, his expression troubled.

Deputy Mansfield approached. "McGrant's on his way," he informed them. "He sent word from town. Jonah, that was either the bravest or the most foolhardy thing I've ever witnessed."

"Had to be done," Jonah replied.

"Well, five families are grateful, that's certain." Mansfield glanced toward the collapsed mine entrance. "Though I suspect McGrant won't share their sentiment. He was explicit about nobody entering."

"Was he now?" Jonah's voice hardened. "Interesting that his primary concern wasn't rescuing his men."

Mansfield's eyes narrowed slightly. "Interesting indeed. We'll talk later." He moved off to help organize the transportation of the wounded down to town.

Abigail touched Jonah's arm, drawing his attention back to her. "You need that wound cleaned," she said firmly. "Come to the parsonage with me."

Too exhausted to argue, Jonah allowed her to lead him away from the chaos of the mine disaster. As they walked down the hill, he glanced back once, his eyes fixing on the thin plume of smoke still rising from the mine opening. McGrant had questions to answer, and Jonah intended to ensure he couldn't avoid them.

# Chapter 33

The parsonage was quiet after the cacophony of the mine disaster. Abigail guided Jonah to a chair at her small kitchen table, then bustled about gathering clean water, clothes, and her medicine box.

"You could have been killed," she said quietly as she prepared to clean his wound.

"So could those miners."

Abigail dampened a cloth and began gently wiping the blood from his forehead. Her touch was light, careful, but Jonah still winced as she cleaned the cut.

"Sorry."

"It's fine." He watched her face as she worked, noting the concentration in her eyes, the slight furrow between her brows. "You were brave today, too. Most women would have stayed far from the danger."

A small smile curved her lips. "I'm not most women."

"No. You certainly are not."

Their eyes met briefly.

Abigail reached for a small jar from her medicine box. "This will sting," she warned, applying a pungent salve to the cut. "But it will prevent infection."

Jonah remained still despite the burning sensation, his mind returning to the mine and what he'd witnessed. "The miners said there was too much blasting powder," he said abruptly. "McGrant's orders, carried out by McCallum despite warnings."

Abigail paused, her fingers hovering near his forehead. "Deliberate negligence?"

"Or worse." Jonah's expression darkened. "The damage I saw inside... it wasn't consistent with normal mining operations. And McCallum's behavior, trying to prevent rescue attempts..."

"You think it might have been intentional?" Abigail's voice was hushed with horror.

"I don't know what to think yet." Jonah sighed heavily. "But Doc Carpenter clearly has suspicions of his own. We should hear what he has to say before drawing conclusions."

Abigail nodded, returning to her ministrations. She applied a clean bandage to his forehead, her fingers gentle against his skin.

"There," she said when she'd finished. "You'll have a scar, but it should heal cleanly."

"Another to add to my collection," Jonah replied wryly, touching the bandage gingerly.

Abigail began cleaning up her supplies, her movements efficient but distracted. "If what you suspect is true," she said slowly, "then McGrant isn't just a ruthless businessman. He's—"

"A murderer. And proving it won't be easy."

"But we must try," Abigail insisted, her eyes suddenly fierce. "For the Griffins, for the Pattersons, for all those who've suffered."

"We will," he promised. "But carefully. McGrant is more dangerous than I realized, and he already sees you as a threat."

"Us," Abigail corrected. "He sees us as threats. Your actions today won't have endeared you to him, either."

A knock sounded at the door. Abigail went to answer it, returning moments later with Deputy Mansfield.

"McGrant's calling it a tragic accident," Mansfield reported without preamble. "Griffins passed from his injuries. McGrant offered condolences to his family, promising compensation. The perfect, concerned employer."

"And the town?" Jonah asked.

"Mixed reactions. Relief for those rescued, grief for the Griffins, but also questions. More than a few are wondering why McCallum tried to prevent rescue attempts."

"As they should," Abigail said firmly.

Mansfield nodded. "I'm heading to Doc Carpenter's now. Thought you might want to come along."

They left the parsonage together, walking briskly through town toward the doctor's office. Main Street was unusually quiet, most residents either still at the mine or gathered at the boarding house, where many of those with minor injuries were being tended to.

Doc Carpenter's office was a small but tidy building near the edge of town. The doctor himself answered their knock, ushering them quickly inside and locking the door behind them.

"Sit," he instructed, gesturing to chairs arranged in his consultation room. "What I'm about to share puts all of us at risk, but after today, I can't remain silent any longer."

He moved to a cabinet, unlocking it with a key from his pocket. From inside, he withdrew a leather-bound journal and several folded papers.

"I've been keeping records," he explained, returning to join them. "For nearly a year now. Pattern of injuries, types of accidents, timing." He opened the journal, revealing meticulous notes in a precise handwriting. "At first, I thought it was just poor management, typical frontier corner-cutting. But then I noticed something."

He turned the journal toward them, pointing to a series of entries. "The serious accidents, the ones resulting in deaths or life-altering injuries, they almost always involve men who've spoken against Mc-Grant in some way. Men who questioned safety practices, who talked about organizing for better conditions, who supported community initiatives McGrant opposed."

"And there's more." He spread out the folded papers—diagrams of the mine's layout, with areas marked in red. "These are the locations of major accidents over the past six months. Notice anything?"

Jonah studied the diagrams. "They're all in the newer sections, the expansion areas."

"Yes. And according to the miners I've treated, those are also the areas where McGrant insisted on accelerated extraction, despite warnings about unstable rock formations and support beams."

"Deliberate negligence at minimum," Mansfield concluded, his face grim.

"But today was different," Jonah said slowly. "The miners mentioned excessive blasting powder. McGrant's specific orders."

Doc Carpenter's expression hardened. "That crosses the line from negligence to something far worse."

"Why would he risk his own mine?" Abigail asked, bewildered. "The silver is his livelihood."

"Not for much longer, perhaps," Doc replied. "There are rumors the veins are playing out. Several miners have mentioned decreasing yields over the past few months. McGrant's been pushing them harder, demanding they work harder and faster."

"Wait... an insurance scheme?" Mansfield suggested. "Collect on a destroyed mine when the silver's gone, anyway?"

"Possibly." Doc shook his head. "But I suspect there's more to it. McGrant's been buying up land around Clear Springs, expanding his holdings significantly. He's planning something beyond silver mining."

Jonah's mind raced, connecting pieces of information. "The town meeting tomorrow. He's using these 'accidents' to consolidate control, presenting himself as the solution to problems he's creating."

"While eliminating those who oppose him," Abigail added, her voice tight with anger.

The room fell silent as they absorbed the implications. It was Mansfield who finally spoke.

"We need proof," he said firmly. "Suspicions and patterns won't be enough. McGrant has too much influence with the territorial authorities."

"The miners who were with me today," Jonah suggested. "They heard the orders about excessive blasting powder."

"Their word against McCallum's," Doc pointed out. "And McCallum is firmly in McGrant's pocket."

"Then we need physical evidence," Jonah decided. "I need to get back into that mine."

"Impossible," Mansfield objected. "McGrant will have guards posted."

"There's another entrance," Doc Carpenter said quietly. "An old shaft from the early days, before McGrant took over. It's overgrown, mostly forgotten, but it connects to the main tunnels. I treated a miner last year who mentioned using it as a shortcut."

"Where?" Jonah asked immediately.

Doc moved to a shelf, retrieving a rough map of the area around Clear Springs. "Here," he said, pointing to a location on the eastern slope of the hill. "Hidden in a stand of pines."

"I'll find it," Jonah stated with certainty.

"Not alone," Abigail insisted. "It's too dangerous."

"Miss Whitaker is right," Mansfield agreed. "I'll go with you. Tonight, after dark."

Jonah nodded his acceptance.

"Look for anything unusual," Doc said. "Signs of tampering with support structures, evidence of excessive blasting materials, documentation of McGrant's orders."

"McCallum's office near the mine entrance," Mansfield said. "We may find evidence there."

They spent the next hour planning, Doc Carpenter providing as much detail as he could about the mine's layout based on what he'd learned from treating injured miners. As they prepared to leave, Jonah turned to Abigail.

"You should stay at the boardinghouse tonight," he said firmly. "If McGrant suspects we're up to something, you could be in danger at the parsonage alone."

"I can't hide while you risk your lives," Abigail protested.

"You're not hiding," Jonah countered. "You're being prudent. The town needs you, Abigail. The church needs you. And..." he hesitated, then added quietly, "I need to know you're safe."

Something in his tone must have conveyed his sincerity, for Abigail's expression softened. "Very well," she agreed. "But you must promise to be careful. Both of you." Her gaze included Mansfield in the admonition.

"We will," Jonah assured her. "And God willing, soon, we'll have evidence."

As they stepped outside, smoke still rose from the mine on the hillside, a somber reminder of the day's tragedy and the greater evil they now sought to expose. Jonah walked Abigail to the boarding house, hyper-aware of every movement around them, every pair of eyes that might be watching.

"I'll see you tomorrow," he said as they reached the boardinghouse steps.

Abigail reached out suddenly, taking his hand in hers. "Jonah," she said quietly, "Those miners are alive because of your courage today."

"One died," he reminded her grimly.

"But four survived who wouldn't have without you." Her blue eyes held his steadily. "That matters. Thank you."

She rose on tiptoe and pressed a gentle kiss to his cheek. "For protection," she whispered.

Then she was gone, slipping inside the boarding house, leaving Jonah standing on the porch, his cheek tingling where her lips had touched his skin. His hand moved to his shirt pocket, where the small wooden cross still rested.

"Protection indeed," he murmured, a small smile touching his lips despite the gravity of their situation.

# *Chapter 34*

Darkness had fully descended by the time Jonah met Deputy Mansfield at the agreed location behind the livery stable. Both men wore dark clothing and carried small packs containing lanterns, tools, and weapons, Jonah with his hunting knife, Mansfield, his service revolver.

"Ready?" Mansfield asked quietly.

Jonah nodded, his expression resolute.

They moved silently through town, keeping to shadows and avoiding the few townsfolk still abroad. Most were gathered at the saloon or the boarding house, discussing the day's tragedy in hushed, somber tones. No one noticed two dark figures slipping away toward the eastern slope of the mine hill.

The night was clear, stars providing just enough light to navigate without lanterns until they reached the tree line. Once among the pines, Jonah struck a match, lighting his lantern but keeping the flame low.

"Doc said to look for an outcropping of rock shaped like a wolf's head," he murmured, scanning the hillside.

They searched methodically, working their way along the slope, pushing through undergrowth that had reclaimed much of the area since the old shaft's abandonment. After nearly half an hour, Mansfield called out softly.

"Here!"

Jonah joined him, holding his lantern higher. Sure enough, a rocky formation resembled a crude wolf's head, and beneath it, partially hidden by scrub and fallen pine branches, was a dark opening barely large enough for a man to enter.

"That's it," Jonah confirmed, already clearing away the concealing brush.

They enlarged the opening enough to slip through comfortably, Jonah leading the way. The tunnel beyond was narrow and low, forcing them to crouch as they moved forward. Cobwebs clung to their faces and clothing.

"Watch your step," Jonah cautioned, his lantern revealing the uneven floor. "Old timbers are rotting."

The shaft sloped gently downward, twisting as it followed what must have been an early vein of ore. The air grew staler as they descended, carrying the mineral scent of rock and the mustiness of long-abandoned passages.

After what seemed like an eternity of careful progress, the shaft widened and intersected with a larger tunnel, clearly part of the current mine's network, with more recent timber supports and the tracks for ore carts embedded in the floor.

They moved with increased caution now, aware that despite the late hour, there might be guards or workers in the mine. The echo of their footsteps seemed unnaturally loud in the oppressive silence.

The damage from the explosion became evident as they progressed. Fallen debris, splintered support beams, and the lingering smell of blasting powder grew stronger. They passed a section where miners had clearly been working to shore up a weakened wall.

"Look here," Jonah murmured, stopping to examine a support beam. He ran his fingers along a crack that split the thick timber nearly in half. "This wasn't damaged in the explosion."

Mansfield leaned closer. "What do you mean?"

"See how clean the cut is? And look—" Jonah pointed to small, regular marks along the crack. "Someone cut partway through this beam with a saw. Deliberately weakened it."

"Sabotage," Mansfield breathed, his expression hardening.

They found similar evidence on two more support beams as they continued, each partially sawn through in a manner that would cause eventual collapse under pressure.

"McGrant's setting up these accidents," Jonah said grimly. "Weakening critical supports, then using excessive blasting powder nearby to trigger collapses."

"But why risk the entire mine?" Mansfield wondered. "Unless Doc is right about the silver playing out."

They reached a junction where the main tunnel branched in three directions.

"Let's check today's explosion site first."

They moved cautiously down the left tunnel, their lantern light revealing increasing destruction as they progressed. The walls showed scorch marks, and debris littered the ground more densely.

"Here," Jonah said, stopping suddenly. He crouched, holding his lantern close to the ground. "Look at these powder residue patterns."

Mansfield knelt beside him. "What am I seeing?"

"Multiple blast points," Jonah explained, pointing to distinct scorch marks. "This wasn't a single charge for ore extraction. Someone set charges along the entire section."

Jonah moved to a fallen support beam, examining it closely. "Same saw marks here. They weakened the supports, then placed charges to ensure catastrophic failure."

They continued their investigation, and found more partially sawn timbers, excessive blasting powder residue, and a discarded barrel marked with the company's name that had contained far more powder than standard mining operations would require.

"Let's check the office."

They retraced their steps to the junction, then consulted Doc's rough map in the lantern light.

"The main tunnel is here," Mansfield said, tracing the route on the map with his finger. "The office is outside and to the left."

"And hopefully unguarded tonight," Jonah added.

They walked along the main tunnel quickly, extinguishing their lanterns before exiting. Relying on the moonlight.

The path leading away from the mine entrance took them to a small building set apart from the mining complex, built partially into the hillside. Deputy Mansfield picked the lock to enter the office.

Inside, the office was crude but functional: a desk, shelves holding ledgers and mining equipment, a safe in one corner, and maps of the mine tacked to the walls.

They moved carefully, alert for any sign of guards. Jonah reached the desk first, setting his lantern down and re-lighting it. He rifled through papers scattered across its surface. Most were mundane: shift schedules, equipment inventories, production reports. But beneath these, he found a folder containing correspondence between McCallum and McGrant.

"Here," he muttered, scanning the letters rapidly. "McGrant ordering accelerated extraction in the west section, despite McCallum's warnings about unstable rock formations. Demands to use whatever means necessary' to meet production quotas."

While damning, the letters didn't explicitly order sabotage or excessive blasting powder. Jonah turned his attention to the ledgers on the shelves, pulling down the most recent volume. He flipped through pages of mining records, production figures, equipment requisitions...

"This is it," he said suddenly, his finger tracing an entry from the previous week. "Blasting powder requisition, signed by McGrant himself, tripling the normal amount for the section that collapsed today."

Mansfield examined the ledger. "That's evidence of negligence, at least. Criminal negligence, given the outcome."

"Payroll records," Jonah murmured, as he continued quickly flipping through various other ledgers. "Production quotas... wait." He held up a letter, wedged into one of the books, his expression darkening as he read. "It's from McGrant, dated three days ago. Listen to this: 'Accelerate extraction in Section 4 regardless of structural concerns. Use whatever means necessary to meet quotas before month's end. Prepare for transition as discussed.'"

"Transition?" Mansfield questioned.

Jonah moved back to the desk and began searching through the drawers. He opened a drawer on the bottom right of the desk to reveal a leather-bound ledger. "This shows declining silver yields for months now, just as Doc suspected."

Mansfield pulled open another drawer, extracting a folded document. "Insurance papers," he said with grim satisfaction as he quickly read the documents. "The mine is insured for three times its current value."

Jonah found a locked drawer in the desk, which he pried open using his knife. Inside was a smaller ledger, its cover unmarked, and several documents were stuffed within the pages.

"Private accounts," Jonah realized as he flipped through it. "Payments to men, not on the regular mine roster. Names I don't recognize."

"Hired muscle, maybe?" Mansfield suggested.

"Possibly." Jonah turned a page and stopped, his expression grim. "Listen to this entry: 'Payment to Harker for special timber work in west shaft, 50 dollars.' Dated three days ago."

"The sawn support beams," Mansfield concluded.

Other documents detailing not only the deliberate sabotage of the mine but also plans for what would follow: using the insurance money to fund a new venture, something called the "Clear Springs Development Company," which would transform the town into what McGrant called a "proper civilized settlement" after driving out the current residents through economic hardship.

"Take all of that," Mansfield said as he started gathering various other documents and ledgers.

"We need to get this information to the territorial marshal," Jonah said. "McGrant has too much influence with local authorities."

They carefully packed the evidence, then consulted Doc's map one final time before extinguishing their lantern.

"The old shaft exit we used to enter the mine is our safest route back to town," Mansfield decided. "We must hurry."

They made their way back through the mine tunnels, moving more quickly now that their mission was accomplished. The return journey through the old shaft seemed shorter, urgency lending speed to their steps.

When they finally emerged into the night air, both men took deep breaths, relieved to escape the oppressive confines of the mine.

They made their way carefully down the hillside, staying within the tree line until they reached the outskirts of Clear Springs. The town was quiet, most lights extinguished as residents sought what rest they could after the traumatic day.

"We should separate," Mansfield suggested as they paused in the shadow of the livery stable. "Less conspicuous. I'll take the evidence with me."

Jonah nodded agreement. "I'll check on Abigail at the boarding house, then meet you at Doc's."

They parted ways, Mansfield taking the stolen documents and slipping away toward Doc's office, while Jonah moved cautiously through the back alleys.

As he approached the boarding house, a movement in the shadows across the street caught his attention. A figure was watching the building, partially concealed behind a water trough. Even in the darkness, Jonah recognized the distinctive silhouette of one of McGrant's hired men.

Cold anger flooded through Jonah.

Jonah approached the boarding house's back entrance. He tapped softly on the kitchen door, relieved when it was Margaret herself who answered.

"Mr. Brooks," she whispered, ushering him inside. "I've been worried sick. Abigail told me what you and the deputy were planning."

"Is she safe?" Jonah asked immediately.

Margaret nodded. "Sleeping upstairs. Though not easily, I'd wager. That girl's got a weight on her heart for this town and for you."

Jonah felt warmth spread through his chest at her words, but he pushed the feeling aside to focus on the immediate danger. "McGrant has a man watching the boardinghouse."

Margaret's expression hardened. "That snake... stationing men to intimidate us."

"We found evidence tonight. The mine disaster wasn't an accident. McGrant deliberately endangered his men," Jonah said quietly.

Margaret's face paled in the dim kitchen light. "God have mercy."

"I need to meet Mansfield at Doc Carpenter's. Can you continue to be observant and not let Abigail leave?"

Margaret nodded firmly. "I'll see to it. And Jonah—" she caught his arm as he turned to leave. "—be careful. McGrant's desperate, and desperate men are the most dangerous kind."

"I know," Jonah agreed. "Lock this door behind me."

He slipped back into the night, keeping to the shadows and circling around to avoid McGrant's watchman.

As Jonah made his way toward Doc Carpenter's office, he noticed unusual activity near the sheriff's office. Two unfamiliar men stood outside, engaged in low conversation. Their posture and the way they surveyed the street spoke of hired muscle, not ordinary townsfolk.

Jonah changed course, approaching Doc's office from the rear instead. He tapped softly on the back window, relieved when the doctor himself pulled aside the curtain. A moment later, the door opened.

A single lamp dimly lighted the office. Deputy Mansfield sat waiting, the incriminating documents spread across Doc's examination table.

"McGrant's got men watching the boarding house and the sheriff's office," Jonah reported.

"He's rattled," Mansfield said, nodding. "Probably escalating."

He moved to the table, glancing over the documents they'd recovered. The ledger showing excessive blasting powder, the payment records for "special timber work," the insurance papers, and the plans for the "Clear Springs Development Company."

Mansfield gestured toward all the documents. "I have more than enough to prove McGrant deliberately sabotaged his own mine. He's been weakening support beams, then using excessive blasting to trigger collapses. The mine's played out. Production's been declining for months, yet he's insured it for three times its value."

"And that's just the beginning," Jonah added grimly. "The plans for this 'Development Company' show he intends to use the insurance money to transform Clear Springs entirely. Drive out the current residents, bring in wealthy investors."

Doc's face hardened as he examined the documents. "So it wasn't just about silencing opposition. He's planning to destroy the town as we know it."

"The mine collapse was meant to be much worse," Jonah said. "If those men had died, if the evidence had been buried, McGrant could have claimed it was a tragic accident while collecting his insurance payout."

"And our rescue efforts weren't part of his plan," Mansfield concluded.

Doc looked up sharply. "Which means he'll be desperate to silence anyone who suspects the truth. Especially after the town meeting tomorrow."

"The meeting's a distraction," Jonah said. "He'll use it to gauge who stands against him."

The three men fell silent, the gravity of their situation settling over them. McGrant wasn't just a corrupt businessman, he indeed was a cold-blooded murderer willing to sacrifice lives for profit.

"I need to get these documents to the territorial marshal," Mansfield said.

"That's at least a half a day's ride," Doc pointed out. "And McGrant's men will be watching the roads."

"You should leave soon," Jonah advised. "Under cover of darkness."

Mansfield nodded. "I'll take the south trail through Miller's Pass. It's a bit shorter and less traveled, but also rougher."

"What about the town meeting?" Doc asked.

"We need to buy time," Jonah said firmly. "Keep McGrant occupied, and protect Abigail."

"She could be McGrant's primary target if he suspects any of us have turned on him," Doc said.

Jonah's jaw tightened. "I won't let him near her."

"We should make copies of the most damning documents," Doc suggested, moving to his desk. "In case something happens to the originals."

While Doc and Mansfield worked on copying the evidence, Jonah paced the small office, his mind working through contingencies. The town meeting presented both danger and opportunity.

"The meeting's at noon tomorrow," Mansfield said as he carefully folded the copied documents. "McGrant will expect you both there."

"And we'll be there," Jonah confirmed. "The more normal everything appears, the better."

"What about the rest of tonight?" Doc asked. "McGrant's men are watching. If they see either of you leaving my office this late..."

"I won't allow them to see me," Mansfield decided. "I can slip away without arousing suspicion. No worries."

"I'll do the same and return to my shop," Jonah added. "If McGrant's watching it, my absence would be noted."

They finalized their plan: Mansfield depart and ride hard. Jonah and Doc would attend the town meeting tomorrow, appearing to know nothing of the mine sabotage. They would protect Abigail and try to keep tabs on McGrant.

"I'll do my best to be back late tomorrow," Mansfield said as he tucked the documents securely inside his jacket. "I'll return with Marshal Carter and enough men to arrest McGrant and his accomplices."

"Be careful," Jonah warned. "McGrant's desperate. He won't hesitate to eliminate anyone who threatens his plans."

The deputy nodded grimly. "I've dealt with his kind before. Men who think money and power put them above the law."

"Above God's law as well as man's," Doc added softly.

They shook hands; the gesture carrying the weight of their dangerous undertaking. Jonah felt the responsibility settling on his shoulders, not just for keeping his eye on McGrant, but for protecting Abigail and the townsfolk.

"I'll go first," Jonah said, moving to the door. "Check if the way is clear."

He slipped outside, scanning the darkened street. The men he'd spotted earlier were no longer visible, but that didn't mean they weren't watching from the shadows. Moving silently, Jonah circled the building, checking all approaches before returning to the back door.

"Two men near the saloon," he reported quietly. "Watching the main street. If you stay in the shadows behind the buildings, you should make it to your quarters without being seen."

Mansfield nodded.

"God be with you," Doc said, clasping the deputy's shoulder.

Jonah and Mansfield left together, separating at the first alley. Jonah made his way toward his smithy shop, hyperaware of every sound.

Abigail's wooden cross still rested in his pocket, his fingers seeking it for reassurance.

When he reached his shop, he paused in the doorway, scanning the street one final time before entering. The familiar smell of coal and iron greeted him. The solitude of his shop that he'd cultivated for so long felt oppressive rather than comforting.

He moved his cot to the wide open doorway of his shop, tucked inside just enough to not immediately be seen in the dark, and knelt beside it. The wooden cross in his hand, he closed his eyes.

"Lord," he whispered, "I don't know if You're listening to me. I haven't given You much reason to. Our town needs Your help. Watch over and protect us."

The prayer felt awkward, halting, but as the words came, something long-frozen within him began to thaw.

"I couldn't save them before," he continued, memories of his family's graves fresh in his mind. "But maybe, with Your help, I can save these people. Save her."

He remained kneeling for several minutes, the surrounding silence a comfort. When he rose he and lay down on his cot, exhaustion claimed him quickly, but his sleep was deeper and more peaceful than it had been in years.

# Chapter 35

Jonah woke instantly, years of wartime vigilance having trained him to transition from sleep to full alertness in seconds. He listened carefully, hearing only the normal early morning sounds of Clear Springs gradually awakening.

The street was empty.

Jonah moved the cot to the back room and built a small fire in his forge, maintaining the appearance of normal routine while watching for any unusual activity.

Jonah worked steadily through the morning, crafting sets of horseshoes while keeping an eye on the comings and goings outside. He noted two of McGrant's men walking past his shop multiple times, their eyes scanning doorways and windows with predatory vigilance.

Shortly before noon, he set aside his work and washed his hands and face, donned a clean shirt, and stepped out onto the street. The town meeting would begin soon, and he intended to be at Abigail's side.

He stood in the doorway of his shop, waiting.

Within moments, Abigail stepped out of the boarding house, accompanied by Margaret. Even from a distance, he could see the tension in her posture, and the determined lift of her chin.

Jonah crossed the street, walking purposefully toward Abigail and Margaret. He noted how Abigail's eyes brightened when she spotted him, a smile lifting the corners of her mouth despite the gravity of their situation.

"Mr. Brooks," Margaret greeted him, her voice carrying its usual warmth, though her eyes held concern. "A fine day for a town meeting, wouldn't you say?"

"Indeed, Mrs. Hale," Jonah replied, falling into step beside them. He lowered his voice. "Did you sleep well?"

Abigail glanced at him, understanding his real question. "As well as could be expected. No disturbances, though I noticed we had... observers."

"They're still watching," Jonah confirmed quietly.

The town hall, actually Tuttle's Café, cleared of tables for the occasion, was already filling with Clear Springs residents as they approached. Mayor Jenkins stood near the entrance, looking uncomfortable as he greeted arrivals. His eyes widened slightly at the sight of Jonah walking alongside Abigail.

"Miss Whitaker, Mrs. Hale," he nodded nervously. "Mr. Brooks... didn't expect to see you at a town gathering."

"Thought I'd make an exception today," Jonah replied evenly.

Inside, the room buzzed with tension. Miners clustered together in one area, their faces somber after yesterday's tragedy. Doc Carpenter sat near the back, pretending to read a medical journal while surveying the room. Silas McGrant had not yet arrived.

Jonah guided Abigail and Margaret to seats beside Doc. As they settled, Abigail leaned close to Jonah, her breath warm against his ear.

"Deputy Mansfield?"

"On his way to get the territorial marshal," Jonah whispered.

Their conversation was interrupted as the door opened and Silas McGrant entered, followed by McCallum and two burly men Jonah recognized as recent arrivals to town. McGrant wore an expensive suit, his posture radiating confidence as he strode to the front of the room. McCallum, by contrast, looked pale and nervous, his eyes darting around the gathering, an unusual sight for him.

Jonah's jaw tightened. McCallum knew what they'd done to the mine. He'd participated in the sabotage that had killed Griffin and nearly killed the others. The man's obvious discomfort suggested he might be a weak link in McGrant's operation.

Mayor Jenkins called the meeting to order, introducing McGrant as "our town's leading businessman and benefactor."

McGrant stepped forward, his expression a practiced mask of solemn concern. "Friends and neighbors," he began, his voice carrying easily through the room. "Yesterday, our community suffered a terrible tragedy. The loss of Jedidiah Griffin weighs heavily on us all, and the injuries sustained by our hardworking miners are a cause for great sorrow."

He paused, scanning the crowd with what appeared to be genuine sympathy. "I've already visited Mrs. Griffin and assured her that the McGrant Silver Mining Company will provide generous compensation for her loss. The injured men and their families will receive full wages during their recovery, and their medical expenses will be covered."

Murmurs of approval rippled through the gathering. McGrant was playing his role perfectly, the concerned employer, the community leader stepping up in a time of crisis.

"However," McGrant continued, his tone shifting subtly, "this tragedy highlights certain dangers facing our community. The mine accident, while devastating, is just one symptom of a larger problem."

Jonah felt Abigail tense beside him.

"Clear Springs stands at a crossroads," McGrant declared. "We can remain a rough mining camp, vulnerable to the whims of fortune and nature, or we can seize the opportunity to become something greater... a proper town with proper amenities, safety, and prosperity for all."

McGrant unrolled a large map and displayed it on an easel. "This is my vision for the future of Clear Springs. New buildings of brick and stone replacing our vulnerable wooden structures. Wider streets. A real school. A hotel to attract investors and visitors. And yes, even a proper church."

At this, he glanced directly at Abigail, his smile not reaching his eyes.

"To achieve this vision, we must work together. The McGrant Silver Mining Company is prepared to invest substantially in Clear Springs' development. But we need unity of purpose. We need to move forward as one community, embracing progress rather than clinging to outdated ways."

Jonah watched the crowd carefully. Many seemed impressed by McGrant's vision, nodding along as he described improvements that would benefit everyone. But others, particularly the miners who had witnessed yesterday's tragedy firsthand, looked skeptical.

"What about the mine safety concerns?" Billy Patterson called out, his head bandaged from yesterday's injuries. "Three men warned about those support beams, and they were fired for speaking up."

McGrant's expression hardened momentarily before he smoothed it into one of sincere regret. "A terrible misunderstanding, Mr. Patterson. McCallum has informed me that those concerns were never properly communicated to management. I assure you, had I known, immediate action would have been taken. Those men will be reinstated with back pay."

"That's not true!" another miner shouted. "McCallum told us straight out that you ordered us to ignore the warning signs!"

McCallum flinched visibly, and McGrant shot him a warning glance.

"Gentlemen, please," McGrant said, raising his hands placatingly. "This meeting isn't about assigning blame for yesterday's tragedy. A full investigation will be conducted, I assure you. Today, we're here to discuss Clear Springs' future."

He turned back to his map, pointing out specific improvements, redirecting attention away from the mine accident. But the damage was done. Doubt had been planted.

Abigail rose to her feet, her blue eyes clear and direct. "Mr. McGrant, your vision for Clear Springs sounds impressive. But I can't help wondering, where do the current residents fit into this plan? Will the miners and their families who built this town have homes in your new Clear Springs? Will they be able to afford to live here once these... improvements are made?"

The room fell silent, all eyes turning toward Abigail.

McGrant's smile tightened. "Miss Whitaker, I appreciate your concern for our working families. Rest assured, there will be a place for everyone willing to embrace progress. Change, however, requires adaptation. Some may need to... adjust their expectations."

"Or leave entirely?" Abigail pressed. "Because your map shows new homes where many current residences stand. Including, I notice, the church."

McGrant's eyes narrowed slightly. "The current structure is hardly adequate. A new, proper church would better serve the community's spiritual needs. Surely, you can appreciate that, given your recent... renovations."

"The current church serves its purpose quite well," Abigail replied steadily. "What makes a church isn't the building but the faith and community within it."

McGrant stared at her for a long moment, calculation evident in his eyes. Then he smiled again, broader but colder. "Perhaps we should put it to a vote. After all, Clear Springs belongs to all of us, doesn't it? Those who support progress and improved safety measures, and those who... prefer things as they are."

The implication was clear, oppose McGrant's plan, and you were choosing danger and tragedy over safety and progress.

Jonah stood up, drawing all eyes to him. His presence commanded attention.

"Before we vote on anything," he said, his deep voice carrying easily, "I'd like to suggest we wait for Sheriff Holden to return from Denver. Major town decisions should have the input of all our officials. Wouldn't you agree, Mayor Jenkins?"

Jenkins looked uncomfortable, but nodded. "That seems reasonable—"

"The sheriff could be gone for days," McGrant interrupted. "Clear Springs can't afford to delay progress, especially after yesterday's tragedy has shown how urgent our safety concerns are."

"Speaking of safety," Doc Carpenter interjected, standing up beside Jonah, "I've noticed some troubling patterns in the injuries I've treated over the past months. Patterns that suggest the mine accidents may not be as random as they appear."

McGrant's face darkened. "Are you accusing someone of negligence, Doctor?"

"I'm simply stating medical facts," Doc replied calmly. "The incidents show remarkable... consistency."

A murmur ran through the crowd. McCallum was now visibly sweating, his eyes darting between McGrant and the exit.

"This is outrageous," McGrant declared, his composed façade cracking slightly. "Unfounded accusations will not help our community heal or move forward. Mayor Jenkins, I suggest we proceed with the vote immediately."

"Actually," Ruth Patterson stood up, her voice trembling but determined, "I think we should wait for Sheriff Holden, as well as Deputy Mansfield, which, by the way, where is he?"

"Official business, I assume," McGrant said dismissively.

"Strange," Jonah remarked, "that our deputy would be absent right after a major mine disaster."

The atmosphere in the room shifted palpably, suspicion replacing the earlier receptiveness to McGrant's vision. McGrant himself seemed to sense it, his expression hardening as he surveyed the crowd.

"I see certain elements in our community are determined to obstruct progress," he said coldly. "Perhaps some of you need a reminder of the economic realities facing Clear Springs. The mine operation can easily be relocated. The jobs it provides, the business it brings to your shops and establishments, all of that can disappear overnight if Clear Springs becomes... inhospitable to development."

The threat hung in the air, explicit and chilling. Some of the townsfolk exchanged worried glances.

"Or perhaps," Abigail said clearly, "we need a reminder of what truly makes a community. Not buildings or businesses, but people standing together. Supporting each other through hardship. Choosing right over wrong, even when it's difficult."

She stood beside Jonah, her shoulder brushing against his arm in a gesture of solidarity that didn't go unnoticed by the watching crowd. Or by McGrant, whose eyes narrowed dangerously.

"Miss Whitaker," he said, voice dripping with false concern, "your dedication to spiritual matters is admirable. But I fear you've been misled by certain individuals with their own agendas." His gaze flicked to Jonah. "Perhaps you should reconsider your... associations."

"I choose my friends carefully, Mr. McGrant," Abigail replied steadily. "Based on their character, not their usefulness to my interests."

McGrant's face flushed with anger. For a moment, Jonah thought he might abandon his façade of civility entirely. Instead, McGrant forced a tight smile.

"This meeting is clearly not productive today. Emotions are running high after yesterday's tragedy. Mayor Jenkins, I suggest we adjourn and reconvene when cooler heads prevail."

Jenkins, looking relieved at the suggestion, quickly agreed and declared the meeting adjourned. The crowd began dispersing, breaking into small clusters of animated conversation.

McGrant strode toward the exit, but paused beside Jonah and Abigail. "A word of advice," he said quietly, menace underlying his tone. "Clear Springs has survived this long because people understand their place in the natural order. Those who disrupt that order tend to encounter... misfortune."

"Is that a threat, McGrant?" Jonah asked evenly.

"Simply an observation of frontier reality, Brooks." McGrant's eyes were cold. "Miss Whitaker, I'd reconsider tonight's prayer meeting if I were you. After such tragedy, surely the town deserves a few days of quiet reflection rather than... public gatherings."

Without waiting for a response, he left McCallum and his men following close behind.

Jonah turned to Abigail, concern evident in his expression. "He's growing more desperate."

"I know," she said quietly. "I will not cancel the prayer meeting. The town needs hope now more than ever."

"To dangerous," Jonah warned. "McGrant clearly doesn't want people gathering, especially not at the church."

Abigail's eyes met his, unwavering. "I won't abandon my mission out of fear, Jonah. You know that."

He did know it, and despite his concern, that steadfast courage was part of what had drawn him to her. Jonah nodded slowly. "Then we'll take precautions. I'll attend the prayer meeting this evening, and I'll make sure others are helping me keep watch."

Doc Carpenter joined them, speaking in a low voice. "McCallum's rattled. Did you see his face when the miners mentioned those warnings?"

"He might be a weak link," Jonah agreed. "If pressed, he might turn on McGrant to save himself."

"Or he might become more dangerous," Abigail cautioned. "Desperate men often are."

They moved outside, where the noon sun cast harsh light on Clear Springs' dusty main street. McGrant and his men were nowhere to be seen, but Jonah remained vigilant, positioning himself protectively close to Abigail.

"I should check on Ruth and Billy," Abigail said. "They took a risk speaking up today."

"I'll come with you," Jonah replied immediately.

As they walked toward the Patterson's' small home, Abigail glanced at him. "You didn't tell Mrs. Hale everything about last night, did you? What else did you find in the mine?"

Jonah hesitated, then spoke quietly. "Evidence that McGrant deliberately sabotaged his own mine. The silver's playing out, but he's insured it for three times its value. He's planning to collect the insurance and transform Clear Springs entirely and drive out the current residents, bring in wealthy investors."

Abigail's face paled. "The collapse really was intentional? Those men... Jedidiah Griffin..."

"Murder."

"Dear God," Abigail whispered, genuine horror in her voice. "How could anyone be so... evil?"

"Greed," Jonah said simply. "I've seen it turn men into monsters before."

They reached the Patterson's home, where Ruth welcomed them with obvious relief. Billy was resting, his head injury causing dizziness but not life-threatening. Their children played quietly in the corner.

As Ruth prepared coffee, she leaned close to Abigail. "McGrant's men came by this morning. Said they were checking on Billy, but it felt like a warning. Their eyes were cold, and calculating."

"You were brave to speak up at the meeting," Abigail told her.

Ruth shook her head. "Not brave. Desperate. If Billy had died yesterday..." Her voice broke. "He only went back to the mine after other incidents because McGrant threatened to evict us if he didn't."

Jonah's expression darkened. "How many others were coerced back after raising safety concerns?"

"Most," Ruth admitted. "McGrant owns most of the housing. Cross him, and you lose your home and your livelihood in one stroke."

The conversation reinforced what they already knew. McGrant's control of Clear Springs was near-absolute, built on economic leverage and fear. Only the church and a few business owners like Jonah maintained any independence.

As they left the Patterson's, Jonah noticed the sun's position. "The prayer meeting is in three hours. I will go to my shop and work while keeping a watchful eye on the town. I'll meet you at the church for the prayer meeting. I do not sense you are in any danger right now. McGrath will lie low for a while, making plans."

Abigail nodded, then reached out to touch his arm. "Jonah... thank you. For everything you've done. For the miners yesterday, for going back into that mine last night, for standing with me today. I... I don't know what I would have done without you."

The sincerity in her blue eyes touched him deeply. He covered her hand with his own.

"You would have managed," he said.

A faint blush colored her cheeks. "Perhaps. But I'm grateful I didn't have to face this alone."

For a moment, they stood there, connected by touch and gaze, the busy street around them fading into insignificance. Then Jonah reluctantly withdrew his hand.

"I'll see you at the church," he promised. "Be careful until then."

As Jonah walked back to his smithy, his mind replayed that moment of connection.

It terrified him. And yet, he couldn't deny the growing certainty that she had become essential to him, as necessary as breath. The thought of anything happening to her was unbearable.

Inside his shop, Jonah moved mechanically through familiar tasks, checking his tools, banking the forge fire, always with an eye on the church and parsonage. His thoughts remained with Abigail, and with the danger McGrant posed to her and the town she was trying to save.

He pulled the small wooden cross from his pocket, running his thumb over its smooth surface.

"Lord," he whispered, "protect her. And help me find the strength to do what needs to be done."

# Chapter 36

Jonah couldn't focus. The half-formed horseshoe lay abandoned on his anvil as he paced the length of his smithy shop, each turn bringing his gaze back to the church and parsonage. The prayer meeting wasn't scheduled to begin for another hour, but unease crawled along his spine like a physical thing.

He grabbed a rag and wiped the sweat and soot from his hands with quick, agitated movements. Jonah tossed the rag aside and strode to the doorway, scanning the quiet street. Two of McGrant's men lounged against a post outside the saloon, their casual postures belied by the alertness in their eyes. They were watching, waiting for something.

Jonah extinguished the forge fire, locked his tools in the cabinet, and closed the wide doors to his smithy with a decisive thud. His long strides carried him purposefully down main street.

Sid Paulson looked up from sweeping the boardwalk in front of his general store, eyebrows rising in surprise at Jonah's determined pace.

"Everything all right, Jonah?" he called.

Jonah barely slowed. "Prayer meeting at the church," he said over his shoulder. "Come now."

Paulson's broom stilled. "Now? But I thought—"

Jonah was already too far to hear the rest, but from the corner of his eye, he saw Paulson prop his broom against the wall and disappear inside his store.

As he passed the boarding house, Margaret stepped onto her porch, a basket of mending in her hands. Her eyes widened at the sight of him.

"Mr. Brooks? Is something the matter?"

"Prayer meeting," Jonah repeated, not breaking his stride. "Starting early. Spread the word."

Behind him, he heard Margaret call to someone inside the boarding house.

By the time Jonah reached the church, several townsfolk had fallen in behind him. Ruth hurried to catch up, little Emma balanced on her hip.

"Jonah? What's happening?" she asked, slightly breathless.

"Just a feeling," he replied, slowing to let her match his pace.

Ruth's expression grew serious. "McGrant?"

Jonah nodded once.

The church doors stood open. Jonah strode up the newly repaired steps and entered, making his way to a back pew where he could watch both the entrance and the side door leading to the parsonage.

Ruth followed him inside, settling Emma on the bench beside her. Within minutes, others began to arrive, the Tuttle's from the café, Doc Carpenter, Timothy Wells and his wife, and several miners still bearing bandages from the recent accident.

Jonah sat silently, his body tense as a drawn bowstring, eyes watching. People nodded to him as they entered, some with surprise, others with understanding. Word was spreading quickly through Clear Springs' efficient gossip network.

The side door opened, and Abigail stepped into the sanctuary, a small Bible in her hands. She stopped short at the sight of the gathering crowd, her blue eyes widening in confusion. Her gaze found Jonah immediately, eyebrows lifting in silent question.

He rose and moved toward her, aware of the curious glances following him.

"Jonah," she said quietly as he reached her. "What's happening?"

"McGrant's planning something. I can feel it," he said, keeping his voice low. "I thought it best to have everyone here early."

Concern flickered across her face, but she nodded, trusting his judgment. "I haven't prepared—"

"It doesn't matter," he assured her.

Abigail glanced at the growing congregation, then back to Jonah. "Reverend Blake—he doesn't know we're starting early."

Jonah hadn't considered the elderly minister. "Stay here with the others," he said. "I'll go fetch him."

"But McGrant's men—"

"Won't bother me," Jonah said with grim confidence. "You will be fine as well with the others here in the church."

Abigail hesitated, then reached out and squeezed his arm. "Be careful."

The simple touch and the concern in her eyes sent warmth through him despite the tension of the moment. Jonah covered her hand with his own briefly.

"I will. Keep everyone here. Don't let anyone leave alone."

He turned to address the congregation, which had grown to nearly twenty people. "Folks, Miss Whitaker will be leading us in some hymns while I fetch Reverend Blake. Everyone stay together, you hear?"

Timothy stepped forward. "Take my buggy, Jonah. It's hitched out back."

Jonah nodded his thanks and headed for the door, passing more townsfolk on their way in. The sanctuary was filling up fast. Word had spread quickly, and Clear Springs' residents had responded.

Outside, McGrant's two watchers at the Saloon had noticed. They'd straightened from their casual poses, one speaking urgently to the other. Jonah kept his pace unhurried but purposeful as he rounded the church to where Timothy's buggy waited.

As he climbed up and took the reins, he heard the first strains of "Amazing Grace" rising from the church, Abigail's clear voice leading the impromptu congregation. The familiar hymn followed him as he urged the horse forward, heading for the outskirts of town, where Reverend Blake's small cottage stood.

# Chapter 37

Reverend Blake's cottage was dark when Jonah arrived, and for a moment, he feared the elderly minister might be out. He leaped down from the buggy and strode to the door, knocking firmly.

"Reverend Blake? It's Jonah Brooks."

Silence greeted him. Jonah knocked again, louder this time. "Reverend?"

A shuffling sound came from inside, followed by the thump of a cane on wooden floorboards. "Coming, coming," called Blake's aged voice. "No need to break down the door."

The door swung open to reveal the minister, looking frailer than Jonah remembered. His rheumatism must have been troubling him more than usual.

"Jonah," Blake said, surprise evident in his watery eyes. "What brings you to my door? Not like you to make social calls."

"The prayer meeting, Reverend. It's starting early."

Blake's bushy eyebrows drew together. "Early? But why—" Understanding dawned on his weathered face. "McGrant's on the move, isn't he?"

Jonah nodded. "I think so. People are already gathering at the church. We need you there."

The old man's expression hardened with determination. "Then let's not keep them waiting. The Lord's work waits for no man's convenience."

Jonah helped the minister down the short path to the buggy, supporting his frail frame as he climbed aboard. Blake's hands trembled slightly as he settled himself, but his eyes were clear and focused.

"You know," Blake said as Jonah flicked the reins and the horse set off toward town, "I've been praying for this day for years."

"What day?"

"The day Clear Springs finds its backbone again." The old man smiled, the wrinkles around his eyes deepening. "And the day you find your way to the Lord's house."

Jonah kept his eyes on the road. "I'm just helping Miss Whitaker."

"Of course you are," Blake agreed. "And I'm just an old man with a bad hip."

Clear Springs appeared ahead, the church windows glowing with light. Jonah could hear singing even from a distance. It sounded as if the congregation had grown considerably during his absence.

"Sounds like the Lord's house is full tonight," Blake observed with satisfaction.

Jonah guided the buggy to the church steps and hitched the horses to the nearby hitching rail, and helped the elderly minister down. Blake leaned heavily on his cane and Jonah's arm as they made their way up the steps.

The scene inside stopped Jonah in his tracks. Every pew was filled, and people were standing along the walls and in the back. Abigail stood at the front, leading the congregation in "Rock of Ages," her face alight with the kind of joy that transcends circumstances. When she spotted Jonah and Reverend Blake in the doorway, her smile widened.

"Reverend Blake is here," she announced as the hymn ended. The congregation turned, many rising respectfully as Jonah helped the minister down the center aisle.

"Bless you all for coming," Blake said, his voice stronger than it had been at his cottage. "What a sight for these old eyes."

Jonah guided him to the front pew, where Margaret quickly made space. The elderly minister sank down gratefully, nodding his thanks to Jonah.

Abigail approached, clasping Blake's gnarled hands in her own. "I'm so glad you're here, Reverend. Would you like to lead us?"

Blake shook his head. "No, my dear. This is your meeting. I'm content to watch the Lord work through you tonight." He patted the space beside him. "Mr. Brooks, join me if you would."

Jonah sat beside the minister, acutely aware of the many eyes upon him.

Abigail returned to the front of the congregation. The candle and lantern light caught the gold in her hair, haloing her in gentle light. She looked both vulnerable and incredibly strong as she faced the packed church.

"Friends," she began, her voice steady and clear, "we've gathered a little earlier than planned, but God's timing is always perfect. Tonight, we come together in community and faith, to share our burdens and lift each other up in prayer."

She opened her Bible. "In John 1:5, we read: 'The light shines in the darkness, and the darkness has not overcome it.' Clear Springs has faced much darkness... tragedy at the mine, uncertainty about our future, threats to our community. But look around you." She gestured to the filled sanctuary. "The light shines still. It shines in each of you who came tonight, in your courage to gather despite fear."

Murmurs of agreement rippled through the congregation. Jonah watched Abigail closely, once again struck by her natural grace and the quiet authority with which she spoke.

"Let us sing together," Abigail continued, "and then we'll open our hearts in prayer for the concerns that weigh on us all."

She led them in "Great Is Thy Faithfulness," her clear soprano rising above the congregation's voices. Jonah found himself silently mouthing the words, memories of his childhood faith stirring reluctantly within him.

Beside him, Reverend Blake sang with surprising strength, one gnarled hand keeping time on his knee. When the hymn ended, Abigail invited the congregation to share their prayers and concerns.

Ruth stood first. "I want to thank God for sparing my Billy in the mine collapse, and ask for His healing on those still recovering, especially Ezekiel Mercer."

Several miners nodded in agreement.

Timothy rose next. "I'd like to pray for guidance for our town. With all these changes and challenges, we need wisdom more than ever."

Others followed—prayers for safety, for justice, for hope in uncertain times. No one mentioned McGrant by name, but his shadow lay across many of the concerns raised.

Finally, Abigail nodded and smiled gently. "Let us bow our heads together and bring these concerns before the Lord."

The congregation bowed their heads. Jonah felt Blake's hand settle on his arm, bony fingers gripping with surprising strength. He glanced at the old minister, who nodded toward Abigail, his eyes conveying a clear message.

Jonah hesitated, his heart pounding against his ribs. Then he was on his feet and moved forward to stand beside Abigail. She looked up at him, surprise and something like hope shining in her eyes.

Jonah reached for her hand, his large, calloused fingers enveloping her smaller ones. The touch anchored him as he turned to face the startled congregation.

"I'm not a man of many words," he began, his deep voice filling the silent church. "And I haven't stood in a house of worship for many years. But tonight... tonight I feel called to pray with you all."

He took a deep breath, squeezing Abigail's hand gently. Her answering pressure gave him courage.

"Heavenly Father," he said, the long-unused words feeling both foreign and familiar on his tongue, "we come before You tonight as a community facing darkness on all sides. We ask for Your protection over Clear Springs and its people. For healing for those injured in the mine. For comfort for those who grieve."

His voice grew stronger as he continued. "We ask for wisdom to know right from wrong, and courage to stand for what's right even when it's difficult. For justice to prevail against those who would harm the innocent for gain."

Jonah paused, feeling Abigail's fingers trembling slightly in his grasp. "Lord, we thank You for sending Abigail Whitaker to us, for her courage and her faith that have inspired so many. Protect her, guide her, and help us to support her mission in this town."

"And Father," he added, his voice dropping slightly, "I ask forgiveness for my years of anger and doubt, for turning away when I should have turned toward You. Help me—help all of us—to trust in Your plan, even when we can't see the way forward."

"In Your holy name, Amen."

"Amen," the congregation echoed, the single word filled with emotion.

Jonah opened his eyes to find many in the congregation wiping away tears. Reverend Blake beamed at him from the front pew, nodding in approval. But it was Abigail's expression that caught and held him—wonder, joy, and something deeper shining in her blue eyes.

She squeezed his hand once more before releasing it.

He nodded, suddenly self-conscious, and moved to step back. Before he could return to his seat, however, a commotion at the back of the church drew everyone's attention.

Through the wide-open doors, Jonah could see Silas McGrant approaching, flanked by McCallum and three of his hired men. Their expressions were grim, purposeful.

Instinctively, Jonah turned and stepped in front of Abigail, his body tensing for confrontation. Behind him, he heard the congregation shifting, murmurs of concern spreading through the church.

"Stay behind me," he said quietly to Abigail.

"No," she replied, moving to stand beside him instead. "We face this together."

Jonah turned back to face the congregation as McGrant reached the church steps, stopping just outside the doorway. His eyes narrowed as he took in the packed sanctuary, the unified front presented by the congregation.

"What's the meaning of this gathering?" McGrant demanded, his voice carrying easily into the hushed church. "This meeting wasn't scheduled until later."

Abigail stepped forward, her chin lifted. "Prayer knows no schedule, Mr. McGrant. The community felt the need to gather early tonight."

McGrant's gaze shifted to Jonah, hardening with barely concealed hostility. "I see. And was this sudden change your idea, Brooks?"

"The church belongs to the town," Jonah replied evenly. "Not to you or me."

McGrant's jaw tightened, but he maintained his composure. "Indeed. And as a concerned citizen of this town, I've come to share some important information with the good people gathered here."

He stepped into the doorway, his men remaining outside. "Friends and neighbors," he began, adopting the same smooth tone he'd used at the town meeting, "I regret interrupting your devotions, but a matter of public safety cannot wait."

Jonah felt Abigail tense beside him. McGrant was too controlled, too calculated. Whatever he was planning, it wouldn't be a direct confrontation—not with so many witnesses.

"This afternoon," McGrant continued, "I received disturbing news from Denver. It seems the territorial marshal is investigating reports of misappropriated church funds in several frontier communities. Funds intended for church construction being used for... personal gain."

A murmur ran through the congregation. McGrant's eyes fixed on Abigail, his expression one of manufactured concern.

"Miss Whitaker, as the administrator of this church's finances, you might want to prepare for some official inquiries. I'm told the penalties for such misappropriation can be quite severe."

Abigail's face paled, but her voice remained steady. "There has been no misappropriation, Mr. McGrant. Every penny donated to this church has gone toward its restoration or to helping those in need, as the church board can attest."

"Board?" McGrant raised an eyebrow. "I wasn't aware this establishment had a formal board."

"Formed last week," Reverend Blake called from his seat, his aged voice carrying surprising authority. "Myself, Doc Carpenter, Timothy Wells, and Ruth Patterson. We've reviewed all expenditures and found everything in perfect order."

McGrant's smile tightened fractionally. "How convenient. Nevertheless, when officials arrive—"

"They'll find nothing but honest books and clear records," Abigail interrupted. "Now, if you've come to pray with us, Mr. McGrant, you're welcome to stay. If not, we were in the middle of our service."

For a moment, McGrant's mask of civility slipped, raw anger flashing in his eyes. Then he smoothed his expression once more.

"I wouldn't dream of interrupting further. Good evening to you all." He turned to leave, then paused, looking back at Jonah. "Oh, and Brooks?"

"Yes?"

"Silas McGrant... you and your men have no further business here," a commanding voice declared from outside.

McGrant, visibly irritated by the interruption, turned and found himself face-to-face with Marshal Carter, who stood flanked by his deputies as well as deputy Mansfield.

McGrant's face contorted with shock. "What is the meaning of this?" he demanded, taking an involuntary step backward.

"Silas McGrant," Marshal Carter announced, his voice carrying clearly through the church doorway, "you're under arrest for sabotage, fraud, criminal negligence resulting in death, and conspiracy to commit murder."

McCallum paled visibly, his eyes darting frantically between McGrant and the lawmen.

"This is preposterous!" McGrant sputtered, regaining his composure. "I demand to know the basis for these outrageous accusations!"

Marshal Carter held up a leather portfolio. "Evidence recovered from your mine office, including payment records for deliberately weakened support beams, orders for excessive blasting powder, and insurance documentation... among other things."

McGrant's expression hardened as he glanced at his men, who tensed in response. "These are private business documents stolen from my property. They prove nothing."

"That'll be for a judge to decide," Marshal Carter replied evenly. "Now, you can come quietly, or—"

"Get them!" McGrant suddenly shouted, lunging forward.

The church erupted in chaos. McGrant's men surged toward the lawmen, while McCallum hung back, terror evident on his face. One of McGrant's hired thugs swung wildly at Deputy Mansfield, who ducked and delivered a precise blow to the man's midsection.

The congregation scrambled to the sides of the church, women gathering children protectively, men moving forward to help if needed.

McGrant himself charged directly at Marshal Carter, but the experienced lawman sidestepped neatly, catching McGrant's arm and twisting it behind his back in one fluid motion.

"That's enough!" Carter commanded, forcing McGrant to his knees.

Two of McGrant's men continued struggling, one managing to land a solid punch on a deputy before Timothy Wells and Billy Patterson joined the fray, helping to subdue them. The third of McGrant's men raised his hands in surrender, clearly recognizing the futility of resistance.

McCallum, seeing the fight turn against them, tried to flee but found his path blocked by Doc Carpenter and another deputy.

"James McCallum," the deputy announced, "you're also under arrest as an accomplice to these crimes."

Within moments, the brief but intense struggle ended. McGrant and his men were restrained.

Marshal Carter hauled McGrant to his feet, keeping a firm grip on his arm. "As I was saying, Silas McGrant, you're under arrest. You have the right to legal representation at your trial. You'll be transported to Denver to face territorial justice for your crimes against the people of Clear Springs."

McGrant's face was livid with rage. "This isn't over," he spat, his gaze finding Jonah and Abigail. "You think you've won, but men like me don't stay down."

"They do when there's enough evidence to hang them," Marshal Carter replied coldly. He nodded to his deputies. "Get them out of here."

As the lawmen marched McGrant and his men from the church, Deputy Mansfield approached Jonah and Abigail. His face was bruised, and he looked exhausted, but triumphant.

"Marshal Carter assembled his men immediately when he saw the evidence," he explained. "We rode hard to get here as quickly as we could. Good thing, too... looks like we arrived just in time."

The congregation began to recover from the shock, murmurs of amazement spreading through the sanctuary.

"Is it truly over?" Abigail asked quietly, her hand finding Jonah's arm.

"The mine sabotage, McGrant's threats—yes," Mansfield confirmed. "Marshal Carter says the evidence is overwhelming, and he's sure they will find more once they search his home and offices. Neither

McGrant nor McCallum will see the outside of a prison for a very long time, if ever."

Reverend Blake thumped his cane on the floor, drawing everyone's attention. "It seems," he said, his aged voice carrying clearly through the now-silent church, "that we have even more to be thankful for tonight than we realized."

A murmur of agreement rippled through the congregation, growing into spontaneous applause.

Abigail turned to Jonah, her eyes shining with unshed tears of relief and joy. "God's timing truly is perfect," she whispered.

Jonah looked down at her, at the faith and courage that had never wavered, even in the darkest moments. "It is," he agreed, his hand covering hers where it rested on his arm.

Reverend Blake rose shakily to his feet. "Friends," he called, "let us continue our service with a hymn of thanksgiving. For surely the Lord has delivered us this day."

As Abigail moved to lead the congregation, Jonah remained where he was, watching her with a heart full of emotions he'd thought long dead. He joined in singing, his deep voice blending with those around him, no longer a solitary figure standing apart, but part of something whole and healing.

The light indeed shone in the darkness, and the darkness had not overcome it.

# Chapter 38

"Hannah," Abigail gasped, grabbing Jonah's arm as the congregation rose to leave the church. The prayer meeting had officially ended, though excited chatter filled the sanctuary as townsfolk processed the dramatic events they'd just witnessed.

Jonah turned to her, confusion crossing his features. "What about her?"

"She doesn't know," Abigail said urgently, her blue eyes wide with concern. "Her father was arrested. Hannah has no idea what's happened."

Understanding dawned on Jonah's face. "You're right."

"We must go," Abigail insisted, already gathering her shawl. "Now..."

Jonah nodded, immediately scanning the departing congregation. "We'll need a buggy."

"Timothy's is still outside," Abigail suggested, moving toward the door with determined steps.

"I'll ask him—"

"Take mine," Ruth interrupted, having overheard their conversation. "It's hitched out back behind my home."

"Thank you," Abigail said, clasping Ruth's hand gratefully.

"That poor girl," Ruth murmured. "Tell her she's welcome in our home if she needs a place."

Jonah nodded his thanks, then took Abigail's elbow, guiding her through the dispersing crowd. Several townsfolk called questions after them, but Jonah simply raised a hand in acknowledgment without slowing.

"We'll explain later," Abigail called back as they hurried down the church steps.

The night air carried a hint of autumn's approach, though summer still held its grip on the land. Stars glittered overhead in a clear sky as Jonah led Abigail to where Ruth's buggy waited behind her home. Without ceremony, he lifted her onto the seat, his strong hands spanning her waist momentarily before he released her and then climbed up beside her.

Jonah took the reins and urged the horse forward, guiding them away and toward the McCallum residence on the far northern edge of town.

"Just what do you plan to do?" Jonah asked as they traveled, the rhythmic sound of hooves punctuating the night air.

Abigail turned to him, her face half-illuminated by moonlight. "I'm going to ask Hannah to come back to the parsonage with me tonight. She shouldn't be alone, wondering when her father will return or what's happened."

"And if she refuses?"

"Then we'll respect her wishes," Abigail said firmly. "But she deserves the dignity of making that choice herself."

Jonah nodded, impressed once again by Abigail's instinctive compassion, wrapped in practical good sense. They rode in silence for several minutes, the town falling away behind them.

The McCallum house loomed ahead, a substantial two-story structure. Unlike the humble cabins of the miners, it boasted glass windows, a wraparound porch, and decorative trim—all meant to announce James McCallum's position and wealth to anyone who passed by.

Tonight, however, it looked strangely abandoned, with only a single lamp burning in an upstairs window.

"That's Hannah's room," he said, nodding toward the lit window.

"How do you know?" Abigail asked, surprised.

"I delivered a repaired stove to the kitchen last winter," Jonah explained. "Hannah was reading by the window in that room."

Abigail smiled, touched that Jonah had noticed such a detail, and remembered it.

Jonah unexpectedly pulled the buggy to the side of the road, a short distance from the McCallum house, and set the brake. He turned to her, his expression unreadable in the dim light.

"Abigail," he said, his voice rough with emotion. "Before we go further, there's something I need to say to you."

Her pulse quickened as he took both her hands in his, his calloused thumbs brushing across her knuckles. The unexpected tenderness of the gesture left her momentarily speechless.

"I'm not good with words," Jonah began, his voice uncertain. "Never have been. But tonight, watching you in that church, seeing your courage when McGrant threatened you these past few weeks and then Marshal Carter arriving with those deputies tonight..." He paused, seemingly gathering his jumbled thoughts.

Abigail waited, scarcely breathing, afraid to break the spell of this moment.

"Everything's changed," he continued finally. "The town. The church." His grip tightened slightly on her hands. "Me. I've changed."

"Jonah—"

"Please," he interrupted gently. "Let me finish while I still have the nerve."

Abigail nodded, her heart pounding against her ribs.

"When you first arrived in Clear Springs, I was certain you wouldn't last a week," Jonah admitted. "I thought you were too gentle, too refined for frontier life. But I was wrong. You're the strongest person I've ever known."

He looked down at their joined hands. "After Emily died, after I lost everyone I loved... I convinced myself I was better off alone. That caring for people only led to pain."

Jonah raised his eyes to meet hers, and the vulnerability she saw there in the moonlight stole her breath. "But you, Abigail Whitaker, have walked right into my heart. Your kindness, your faith, and your stubborn determination to see good in everyone... even in me, has done something to me."

"There is good in you, Jonah," Abigail whispered. "There always has been."

He shook his head slightly. "Maybe. But it was buried so deep I couldn't find it myself. You showed me the way back... not just to faith, but to living again. To caring again."

His hands trembled slightly around hers. "What I'm trying to say, very badly, is that I love you, Abigail. I think I've loved you since that day you stood up to McGrant over the Dawson family, fearless and righteous, despite the danger."

Tears welled in Abigail's eyes, but she made no move to wipe them away, unwilling to release his hands. "Oh, Jonah."

"I know it's sudden," he continued quickly. "And I know I'm not the kind of man your parents might have chosen for you. I'm rough-edged and battle-scarred, with nothing much to offer except a blacksmith shop and a heart that's learning to trust again."

"Stop," Abigail said gently but firmly. She freed one hand to touch his cheek, her fingers light against his stubbled jaw. "Jonah Brooks, my parents would have adored you. They valued courage, integrity, and faith above all else... and you embody all three, whether you recognize it or not."

Hope flickered in his eyes. "Abigail—"

"I love you too," she said simply, her voice clear and certain. "How could I not? You've risked your life repeatedly for this town, for me. You've protected me, challenged me, supported me through every trial. And tonight, watching you pray in the church after so many years of silence... that was the bravest thing I've ever witnessed."

A smile, rare and unguarded, transformed Jonah's face. Without words, he leaned forward, hesitating just a breath away from her.

"May I?"

Abigail closed the distance between them, her lips meeting his in a kiss that felt like coming home after a long journey.

His hand cradled her face with exquisite gentleness, as though she were made of the finest porcelain. When they finally parted, Abigail found herself breathless, and her heart singing with joy.

"So," Jonah said softly, his eyes never leaving hers, "what happens now?"

Abigail smiled, reaching up to smooth a strand of his dark hair. "First, we help Hannah. Then... we continue rebuilding—the church, the town." She laced her fingers with his. "And us."

Jonah nodded, bringing their joined hands to his lips.

"Together," Abigail added.

"Together," he agreed, the word a promise.

With visible reluctance, Jonah released her hands, adjusted the brake on the buggy, and took up the reins again.

As they approached the McCallum house, Abigail felt a curious mixture of nervousness and determined resolve. Hannah had lost so much already, her mother years before, and now her father to his own greed and corruption. Tonight would change the course of her young life again forever.

The buggy came to a stop before the front steps. Jonah jumped down first, then turned to help Abigail, his hands steady at her waist. Together, they approached the imposing front door.

"Should we knock?" Abigail whispered, suddenly uncertain. "What if there are servants?"

"McCallum kept only a cook who leaves at sunset," Jonah replied quietly. "Hannah is likely alone."

Abigail nodded and raised her hand to the brass knocker, letting it fall with three decisive taps.

Silence followed, broken only by the distant hoot of an owl. Abigail was about to knock again when a flicker of movement appeared behind the etched glass panels of the door. It opened cautiously, revealing Hannah's apprehensive face.

"Miss Whitaker?" Surprise replaced her wariness. "Mr. Brooks? What are you doing here?"

Hannah wore a simple faded cotton dress, her dark hair loose around her shoulders. She looked much younger than her fourteen years, vulnerable in a way that made Abigail's heart ache.

"May we come in, Hannah?" Abigail asked gently. "We need to speak with you about something important."

"Father isn't home yet. He said he had business in town, but he should have returned hours ago."

"That's what we've come to discuss," Jonah said, his deep voice gentle.

Hannah hesitated, then stepped back, opening the door wider. "Come in, then. But we should speak quickly and then you must go. Father doesn't approve of visitors when he's away."

The interior of the McCallum house was opulently furnished with imported carpets, heavy draperies, and polished furniture that spoke of wealth—wealth extracted from the suffering of miners. Despite the luxury, the house felt cold and unwelcoming.

Hannah led them to a formal sitting room, lighting additional lamps with practiced efficiency. "Please, sit down," she said, gesturing to a velvet-upholstered settee.

Instead of sitting, Abigail moved to Hannah's side, taking the girl's hand in hers. "Hannah, I'm afraid we bring difficult news. Your father has been arrested."

Hannah's face drained of color. "Arrested? But that's impossible. Father is with Mr. McGrant."

"Mr. McGrant has been arrested as well," Jonah said. "They're both facing serious charges related to the mine collapse."

"I don't understand," Hannah whispered, her voice small and confused.

Abigail guided her to a chair, sitting beside her while still holding her hand. "Evidence was discovered proving that Mr. McGrant and your father deliberately weakened support beams in the mine and used excessive blasting powder. They caused the collapse that killed Jedidiah Griffin and injured the others."

Hannah's eyes widened in horror. "No. That can't be true. Father wouldn't—" She stopped, her expression shifting as though pieces of a puzzle were suddenly fitting together in her mind. "What's going to happen to him?"

"He'll be taken to Denver to stand trial," Abigail explained gently.

"And me?" Hannah asked, her voice breaking. "What happens to me?"

The question hung in the air, heavy with implications. Hannah, at fourteen, was too young to live alone, yet old enough to understand the gravity of her situation.

"That's why we're here," Abigail said, squeezing Hannah's hand. "I'd like you to come stay with me at the parsonage tonight. You shouldn't be alone right now."

Hannah looked up, genuine surprise in her tear-filled eyes. "You want me to stay with you? Even after what my father did?"

"You are not your father, Hannah," Abigail said firmly.

"But the town will hate me now," Hannah whispered. "Everyone will look at me and see James McCallum's daughter."

"At first, perhaps some might," Jonah acknowledged, his honesty tempered with compassion. "But Clear Springs is changing. Today proved that. The people who gathered at the church tonight aren't looking for someone to blame, they're looking to rebuild their community."

"And you can be part of that rebuilding," Abigail added. "If you choose to be."

Hannah wiped at her tears with the back of her hand. "I don't even know if I can stay in Clear Springs. The house, Father's accounts... everything will be seized, won't it?"

"Likely," Jonah confirmed. "But you won't be without options or support."

Hannah looked between them, confusion evident on her young face. "Why would you help me? After everything Father and Mr. McGrant did to you, to the church, to the town..."

"Because that's what community means," Abigail said simply. "We carry each other's burdens. We don't abandon one of our own in their time of need."

"And you consider me... one of your own?" Hannah asked incredulously.

"Yes," Abigail and Jonah answered simultaneously, their voices blending in perfect harmony.

Hannah cried, years of suppressed emotion breaking free. Abigail wrapped her arms around the girl, holding her as she wept.

"You don't have to decide everything tonight," Abigail murmured, stroking Hannah's hair. "Just come with us to the parsonage. Get some rest. Tomorrow is soon enough to consider what comes next."

After a few moments, Hannah's sobs subsided. She straightened, wiping her face with embarrassed dignity. "I'd like to gather a few things, if that's all right."

"Of course," Abigail nodded.

Hannah disappeared upstairs, leaving Abigail and Jonah alone in the formal sitting room.

"You're remarkable," Jonah said, moving to sit beside her on the settee. "Most people would be celebrating McGrant's downfall, not worrying about the daughter of his accomplice."

"Hannah is innocent in all this," Abigail replied. "And she's been isolated for so long, forbidden from the church, from normal friendships. She needs community now more than ever."

Jonah reached for her hand, his callused fingers gentle against her skin. "You've created that community, Abigail. In just a few weeks, you've transformed Clear Springs from a collection of frightened individuals into people who stand together."

"We did it together," she corrected him. "All of us."

Hannah returned carrying a small valise. Her face was composed now, though her eyes remained red-rimmed.

"I'm ready," she said, her voice steady despite the circumstances.

They left the McCallum house without looking back, Hannah locking the door behind them with a decisive click. As Jonah helped both women into the buggy, Abigail noticed Hannah's backward glance at the home.

"It was never really home," Hannah said. "Not since Mother died. Just a house where Father and I lived separately under the same roof."

The ride back to town passed in thoughtful silence, each absorbed in their own reflections on the day's momentous events. When they reached the parsonage, lights flickered from inside.

Margaret rose from a chair on the parsonage porch, a covered basket in her hands. "I thought you might need some food," she explained as they approached. "And I've prepared a cot on the floor for Hannah in your room, Abigail. Ruth sent word about what you were doing."

Hannah hung back shyly as Jonah helped Abigail down from the buggy.

"Thank you, Margaret," Abigail said.

"Welcome, child," Margaret said, extending a hand to Hannah. "You've had quite a shock tonight, I imagine. Nothing settles the nerves like hot tea and fresh bread."

Hannah took the offered hand tentatively. "Thank you, Mrs. Hale."

"None of that 'Mrs.' business," Margaret insisted, guiding Hannah toward the door. "Margaret will do just fine. Now come inside where it's warm."

As Margaret ushered Hannah into the parsonage, Jonah moved to unhitch the horse.

"I'll return Ruth's buggy," he said. "And I should check on things in town. Marshal Carter might need help to organize watches over McGrant's properties until more official arrangements can be made."

Abigail nodded, understanding the practicalities that required attention despite the emotional revelations of the evening. "Will I see you tomorrow?"

Jonah stepped closer, his eyes warm in the lamplight spilling from the parsonage windows. "Try keeping me away," he said softly.

He glanced toward the doorway to ensure they were momentarily unobserved, then leaned down to brush a kiss against her lips, brief but tender.

"Get some rest," he murmured. "Tomorrow will bring new challenges."

"And new joys," Abigail added, her heart full, as she watched him climb back into the buggy and leave.

Her thoughts drifted to the unexpected declaration of his feelings and the promise of a future together. She had arrived in this frontier town alone and still grieving, determined to honor her parents' legacy but uncertain of her ability to fulfill their vision.

Now, she stood at the threshold of a life she hadn't dared imagine. A thriving church, a community finding its voice, and a love that had blossomed in the most unlikely circumstances.

"Thank you," she whispered into the night, her prayer simple but heartfelt. "For bringing me here, Lord. For everything."

# *Epilogue*



Frost crunched beneath Jonah's boots as he crossed Main Street, his breath forming clouds in the crisp December air. Clear Springs had transformed in the months since McGrant's arrest, not with grand buildings or fancy improvements, but with something more profound—a sense of ownership and community that had been missing under McGrant's shadow.

The mine operated again, now under the management of a consortium formed by the miners themselves, with Billy Patterson serving as their elected foreman. Production was modest but sustainable, as they continued to find small deposits of silver and focused on safe extraction rather than maximum profit.

Jonah's smithy had never been busier, as those ranchers and settlers from outside of town who had previously avoided Clear Springs, now came freely to trade and conduct business. He'd taken on a second apprentice, whose aptitude for metalwork showed promise.

But the most visible transformation was the church, which stood proudly at the edge of town, its white clapboard siding gleaming in the winter sunlight. The bell tower rose toward the sky, housing a new bell that now rang more loudly every Sunday morning, calling the faithful to worship.

Jonah smiled as he approached the church, memories of countless hours spent working alongside the townspeople to complete the renovation washing over him. It had become a true community project, with everyone contributing what they could—time, materials, skills, or simply encouragement and food for the workers.

Today, pine boughs and red ribbons adorned the entrance, a festive touch for the church's first Christmas service since its restoration. Inside, the scent of fresh greenery mingled with beeswax candles, creating an atmosphere both sacred and welcoming.

Hannah McCallum—now Hannah Miller, as she'd chosen to use her mother's maiden name—stood on a ladder, carefully hanging the last of the ornaments on the towering pine tree near the altar. She had blossomed in the months since her father's arrest and conviction, finding purpose as Abigail's assistant and unofficial sister.

"Careful there," Jonah cautioned as he entered, noticing the ladder's slight wobble.

Hannah glanced down, her face breaking into a warm smile. "Hello, Jonah! Don't worry, I'm nearly finished."

"It looks beautiful," he said, genuinely impressed by the transformation of the sanctuary. "Abigail's vision?"

"Partly," Hannah admitted, descending the ladder with the confidence of youth. "But everyone contributed ideas. Mrs. Hale insisted on the pine cones dipped in silver paint, and Reverend Blake made star ornaments from small pieces of twigs that he remembered from his childhood church."

Jonah nodded, noting the handcrafted wooden star atop the tree, his own contribution, carved during long evening hours in the smithy. "Where is Abigail?"

"In the parsonage kitchen with Ruth and Libby, finalizing plans for the Christmas Eve celebration," Hannah replied, a knowing glint in her eye. "She said you'd be by soon."

"Did she, now?"

"Mmm-hmm," Hannah hummed, pretending to adjust ornaments while watching him from the corner of her eye. "She seems particularly excited today. Almost nervous, even."

"Nervous?" Jonah echoed, suddenly concerned. "Is something wrong?"

Hannah laughed, the sound bright in the quiet sanctuary. "Nothing's wrong, Jonah. Quite the opposite, I think. Don't keep her waiting."

With a nod of thanks, Jonah crossed to the side door, exited the church, and walked toward the parsonage. As he approached, he heard women's voices raised in laughter and conversation.

He knocked lightly before entering, not wanting to startle them.

The kitchen was warm and fragrant with the scents of cinnamon, nutmeg, and fresh bread. Ruth and Libby sat at the table, cups of coffee before them, while Abigail stood at the stove, stirring a pot of what smelled like apple cider.

She turned at his entrance, her face lighting up in a way that still caught his breath. "Jonah!"

In the months since their first kiss in Ruth's buggy, Jonah had watched Abigail flourish. The soft-spoken missionary who had arrived in Clear Springs had grown into a confident leader, beloved by the community she'd helped heal. Yet, she retained the gentle compassion that had first drawn him to her, the unwavering faith that had inspired his own return to belief.

"Ladies," he greeted the others with a nod. "Something smells delicious."

"Abigail's spiced cider," Libby explained. "A secret family recipe, apparently."

"Not so secret anymore," Abigail laughed. "I've shared it with half the town."

Ruth rose from her seat, exchanging a meaningful glance with Libby. "I should be going. Billy's watching the children, and heaven knows what state the house will be in if I don't return soon."

"And I promised to help Doc Carpenter organize the medical supplies that arrived yesterday," Libby added, also standing. "So many wonderful donations from Denver since Marshal Carter spread the word about our needs here."

Their departures seemed suspiciously hasty to Jonah, but he said nothing as Abigail showed them out, with promises to continue their Christmas Eve planning later. When she returned to the kitchen, a slight flush colored her cheeks.

"Was there something you needed to discuss with me?" he asked, puzzled by her unusual demeanor.

Abigail nodded, wiping her hands nervously on her apron. "Yes, actually. Would you mind sitting down?"

Jonah complied, taking a seat at the kitchen table while Abigail poured him a mug of the fragrant cider. She placed it before him, then sat opposite, her hands clasped tightly in her lap.

"Jonah," she began, then faltered.

"Abigail?" he prompted gently, concern growing. "What is it?"

She took a deep breath, visibly gathering her courage. "I've been thinking about the future. Our future."

His heart quickened its pace. Over the past months, their courtship had progressed with the blessing of the town and Reverend Blake, who had taken particular joy in watching their relationship develop. They had spent countless hours together, working on the church, walking through town, and sharing quiet moments on the parsonage porch.

They had spoken of marriage in general terms, agreeing that it lay in their future, but neither had pressed for specific timing.

"I've received a letter," Abigail continued, reaching into her pocket to produce a folded document. "From the Mission Board in Boston."

Jonah felt a cold knot form in his stomach. Was she being called back East? Had her superiors decided Clear Springs was now stable enough to continue without her?

"They've approved permanent funding for the Clear Springs church," she explained, sliding the letter across to him. "It's officially recognized as a successful mission outpost now, largely due to the monthly reports I've been sending."

Relief washed through him. "That's wonderful news."

"Yes," Abigail agreed, though her expression remained serious. "But there's more. They've offered me a choice."

"A choice?" Jonah repeated, the knot returning.

Abigail nodded. "I can remain here as the mission representative, overseeing the church until a permanent minister is appointed, or..." she hesitated. "Or I can recommend someone else for the position and be reassigned to a new frontier mission that needs establishing."

Jonah's hand tightened around the mug of cider. "I see."

"No," Abigail said quickly, reaching across to cover his hand with hers. "I don't think you do. I've already made my decision, Jonah. I'm staying in Clear Springs."

The tension drained from his shoulders. "You're staying."

"Of course I'm staying," she said softly. "This is my home now. Our home."

The simple declaration, spoken with such certainty, filled Jonah with a warmth that spread through his entire being.

"But," Abigail continued, nervousness returning to her features, "there's a complication. The Mission Board has certain... expectations for their representatives. Standards of conduct and living arrangements."

Jonah frowned slightly, not following her meaning.

Abigail's cheeks flushed deeper. "They expect unmarried female missionaries to live in approved housing with proper chaperonage. Now that Hannah is considered my ward rather than simply a houseguest, that requirement is technically met, but..."

Understanding dawned, and with it, a surge of something like amusement and tenderness combined. "But you'd prefer a different solution to the housing situation?"

"Jonah Brooks," Abigail said, exasperation coloring her tone, "are you going to make me do this entirely myself?"

He couldn't help the smile that spread across his face. "Do what entirely yourself, Abigail?"

She stood abruptly, moving to the window to stare out at the church. "I had a plan, you know. I was going to be dignified and articulate. Ruth and Libby helped me practice what to say."

Jonah rose and moved to stand behind her, close enough to catch the scent of lavender in her hair. "And what was it you planned to say?"

Abigail turned to face him, her blue eyes meeting his directly despite the color in her cheeks. "That I love you. That these past months have been the happiest of my life, despite all the challenges and changes. That I can't imagine my future without you in it."

Jonah's heart swelled almost painfully in his chest. "I feel the same way."

"Good," Abigail said with surprising firmness. "Then there's only one logical conclusion."

"Which is?" he prompted, enjoying her determination despite knowing exactly where the conversation was leading.

"Jonah Brooks," Abigail said, squaring her shoulders, "will you marry me?"

For a moment, he could only stare at her, struck speechless by her boldness. Then a laugh escaped him, rich and genuine.

"That's not the reaction a woman hopes for when proposing marriage," Abigail said, a hint of hurt in her voice.

Jonah shook his head, still smiling, as he reached into his pocket. "I'm not laughing at you, Abigail. I'm laughing at both of us."

He withdrew a small wooden box, carved with delicate patterns of intertwined leaves and flowers. A labor of love completed over many evenings.

"What's this?" Abigail asked, her eyes widening.

"Open it," Jonah urged, placing the box in her hands.

With trembling fingers, Abigail lifted the lid. Nestled inside on a bed of soft fabric lay a ring. A simple band of polished silver, set with a small but perfect sapphire that matched the blue of her eyes.

"I made it," Jonah explained. "Melted down a silver dollar from the first payment I received in Clear Springs years ago. Found the stone in Denver last month when I delivered those special hinges to the territorial office."

Abigail looked up at him, tears glistening in her eyes. "Jonah..."

"I was planning to ask you tomorrow, after the Christmas Eve service," he admitted. "I even spoke to Reverend Blake last week for his blessing."

A tear slipped down Abigail's cheek. "You asked Reverend Blake?"

"He said your father would have approved," Jonah said. "That a man who protected his daughter and helped rebuild the church her parents founded would have been welcomed as a son."

More tears followed the first, but Abigail's smile was radiant through them. "That means everything to me, Jonah."

He gently took the ring from the box, holding it between them. "So, since you've already proposed to me, I suppose I should answer your question first. Yes, Abigail Whitaker, I will marry you."

She laughed, the sound like music in the warm kitchen. "And my answer is yes as well."

Jonah slipped the ring onto her finger, where it fit perfectly. "I measured using a piece of string while you were sleeping on the porch swing this past fall," he admitted at her questioning look.

"You've been planning this that long?" Abigail asked, wonder in her voice.

"I've been planning this since the night we drove to tell Hannah about her father," Jonah confessed. "I just needed time to become the man worthy of asking."

Abigail placed her palm against his cheek. "You've always been that man, Jonah Brooks. Even when you couldn't see it yourself."

He leaned down to kiss her, a gentle promise of all the years to come. When they parted, Abigail's eyes sparkled with happiness.

"When shall we tell everyone?" she asked.

"They already know," Jonah chuckled. "The entire town has been waiting for this announcement."

"The entire town?" Abigail repeated, incredulous.

"Billy Patterson has been running a betting pool on the date," Jonah confirmed. "I believe Doc Carpenter just won a considerable sum, having selected 'before Christmas.'"

Abigail's laughter filled the kitchen again. "So much for our private moment."

"We'll have plenty of those," Jonah promised, drawing her close. "A lifetime of them."

The church bell began to ring, its clear tone carrying across Clear Springs—not summoning worshippers, but celebrating.

"Hannah, I assume? Shall we go greet our well-wishers?" Jonah asked, offering his arm.

Abigail took it, her ring catching the light. "Together," she said, the word both a statement and a vow.

"Together," Jonah agreed, and they stepped out into the bright winter day, toward the future they would build—together.

# Leave A Review

If you enjoyed this book, please consider leaving an honest review on Amazon

Visit Our Website:

www.vivianbelle.com

Visit Our Amazon Author Page HERE

Find Us On Social Media:

Facebook

Facebook Author Page

Instagram